ERIN
GO BRAGH
III

ERIN

GO BRAGH
III

THE END OF AN ERA
1995-2002

RUAIRI O' CASHEL

Library of Congress Control Number:		2013907853
ISBN:	Hardcover	978-1-4836-3154-7
	Softcover	978-1-4836-3153-0
	Ebook	978-1-4836-3155-4

A special thanks to my wife, the Orange woman of my life, who offered help and corrections; but any mistakes are mine alone.

This book was printed in the United States of America.

Rev. date: 08/08/2013

To order additional copies of this book, contact:
Xlibris LLC
1-888-795-4274
www.Xlibris.com
Orders@Xlibris.com
134167

CONTENTS

DEDICATION

To all the victims of the 'Troubles' in the North of Ireland, and in the Republic, victims of bullets, bombs, incendiaries, car crashes, knifings, slashes, and various other examples of war. Some were victims of sectarian, political, and individual attacks, some were in the wrong place at the wrong time, and others were tortured or massacred on purpose to instill 'fear,' 'terror,' 'vengeance,' 'punishment,' or, simply as an 'example' for others to heed.

HISTORY:
THE START OF THE TROUBLES

*I*n the middle of the 12th century an English Pope (Adrian IV, the only *Pope of English lineage) and an Irish king (Dermot of Leinster) gave the English monarch (Henry II) the opportunity and excuse to meddle in Irish affairs. The English crown and its government has continued to interfere and be involved in Ireland ever since.*

The English crown sought to offset any Irish resistance to this state of affairs by settling English and then Scottish colonists on plantations and in cities around Ireland, with the exception of the far west of the island, in the rather barren province of Connacht. After William of Orange, defeated his father-in-law King James II at the Battle of the Boyne (1690) while flying the Papal flag among others, becoming King William III, his army followed up with victories over James's Irish allies at Athlone and Aughrim, and the siege of Limerick. The Treaty of Limerick promised religious and ownership of land rights to the Irish. But the Catholic Irish soldiers didn't trust the victors and some 11,000 fled Ireland for the continent (The Wild Gueese) becoming the famous "Irish Brigades" of several European armies.

The Irish soldier's suspicions proved correct, for over the next thirty years the 'victorious' Protestant English Parliament established a ruling class in Ireland known as the "Protestant Ascendancy," and passed a series of enactments called the "Penal Laws" that punished any one for practicing Catholicism: the Irish Catholics couldn't possess, sell, or buy certain amounts of land, they couldn't practice certain professions, possess arms, or own a horse worth 5 pounds sterling.

Eventually, a law said Irish Catholics had to split up land among their descendants (reversing the English practice of primogenitor), thus rendering each generation smaller and smaller plots hardly able to sustain a family unless they raised potatoes. In the nineteenth century this dependence on potatoes, because of English law and English political and economic policy, led to the "Potato Famine."

After centuries of riot, revolt, rebellion, and revolution by the native Irish, blight, disease and emigration further reduced their numbers in the millions. The English augmented this further by instigating famine, imprisonment, and deportation. The British government in the later half of the nineteenth century considered a scheme of limited self-government for Ireland, except in the areas of allegiance to the English crown, military security, and foreign affairs. The British government had dropped taxing the Irish for Anglican Church tithes, they had started land reform (fair rents, fixity of tenure, freedom to buy and sell), and now they had of late talked of 'home rule,' to calm Irish rebels.

One faction of Irish Nationalists sat in the British Parliament as a block of about 86 members. The British Liberal Parliamentary Party need the eighty-six Irish votes to form a 'Liberal Government,' and the price for this coalition was at the very least 'Irish Home Rule.'

To the most radical of Irish nationalists, this offer of 'Home Rule' was too little, too late. This minority of Irish extremists called for total Irish independence. This radical faction belonged to a militant group called the Irish Republican Brotherhood (IRB), inspired by late eighteenth century leaders who looked to the 'Republics' produced by the French and American Revolutions. They saw a chance of, if not success, then heroic martyrdom to the cause of Irish freedom and independence during WW I.

The Irish had held steadfast to the maxim, 'Britain's distraction is Ireland's advantage.' So in 1914 the stage was set for Ireland to benefit from Britain's entry into the 'Great War.' What compounded the sense of expectation was the fact that several counties up in Ulster Province had threatened armed rebellion against the British Government because the British Parliament had passed a 'Home Rule' Bill that was to have taken effect in 1914.

A Protestant 'Ulster Volunteer Force' numbering tens of thousands, were prepared to resist the enactment of the 'Irish Home Rule Act' claiming to be

"Loyalists" to the British Crown, British language, customs and traditions, and last but not least, to their Protestant heritage. They claimed their 'Loyalty' transcended an act of Parliament that squarely attacked the British Empire, the United Kingdom, and loyalty of British subjects whose families had lived in Ireland for hundreds of years. Some notable English families and Parliamentarians in the British Conservative Party openly supported the UVF in their threat of rebellion, including Winston Churchill's father Randolph. The UVF was armed with German Mauser rifles and ammunition.

Parliamentary Nationalists formed the 'Irish Volunteers" who believed their joining the British Army would guarantee that 'Home Rule' would be enacted once victory was secured by the British in WW I. The Ulster Volunteer Force offered their services to the British Expeditionary Force (BEF) heading to Europe to guarantee through their loyal commitment to the BEF that the 'Home Rule' bill would be amended to exclude part of Ulster.

The British Army accepted individual Irish recruits, but they hesitated accepting the 'Irish Volunteers' until acts of loyalty were professed and a gold crown was displayed on the top of the golden harp on their regimental flag. Since the IRB had thoroughly infiltrated the Irish Volunteers the British were not groundless in their concern.

But there was concern a plenty at this time. Nationalists were concerned that if things went badly for the BEF, the British might conscript Irishmen into the army. Also, if the Germans appeared to be on the brink of victory, this alone might be a sign for drastic action by the IRB. If either, or both conscription and German victory happened simultaneously, the IRB was committed to a rebellion.

As WW I dragged into its second year there was no sign of either side winning, and in 1916 there were rumors of 'conscription' because of the massive loss of life. The IRB, who had infiltrated the Irish Volunteers, and the socialist 'Citizens Army' of James Connolly, prepared to initiate a 'Rising' during Easter week of 1916. Under the leadership of Patrick Pearse, Thomas Clark, Connolly and others, and after confusion, miss-coordination, and blunder at getting sufficient arms and ammunition from Germany, Pearse proclaimed the Irish Republic from the steps of the General Post Office in Dublin on Easter Monday.

By the end of Easter Week, the "Easter Rising" seemed a total failure. But the British overplayed their victory and in a show of overkill, executed the leaders of the rising, turning them into martyrs.

———•◦●◦•———

From the blood of these rebels two important movements emerged. The first was a transition from a nationalist movement into a political party in 1917 called 'Sinn Fein' (Ourselves Alone) under the leadership of Eamon DeValera, that won a lopsided election in 1918 advocating Irish independence and withdrawal from the British Parliament. On January 21, 1919 a Declaration of Independence (drafted on January 8th) was read at a meeting of the first rebel non British Irish Assembly, "Dail Eireann."

The second movement was the transition from the IRB to the 'Irish Republican Army' (IRA) that initiated a war to ensure that British administration of government in Ireland would be impossible. The British responded by proclaiming martial law and reinforced the Royal Irish Constabulary with 'auxiliary' ex-servicemen collectively known as "Black and Tans."

Michael Collins carried on a brilliant guerilla war against the crown forces. The RIC, the British Military, and especially the 'black and tans' conducted a vicious war of attrition on the Irish nation between 1919 and 1921.

The British Government passed the Government of Ireland Act in 1920, that partitioned Ireland: six counties of the Province of Ulster (Antrim, Down, Armagh, Derry, Tyrone, and Fermanagh) remained within the United Kingdom in accordance with the Loyalist leaders, led by the intransigent Edward Carson and William Craig with their own form of 'Home Rule' and their own parliament. The other twenty-six counties were to have dominion status.

The British Prime Minister, David Lloyd George, threatened Michael Collins and other members of a peace commission with 'total war'. Since Collins knew the dire straights of the IRA by this stage of the 'Tan War,' he accepted the peace treaty. DeValera, as head of the Dail, rejected the deal.

The Dail, Sinn Fein and the IRA split over the Treaty, and the 'partition' of the North, and an oath of allegiance to the British crown became especially heinous. The British government and its military forces left the 26 counties, now called the "Free State." Collins and his 'pro-Treaty' Free State Army made up of his supporters in the IRA fought the followers of DeValera, the anti-Treaty segment of the IRA in what became known as the Irish Civil War between 1921 and 1923.

Atrocities, assassinations, murders were committed by both sides, and Michael Collins among many was killed during the hostilities. At the conclusion of the Civil War, 'partition' was a fact, formally accepted in 1925. Earlier, King George V on June 22, 1921 opened the 'Northern Ireland' Parliament. The Catholic-Nationalist minority, in the North of Ireland, were at the mercy of the Protestant-Unionist majority and their great organization of the new twentieth century "Protestant Ascendancy," the Orange Order. The Orange Order organized marches, bands, and established Halls that 'celebrated' King William's victory in 1690 over the Catholic James II and his Catholic allies, by marginalizing, intimidating, humiliating, and isolating Catholics.

Sir James Craig became the Prime Minister and virtual dictator of the six counties in 1921 until his death in 1940. He ruled through the Orange order, which was the popular expression of the new Protestant Ascendancy, and the political expression of the Unionist Party that ran the new 'home rule' government in the North of Ireland. The British Parliament made a deal with the MPs and Peers from the six counties that in affect gave the Northern Ireland Parliament total control over any and all concerns in the North of Ireland, so England could wash their hand of the "Irish problems" (the Stormont government, the Brits felt, would know best how to handle situations in the six counties of 'Ulster,' thus relieving England of primary responsibility; the English didn't want to know of problems nor were they interested in how they were addressed). Each year a Parliamentary committee in Westminster received a 'report' on Northern Ireland.

Through the Special Powers Act of 1922 (made permanent in 1933 the year that the Stormont Parliament Building was dedicated, thus establishing "Stormont" as the seat of what Craig called "a Protestant Parliament and a Protestant state"), the newly reconstituted RIC became the Royal Ulster Constabulary (RUC), and their all Protestant auxiliaries, the "Ulster Special Constabulary," the "B-Specials" (or "B-men" to Nationalists), the Protestant Ascendancy controlled the six counties. The new security forces cracked down on any perceived threat to the status quo. In the 20s and in the 30s there were demonstrations by Catholics because of the harsh unemployment policies aimed at depriving Catholics of good paying jobs that in turn became sectarian riots by Protestant mobs, the RIC and the B-men.

———•◦•———

During WW II there was a fledging IRA attempt to take advantage of England's distraction in Europe, North Africa and the Far East, which came to a few bombs in London and arrests, beatings and at least one exemplary execution. The normal conditions continued after WW II within the new Labor Governments' social plans: new government housing was clearly provided to families based on religion; employment clearly discriminated against Catholics; and voting districts were gerrymandered favoring the Protestant Unionist Party thus marginalizing the Catholic population and their crowded neighborhoods.

However, the Labor government introduced a new education act shortly after the end of WW II to provide all youth with an opportunity for higher education. For the first time Irish Catholic youth qualified for college and university positions. Knowledge was not only power, it proved to be a threat to the status quo.

———•◦•———

INTRODUCTION
TO THE END OF AN ERA

It seemed like only yesterday and at the same time a lifetime ago that I had been in the North of Ireland, where I had so many memories of both good and bad times. It also seemed that everything in the North was shaped by the Troubles. So much in the North was the same, yet in different ways I was always having trouble sorting it all out. I had 'trouble' sorting out the setting of the 'troubles,' the 'modern troubles,' as some liked to say, in the North of Ireland.

Actually the 'troubles,' modern or those dating back hundreds of years ago, were a way of life in the North of Ireland. And those 'troubles' shaped the soul and character, the health and posture of people in and from the North. And in my case those characteristics were passed on from one generation to the next, from generation after generation, from century to century, down to our own time.

Not only did I have family from the North, in Ulster or Northern Ireland as Loyalists called it, as well as the South, that is the Free State, the Republic, or the Twenty-six Counties as some Nationalists call it, but I also had family from and on both sides of the great social divide there, that is Catholics and Protestants.

I had personally participated in the modern Troubles, I had done things that led some foes to their deaths. Yet at the same time I longed for peace with all my being. I had taken sides, demonstrated full commitment to the cause, for I yearned for undoing the wrongs committed against the Nationalist society for years, decades, centuries. At the same time recognized there were two sides to the story. There were two traditions, heritages, and histories. Although I was committed to peace, it would be a demanding, hard sought, brutal endeavor.

I was messed up, not because I was a hybrid, or half-and-half, some of this and some of that, or a little of this and a little of that. Don't misunderstand me, I wasn't confused, I was a mess up. And coming back to the North from America would bring it all home to me. Oh, I knew who I was and what I was, and why it was I was that way; I also knew that I had had options, and I chose to be who I'd been in the past. That was then, but I was a mess of commitments in the here and now. What a mess.

I couldn't and wouldn't deny my past nor could I ignore it. Some people knew my past, some knew of only parts of my past, and some knew none of my past. That was not only a mess, but it was messy. I had been able to decide who knew what of my past, but the problem was I was married to an Irish girl and thus related intimately to my past. My relatives, starting with my wife, only knew some of my past. My own mother was another issue, as I will explain later. All of this was oh so messy.

The one person who knew the most of my past in Ireland and my Irish undertakings, besides my mother who seemed to know quite a bit about the whole of my past from sources other than myself, was not family and had been a complete stranger to me for the first twenty-one years of my life, that is, before I set foot in Ireland. But he had become one of my best friends, if not THE best friend outside the family, both immediate and extended.

Note, I said "the most," not "all." Even I tried to forget some of my past, and some of my past was forgotten with the dying of brain cells as I aged, quite naturally, without my trying to forget. I've no doubt that some of what was lost through this process was both 'good' and 'bad' as the case may be. But obviously, I don't know for sure.

But I digress. Ireland, the North of Ireland, was and is my main concern, for I was planning to bringing students to the North to 'experience' the 'Troubles.' Part of that experience would be to meet and learn from my friend in the North, 'Denny.' He had experienced it all, so he knew it all. Denny was my earliest contact, confident, confessor, controller, and coordinator in the North, in what seems like a lifetime ago, and just yesterday as I mentioned earlier. I must admit, I always miss him, my old friend.

————◆•◆•◆————

But the separation from Ireland was coming to an end with the conferences I attended in the North in the 1990s. There was a fourteen-year stretch between 1981 and 1995 that I did not go North. Events in nineteen eighty-one had jeopardized both my health and cover, and thus with my well being at issue I took leave of the North for fourteen years.

But the yearning was so strong that I took up my avocation once again. I told Barbrie, my wife, that I had plenty of insurance for her and the girls, so she didn't have to worry. That nearly put an end to it right there. I told her I was kidding of course, but I did have plenty of insurance, just in case.

Barbrie told my mother about my plans and my "comments," resulting in a forceful lecture about my impertinent comments from my mother.

"You don't fool around about 'if I don't make it back,' and the 'cause of Irish freedom.' Your family and the cause are serious, Rudy. You of all people should know that," mom scolded.

"I was trying to make light of the situation, that was all."

Mom ignored my impertinence and didn't let up, "Let me say it again Rudy, your family and Irish freedom are not to be made light of, never again. I don't ever want to hear of you clowning around about them. This conflict has gone on for so long, has cost everyone so much, physically, emotionally, and spiritually, it is not funny. It is not a kidding or laughing matter. When your man Adams called for the 'Long War' in '76, I doubt that any one thought it would, or could, last this long.

"Its like the Brits are just defiantly waiting us out. Their 'imperial pride' won't allow them to admit that they cannot win this time. Our army can nearly match their arms and technology from what I hear. Well, they can wait until hell freezes over, this time we will not loose or quit. We will persevere to the end."

'Aye, mom, don't you know that I know it? Once the 'Northern Command' took over operations in the North for the war, they had new and different ideas and strategies. Much of it came out of the Long Kesh prison, the Maze. Not by arms alone, but also by politics will we win the war," I added.

"As my friend 'The Dark,' Brendan Hughes, was saying before he went into the Maze Prison, we needed a mass movement with involvement in politics, along with the armed struggle, to win this war. The 1981 hunger strike gave it to us on a platter at a terrible price. But thank God for the dumb ass Brits and their pride and intransigence. As Danny Morrison put it in October of '81, we'll take power with an armalite in one hand and the ballot box in the other," I agreed and ended the lesson.

Yet I wondered about her comment of matching the Brits "arms and technology from what I hear." Where did she hear that? Who told her about that? She obviously had contact with sources in the know, and would occasionally let me in on her secrets. I was let in on those secrets if I was on my toes and listening very carefully to not only what she was saying, but also I had to read between the lines and words to keep up. My mother never ceased to amaze me and constantly caused me to pause and wonder.

◆◆◆

The old and new circumstances that shaped my life revolved around the recent conflict that was being waged primarily in the North of Ireland and my involvement in it. My maternal side of the family had been Republicans for over two hundred years, and some had been actively supporting the Republican cause since the early twentieth century. My mother's immediate family ended up in the United States because after the "Tan War" against the British in 1919, 1920 and 1921, the

Republican Movement split over the 'peace' the British Prime Minister offered the Republican Provisional Government and Army.

The crux of the "peace" and subsequent "treaty" was the detachment of six counties in the northeast of Ireland and their retention in the United Kingdom. Those six counties (Antrim, Down, Armagh, Derry, Tyrone, and Fermanagh) were heavily Protestant and Unionist in some areas, and they wanted to remain loyal to the crown and thus remain within the UK.

A little more than half of the Dial, the 'Rebel' Parliament, went along with this 'Partition' of the North from the rest of Ireland. The majority of the population were tired of the war between the Republican Army headed by Michael Collins and the British. Collins saw the treaty and peace as necessary, and this 'Partition' as temporary. His group, that constituted the majority of the Dial members and the population, were known as the 'pro-treat' forces, while their opponents who rejected the treaty and the 'Partition' were called the 'anti-treaty' forces.

My grandfather, being from the North, opposed 'Partition' although he admired and had fought under Michael Collins. Granda knew that the new government in the North would not only be 'loyal' to the crown, but biased against Catholics. Although he was not Catholic himself, his family had a long history of non-sectarianism. They had roots in the 1790s United Irishmen of Theobald Wolff Tone and their non-sectarian Republicanism.

The 'Civil War' that ensued between the 'pro' and 'anti' treaty Republicans lasted just over a year. It was vicious, turning brother against brother, father against son, etc., etc, It was so terrible that the Irish still cannot discuss it openly. Horrendous atrocities occurred, executions, and the assassination of Michael Collins and other leaders from both sides. It also saw my grandfather "go on the run," hiding out down in the Free State, marrying and emigrating to Canada and then to the United States, settling in Hartford, Michigan.

Although my mother had traveled between the USA and Ireland during the thirties and early forties, I was the first to contact the family remaining in Ireland, both North and South, while I was a student in

Belfast. As a result of my contact with the family I was able to have my mother and my Irish wife, her sister and husband connect with our family in the North.

A couple of the younger generation from our County Down family came over to Canada during the summer one year to avoid the conflict. Although they were Protestants, as my mother always said, "They are family, so they are our Protestants," and they were treated as family. They visited Hartford, and one high school aged girl stayed in Hartford with us and attended school for several years.

My family in Michigan, and to a lesser degree in Canada, knew to varying degrees, of my involvement with the Provisional IRA (PIRA; after the mid 70s the designation "P" could be dropped since the only IRA was the Provisional wing) since my time in graduate school in Scotland and in Belfast. Further, my brother-in-law was on the run from the Brits for his activity as a sniper for the PIRA. Our paths had crossed 'professionally' a time or two over in the North. But he was now 'unofficially' residing in the USA, having married the daughter of an Irish friend in Hartford.

My last extended stay in the North had been during the height of the 'hunger strike' in 1981, and it had not been cordial. I had been arrested on trumped up charges and roughed up while in Crumlin Road Jail in Belfast. After a week of internment, I left the North for what I imagined to be a long time after getting even with the man who had set me up. For all I knew there was a price on my head.

My brother-in-law, Danny Conlon, had dished out some payback to three Special Branch men who had been responsible for my harsh treatment in the 'Crum.' He had a price on his head in the North, and would be arrested in the Republic and could be extradited from the USA back to the UK. I was sure that in nothing more than guilt by association, let alone actions on my part, probably I had his curse extended to myself.

But after a friend checked on my status after a several year absence from the North, I got a clean bill of health and was given the green light to attend a couple of conferences in the North on the 'Troubles.' I participated through the Council on International Educational Exchange (CIEE) in their Northern Ireland program a couple of times in the 1990s. CIEE put together great programs where I was introduced to several scholars studying various aspects of the Irish Troubles, and also some participants from the Loyalist community who were former paramilitaries.

It was all good cover. I got to visit with family in Saintfield, County Down. I got to visit with my best friend in the North, Denny. I also got to bring things into the North, like letters, contracts and money. The conferences were short stays of about six days in length, and they often had a schedule to follow. Making my private contacts was often difficult to say the least.

I pretty much had to go along with the program, if for no other reason to avoid drawing attention to myself. Several of the CIEE people in the North were associated with the University system there, usually from the Coleraine campus. I had them pegged as Unionists who, could sick the RUC (later called the PSNI), Special Branch, British Military and/or Loyalist paramilitaries on me.

I truly wanted to avoid attention. My extracurricular missions depended on it. I was sure that some one else could step in and replace me if necessary. I'd had experience with the security forces in the North, and I was getting too old for any rough stuff.

With my personal background and now the diverse sources I was introduced to through the CIEE conferences, I was ready to embark on my own Irish Foreign Studies Program. I could adjust the schedule to allow more free time for me to meet with those I had things for, and to retrieve things to bring back to the US.

Some of the original talks I had with one of my professors from Queen's University on setting up a program involving Queen's did not meet the conditions of students I was to bring to Ireland. Costs and the amount of time involved in meeting Queen's conditions was prohibitive. So running my program through my US community college was the answer.

I proposed courses that fit our curriculum, our tuition costs, and our time frame. We would do class work in May, then take residency in Ireland in June. Having cleared all the hurdles I was poised to bring students North to study the 'Troubles' first hand after a year of jumping through all the community college's hoops.

———◆•●•◆———

So, here I was with about thirty young American students, most with Irish nationality in their background, planning to spend about a month in the North. We were to take up residency at Ti Cuchulainn (Cuchulainn's House), at Mullaghbane, South Armagh. It was a new local youth center in need of cash and exposure. Our group would provide both. In return we received a beautiful venue for our history lectures, archeology talks and starting place for our tours, and political talks by local experts.

Being close to the M1 and A1 motorways we had easy access to many points of interest. We visited museums, cultural centers, archeological and geological sites, ancient cities, and the political center in the North of Ireland, "Stormont" in Belfast, and the "Northern Ireland" Parliament building.

Unofficially, we also visited and witnessed the IRA stronghold of west Belfast (the Falls, Clonard, and Andersonstown) and the Ardoyn, the Loyalist centers of the Shankill and east Belfast (including Tiger Bay), and British Military roadblocks, helicopters hovering overhead, forts and militarized camps (especially in South Armagh and Derry City), and hilltop listening and observation posts and camps. The Royal Ulster Constabulary (RUC), and later the Police Service of Northern Ireland (PSNI), and the Ulster Defence Regiment (UDR), were observed in various facets of their duties. The students got an eyeful.

When local leaders of the various political parties addressed the students they heard diametrically opposing points of view. I was able to arrange visits by the Ulster Unionist Party (UUP), the Democratic Unionist Party (DUP), and the Progressive Unionist Party (PUP) representing shades of Loyalism. The middle of the road Alliance Party was also invited to make a presentation. The Social Democratic and Labor Party (SDLP) and Sinn Fein (SF) spoke for the Republican cause.

Eventually I was able to enlist former paramilitaries from several organizations representing the two sides of the 'Troubles,' along with PR people from the RUC/PSNI, the British Military, the Ulster Volunteer Force and the Ulster Defence Association, and 'Official' IRA and "Provisional' IRA. I was not able to get anyone from British Paratroop Regiment (Paras), the Ulster Freedom Fighters (UFF), or the Red Hand Commandos. Neither was I able to get a representative of the Irish National Liberation Army (INLA).

Logistically it was a nightmare, but with some last minute shifting we eventually got everything and everybody in. Clearly the most cooperative were the Nationalist groups. On the national level we met with Gerry Adams, Martin McGuinness, Conor Murphy, Michelle Gildernew, Jerry Kelly, Monica Williams, and Mitchell Mc Laughlin from Sinn Fein. Conor Murphy and his brother Des seemed willing and able to talk to our group, and he was constantly making arrangements to meet many of the other Sinn Fein delegates.

We met with John Hume and Sean Farren from the SDLP. They took time from their very busy schedules to accommodate us. Since Hume was starting to show the wear and tear of all the years of service to the people of the North, it was often Sean Farren with whom we met. Like Hume, he was gentle, calm, and committed to peace, he talked peace, and he helped American students from Michigan understand the complexities of the peace process.

The Nationalists were playing to the choir, because my students like most Irish-Americans are "Green," that is, they are sympathetic with the nationalist cause. As Reverend Ian Paisley (of DUP) once said to me, "Aye, Mr. Castle, you come here green as the grass, but you've a thing or two to learn." He said it to me, but it was understood that I represented most Americans. I heard this same sort of comment uttered by many Loyalist representatives. Indeed it has been my experience that most people visiting Ireland, both North and South, are sympathetic and empathetic toward the Nationalist position.

I think for this reason Reverend Paisley was generous and gracious to meet with my students when his calendar allowed, and once when he was busy he arranged for us to meet with his son, Ian Jr., also a DUP Assembly member. Everyone was disappointed in missing senior, but as one might have expected, junior did not disappoint ideologically and was as slanted as his father.

Ian Sr. once told me, "Americans come here and they are so green, they don't recognize the other two colors in the tricolor flag they identify with, one of which is 'orange.' You at least bring your students around to let us Loyalists talk to them. I know your loyalties Mr. Castle, but you let them hear us Unionists, you are one of the few, I'll give you that."

That seemed pretty straightforward and accurate. I was impressed with his precise observation and his compliment. I wondered if this was an accident. Most of the time, he seemed to aggressively generalize, blindly distort, and universally condemn at will.

What an anomaly Paisley was; his comments to me proved he could be an accurate observer and analyzer on one the one hand, and a leading bigot on the other. It seemed that his latter stance far out weighed the former. At rallies, meetings, in front of a crowd of his followers, it was as if he was obsessed by a fanaticism that knew no limits. He seemed possessed when he was in his 'Moses' impersonation, admonishing those outside the 'covenant', his 'covenant,' and his antipapal rants, his Catholic bashing, his condemnation of Rome and "Roman Catholics," never just "Catholics."

A Catholic acquaintance from the North once told me, "Most Irish Catholics no longer follow the Papal line blindly. And most of us no longer see Rome as an infallible source of truth. We go to church on Sunday out of habit, not conviction. Our demonstrations of faith are more communal defiance of their bigoted system. We have our kids baptized, see to it they go to confession and communion, are confirmed, married and buried in the church out of an conscious tradition of belligerence for a lot of us, not blind faith.

"Some Protestants think we are still robots or pawns of the priests. But those days are gone. Our blind tribal confidence of olden days in the church is by and large generally gone. Men like Paisley think we are frozen in time. The Pope, Rome, and the Catholic hierarchy are more important to Paisley than they are to us Irish Catholics. Without them, Paisley would be lost!"

As Denny once told me, "No Nationalist shoots Paisley because he's more useful to us alive than dead. Dead he becomes a hero, a martyr, and an icon. Alive he is the prototype of the Loyalist lunatic bigot, the ultimate Protestant sectarian, the premier Unionist hate monger. We pray, 'God let him live, let him speak, let him lead people to Nationalism.'"

Denny was correct. I let my students see Paisley at his best and at his worst. Actually, his best occured when he was at his worst: his anti-Catholic, anti-Papal, anti-Irish Nationalist condemnation and bashing. Students felt, to a person, that the judgmental, damning, fire and brimstone bigot was the "real Paisley."

I cautiously had to admit that I had come to that same conclusion too. I only hesitated because of his comments directly to me as recounted above. But I let the students come to that consensus from what they saw of the man, not just when he posed for pictures with us at Stormont and he was reserved and polite, but what they saw and heard him do and say on the news reports, filmed at rallies, police barricades, marches, and demonstrations.

The irony was, clearly half of my students were not Catholics, but they sided with the Catholics because of the historical bigotry played out in the North, and the continued sectarian attacks on individual Catholics, the confrontational parades through their neighborhoods, and the insulting and provocative assaults on Catholic institutions, churches, parish halls, schools, and Catholic parents, students, and parishioners.

There was also the clear overlap between the Nationalist movement and the Catholic community, and students recognized the symbiotic relationship between the two groups.

Students were receptive to the claims that not all Protestants were anti Catholic in their behavior or in their beliefs. I warned students not to fall into the trap of generalizing about people's beliefs, attitudes, and practices, because they were of a certain nationality, social class, religious persuasion, ethnic group, or occupation.

Most students were receptive to these cautions, and I credit this to their upbringing and education back home in the United States. Not that we Americans are perfect or that we do not have people who exhibit antisocial behavior toward people of different races, creeds, gender, nationalities, ethnic groups, etc. But as a nation, our schools, courts, legislatures, and courts make an effort to practice that which endeavors liberty and justice for all. Though it might be argued that these ideals were ignored and non-existent at times in some places in our history, we at least give lip service to these ideals, and generations of Americans are brought up on these principles and standards.

Americans, quite often, naively judge the actions and policies of foreigners on the basis of our professed ideals. This was no more apparent than in the North of Ireland. The British and the Stormont governments where held up to the prism of American standards, and were found wanting. I sometimes reminded students that the same could be said of clubs and institutions, communities, state governments and national administrations back home, and they would say, "OK, its wrong back there too."

I would think, *Innocence and idealism, the badge of honor of youth. Yet, I couldn't really mock or criticize them for it, for they were on the right track. This was what I had hoped for students when I set up this Irish Studies Program.*

————•◦•————

But I am getting ahead of myself. Let me first of all explain some background to the modern 'Troubles.' Then I'll tell some things about the CIEE conferences I attended in the late 1990s.

HISTORY:
THE MODERN TROUBLES

*T*he post WW II Labor Government of Clement Attlee past educational reform allowed Irish Catholics to qualify for college and university education for the first time in history. The effect was devastating for the Orange government and society in the North of Ireland.

In the 1960s educated Irish youth began the Northern Ireland Civil Rights Association (NICRA) that aimed to end the obvious political and economic discriminations calling for 'one man one vote,' (instead of basing the vote on tax paying), ending gerrymandering, putting a stop to discrimination in hiring for local government employment, fair allocation for housing, repeal of the Special Powers Act and the all Protestant B-Specials. For this challenge to the heavily biased Orange state many Protestants felt NICRA was an IRA front aiming at a united Ireland, which it clearly was not.

The IRA at this time was based in Dublin and had become indoctrinated with leftist leanings focusing on class struggle. In short, the IRA was neither a force in the six counties nor was it interested in the struggle for Irish unity. But some hardcore Loyalists, under the leadership of ex-British servicemen were sure that 1966, the Fiftieth Anniversary of the 1916 Easter Rising, would signal a new IRA offensive in the North.

They resurrected the UVF and decided to make preemptive and provocative strikes to preserve the Protestant six counties. First they sought to assassinate an old IRA man, but failing in their attempt, they decided any Catholic would do, thus initiating a new policy of indiscriminate murder of Catholics. Next *they destroyed some electric facilities, and then blamed Catholics in the hope of putting the RUC and B-men in a fowl mood and on heightened guard for any Catholic Nationalist activity.*

In 1968 the Derry Housing Action Committee planned a march that the NICRA paralleled, and the RUC harassed them, detained and arrested some, and bludgeoned many more, sparking riots in Derry. This was a 'Civil Rights' movement according to the student who began it, but it was labeled an IRA riot according to the RUC and their backers, the Orange order, the Unionist Party, and Reverend Ian Paisley, the unofficial spokesperson for Loyalists.

"Peoples Democracy," a left wing student group calling for civil rights for Catholics and calling for all the NICRA demands as described above sponsored marches in 1969. Loyalist thugs attacked one group outside of Derry City while the RUC stood by and egged them on. One of their members, Bernadette Devlin, was elected to Parliament and in a blistering speech attacked her Parliamentary colleagues who were supposed to represent all people in Ulster, but who in fact stood "for fifty years of neglect, apathy and lack of understanding."

By August of 1969 sectarian riots by Protestant mobs, RUC and B-men led to the infamous "Battle of the Bogside" in Derry. To protect themselves the Nationalists erected barricades, flung petrol bombs from the top of the Rossville Flats, and established "no go areas" for traffic, and proclaimed "Free Derry" in the Catholic Bogside. Rioting soon spread to Belfast, and fires destroy hundreds of houses, especially on Conway Street and half a mile away on Clonard Gardens, Kashmir, Cupar and Bombay streets in the Catholic Clonard area.

Two hundred Protestants came down Percy Street, crossed Divis Street and petrol bombed a Catholic school and some neighboring houses. Saint Peters church next door looked to be next. But three IRA men entered the burning school and held off the sectarian mob with an old Thompson machine-gun and two pistols. This was the only IRA action during the rioting, strictly in defense. The man with the Thompson shot over the rioters heads even though some people called for him to shoot into the crowd.

The future Provisional Commander and leader of the 1980 hunger strike in the Maze, Brendan Hughes watched the three old time IRA men defend his school, church and neighborhood! The modern "Troubles" were on, and the

British Army was sent to the six counties. The Prince of Wales Own Regiment was deployed in Derry, and the Third Battalion of the Light Infantry Regiment went to west Belfast. These were just the first of over thirty years of deployment in the North of Ireland by the British Military.

By 1969 the three major elements for conflict were present in the six counties. First there were the Loyalist paramilitaries, Protestants who fought to retain union with Britain. Next the Republican, at first the 'Official' IRA and then the 'Provisionals,' and the Irish National Socialist Army. Last, the British Army, including the notorious Paratroop Regiment.

The IRA split with the "Officials" retaining their Marxist lean and headquarters in Dublin, and the "Provisionals" taking the lead in the traditional 'defender' role, with their focus in the North. Sinn Fein also split along the same focus lines in 1970.

In 1970 the Loyalist attacks in East Belfast on St. Mathew's Church in the Short Strand and British Army's curfew in the Falls area led to momentous support for Provisional IRA.

The next year, after demands from Unionists, "internment" without trial was introduced. The Ulster Defence Force (UDA) was founded with British Military Intelligence involvement, and competed with the UVF for Loyalist loyalty.

In 1972 "Bloody Sunday" resulted when British Paratroops shot dozens and killed 14 unarmed Civil Rights demonstrators at a Peace Rally in Derry.

The Nationalist community saw significant volunteers flock to the Provisional IRA.

The British Government, in favor of 'direct rule,' prorogued the Stormont Government. Nine people were killed in Belfast during bomb attacks in what became known as "Bloody Friday."

The IRA bombed London in 1973, and the next year Loyalist paramilitaries set off bombs in Dublin and Monaghan in the Republic. There were accusations that the British Military were involved in assisting and planning these bombings.

In 1974 a 'power sharing' government experiment in the North was brought down by a Unionist 'General Strike.' The PIRA and British Army continue their war at a vicious pace. The next year, the British government introduced its "Ulsterization," "Normalization," and "Criminalization" strategy, hoping to return security to the RUC.

In 1976, as Republican prisoners were denied political status they begin their H-block protests at Long Kesh Prison. Accusations of torture by the RUC and prison guards continue, and two years later the European Court of Human Rights found Britain guilty of using degrading and inhumane interrogation techniques. That same year twelve people were killed at the La Mon Hotel by PIRA bombs.

Margaret Thatcher became British Prime Minister in 1979, and Lord Mountbatten and three others, and 18 British soldiers were killed in separate attacks by PIRA as reprisals for "Bloody Sunday."

A 'Blanket Protest' and a 'Dirty Protest' by Republican prisoners at the Long Kesh Prison (also known as the Maze Prison and the H-Blocks) in 1980, over several demands, turned deadly during a second 'Hunger Strike' in 1981 with ten hunger strikers dying during the second strike. Bobby Sands, leader of the 1981 strike was elected as a Member of Parliament on his deathbed. Protests escalated across the North and become ever more violent.

In North Armagh three PIRA men were shot dead in 1982. This attack was the first of many 'shoot-to-kill' incidents that occurred in the county. The next year Gerry Adams was elected Member of Parliament and President of Sinn Fein.

Adams was shot five times in a Belfast attack by Loyalist gunmen. The Conservative Party conference in Brighton, England, was bombed narrowly missing Margaret Thatcher. Adam's said she was lucky to have been missed and would have to remain lucky all the time, whereas the IRA would only have to be lucky once!

Also in 1984 an "Anglo-Irish Agreement" provided the Dublin government a consultative role in the administrative affairs in the North. Loyalists felt betrayed by the British Government.

Brian Nelson, a UDA member and a British agent, went to South Africa to negotiate arms buying. Yet an Anglo-Irish Agreement between the British and Irish governments was signed this same year (1985).

————◆•◆————

Through Father Alec Reid of Clonard monastery, Gerry Adams of Sinn Fein and John Hume of the SDLP met to discuss a way forward towards peace. Although the British Government and the Loyalist political groups refused to openly meet with Sinn Fein, John Hume of the SDLP believed Adams was sincere and was honestly trying to convince the IRA of a political approach alone to end the Troubles.

The British SAS (Special Air Service) killed 8 IRA men and one civilian at Loughgall. Meanwhile the ship Eksund was captured with 150 tons of weapons for the IRA from Lybia in 1987. And a bomb killed eleven civilians in Enniskillen.

In 1988, shortly after the first public meeting between John Hume and Gerry Adams took place, three unarmed IRA volunteers, Mairead Farrell, Dan Mc Cann, and Sean Savage were killed at Gibraltar, victims of the controversial "shoot-to-kill" policy of the British Army. Then at the burial at Milltown Cemetery in Belfast, a Loyalist mad man, Michael Stone, attacked the mourners with a gun and grenades. At the funeral procession of one of Stone's victims, Caoimhin MacBradaigh, members of the funeral cortège killed two British corporals, thought to be provocateurs or at least spies on the procession. Just a year earlier there had been ugly incidents by the authorities at the funeral of Larry Marley.

Even with continued talks between Sinn Fein and the SDLP, and later with the Republic's Fianna Fail, the IRA avenged the 1988 British and Loyalist actions by killing six soldiers in Lisburn and eight more in County Tyrone, and they shot down a British helicopter.

The Loyalists reacted by first killing a prominent Human Rights lawyer who often represented IRA volunteers, Pat Finucan, at his dinner table in front of his family, and the Sinn Fein councilor John Davey. In a turn of events, the UDA-UFF (Ulster Freedom Fighters), released to the public thousands of photos and files, provided to them by the RUC and British Military, of

*Republicans and Nationalists, thus confirming the charge of "collusion"
that Republicans had known for years and had accused the security forces of
sharing with Loyalist murder gangs.*

*In another turn of events, Peter Brooke, the new British Secretary of State
for Northern Ireland, admitted that there was a military stalemate in the
North. The next year, 1990, while speaking in London, he said, "The British
Government has no selfish strategic or economic interests" in the North of
Ireland.*

*The second message of 'good news' coming out of England that year was that
Margaret Thatcher was forced to step down from the leadership of the British
Conservative Party, being replaced by John Major, who also became Prime
Minister. The 'good tidings' merited a Christmas cease-fire by the IRA, the
first in fifteen years.*

*In 1991 the IRA pulled off one of the 'spectaculars' by mortar bombing 10
Downing Street, home of the British Prime Minister in Westminster near
Parliament. But Eddie Fullerton, a Sinn Fein councilor was shot to death in
his home in Donegal.*

*Eddie's son carried on a campaign to have investigations carried out a probe
of the probability that the Loyalist gunmen got help from not only the RUC
but also the Gardai (police) in the Republic of Ireland. Yet there was another
three-day cease-fire at Christmas announced by the IRA.*

*Nineteen ninety two saw cases of multiple killings: eight workers refurbishing
an RUC base were killed by the IRA for their labor. In turn at the Falls
Road Sinn Fein office three were killed in a Loyalist shooting. On the lower
Ormeau Road at a bookie establishment five more Nationalists were gunned
down. But the IRA announced another three day Christmas cease-fire.*

*The following year the IRA told the British Government that to facilitate
peace talks between Sinn Fein and the British Government, they would
suspend military operations. While the British mulled this offer over, Gerry
Adams' home was bombed by Loyalist paramilitaries. After the British rejected
the offer by the IRA to suspend operations, an IRA bomb on the Loyalist
Shankill Road kills nine and the IRA man placing the device. Later, in the*

fall, seven were killed at the Rising Sun bar in County Derry when Loyalists came in wearing Halloween masks and yelling, "Trick or treat."

This same year (1993) the 'Downing Street Declaration' between the leaders of the United Kingdom and the Republic of Ireland, stated categorically that Britain had no selfish, strategic, or economic interest in 'Northern Ireland,' and that the principle of self determination exercised by all the people of Ireland had to be accepted, achieved, and exercised with the agreement and consent of the majority of the people in 'Northern Ireland.'

In 1994 Adams asked John Major for some clarifications on the 'Declaration,' but Major refused. The Irish government provided some clarification, and both Gerry Adams and later Joe Cahill, a prominent IRA leader, were granted visas to the United States amid British protests.

The IRA announced a three-day cease-fire at Easter, and then pulled off another 'spectacular' by mortar attacking London's Heathrow Airport. In County Down the UVF killed six at a bar at Loughinisland.

The British Government finally got around to offer their clarifications on the 'Downing Street Declaration.' The IRA responded with the announcement of a cessation of hostilities. Some time later the Loyalists also called for a cessation of war.

Just as progress seemed to be making headway with cessation of the "armed struggle" on the one hand and "protecting Ulster's British heritage" on the other hand, in early 1995, the British threw a monkey wrench into the public peace discussions between Sinn Fein and London, by raising the issue of "decommissioning" as a precondition to Sinn Fein's involvement in the peace process. The IRA felt that the reward for their cessation of operations was inclusion in talks with the British and progress arising from those talks.

Adams was invited to Washington for a St. Patrick's Day event at the White House with President Clinton, the US government was about to end restrictions on Sinn Fein fund raising in the US. So it was no coincidence that Sir Patrick Mayhew, former British Attorney General and now Secretary of State for Northern Ireland, announced in Washington three conditions for decommissioning and thus allowing Sinn Fein into 'all party talks': the IRA had to "disarm progressively," they had to agree how decommissioning would in practice be carried out, and finally and most controversially, as a "tangible, confidence-building measure," it had to decommission some of its weapons at the start of the talks. This last demand became known as the "Washington Three."

The IRA, Albert Reynolds, former head of the Irish Government, and even Sir Hugh Annesley, Chief Constable of the RUC, said decommissioning was never a precondition in any of the talks leading up to Sinn Fein's inclusion in all party talks. Further, it would be a symbolic "sign of surrender," which was not the case. Also decommissioning had never happened in Irish history (the IRA had "dumped" their weapons after previous conflicts), and it had not been a precondition in 'conflict resolution' in South Africa, the Middle East, or Bosnia. Arms weren't handed over until the final settlement had been reached.

Adams met with Mayhew in Washington for clarification of the "Washington Three," and a Sinn Fein delegation met with President Nelson Mandela in South Africa. The traditional Orange march at Portadown became a confrontation between the RUC and Orange marchers trying to march along the Garvaghy Road that runs through a Nationalist area (to be known as the "siege of Drumcree"). Ian Paisley and the soon to be leader of the Ulster Unionist Party, David Trimble, did a little dance the last few yards down the Garvaghy Road.

With tensions running high, President Clinton, the first US President to do so, visited the North of Ireland. It was decided that there would be a 'twin track' to the all party talks and the issue of decommissioning. As Gerry Adams was later to describe the 'twin tracks' approach, it was "an international body . . . . [with] substantive bilateral and trilateral talks between the parties and the government . . . ." Negotiations on the peace and on decommissioning would happen simultaneously, with the US Senator Mitchell heading a commission on arms decommissioning and Sinn Fein made a concession to the commission on arms.

———•◦•———

COMING 'HOME'
AFTER FOURTEEN YEARS

The CIEE Program had scholars from all across the USA fly into the North of Ireland on a Saturday or Sunday in June. A van was available to bring participants from Belfast International Airport to Coleraine, a University of Ulster town since 1968, and the host to the CIEE Conference. My college had a faculty grant program that instructors could apply for under competitive rules. A committee of teaching faculty and administrators judged the applications and awarded sums of money on the budget submitted along with the application. I had the cost of the airline ticket, the conference room and board, plus a car rental. I worded my proposal in such a way that taking in the conference was only part of my rational.

The other part was to make contacts for establishing our own study program in the North of Ireland. I kept the expected budget costs reasonable as well. I had three years of discretionary money from my department at the college saved for extras.

When I got the grant, I was surprised that my budget was not chopped at all. I received everything I requested. When I added my departmental funds I had more than enough to do everything I wanted to accomplish. The only drawback would be time. I didn't think there would be enough time to fit everything into my schedule.

Participants were put up at a new motel some distance out side of Coleraine. Participants were isolated unless they were strong walkers or had funds to hire a taxi. Because I had work besides the conference, I had rented a car at the airport. I was the only participant to do so; I kept the rented car something of a secret as long as possible since I envisioned becoming the resident taxi to fellow participants.

Neither did I advertise presently my rather extensive knowledge of the North, it's geography, politics, paramilitaries, or security forces. I spent Saturday evening at the hotel in the company of some of my new comrades. I had met two women at Kennedy Airport in New York who were carrying their CIEE Itinerary out in the open. I introduced myself to them. One, from Wisconsin, a librarian at a small college. The other was an attorney from Florida who taught some law classes at a major university there.

After showing the ladies pictures of my attractive Irish born wife and beautiful daughters, they were suitably at ease with me to form an informal low-key clique of pro-Nationalists, sympathetic IRA, Republican supporters.

Sunday morning we found a Catholic church north of Coleraine near Portstewart. So it happened we were also pro-Catholic. We were the "A-typical 'green' Americans come to the North to study the Troubles." As it turned out, about fifteen of the eighteen participants were the same.

After Mass we spent a good part of Sunday driving along the coast as far as Dunluce and the Giants Causeway, before heading back to the motel and the 'Introductory Banquet" where introductions by the University of Ulster staff were made. The introduction of participating members was also given.

Although we had a participant's list, indicating their colleges and universities, subjects taught and topics of interest, it was interesting to put faces to the names and information. Some were from as far west as California, a few from the mid-west like myself, but most from the east, from Boston to Florida.

I was one of two from a community college. I didn't feel any misgivings or prejudice against the two-year community college, and over the next week I quietly and slowly established my expertise on several topics of study, thus enhancing the prestige of some faculty of two-year community colleges. My Queen's University degree stood out, especially with my mid-west American accent. No one, not even my two lady friends, could quite make me out.

I explained that my doctoral interests were officially literary, dealing with legends, myths, and history of medieval and early modern shipping, trade and piracy. My purpose in returning to the North and participating in this program was an extension of my earlier interests to include the twentieth century 'Troubles.'

————————◆•◆••◆————————

Immediately after the introductory banquet, everyone retreated into the bar and lounge to forge friendships and to follow up with discussion and inquiry into each others background, possible acquaintances at schools, and further subjects of interest. My antennas were out and trying to pick up anyone too interested in political backgrounds and personal contacts in the North, contacts that clearly would interest security personnel. Although I was focused on the University of Ulster staff, I was sensitive to my American colleagues as well. I denoted no obvious prying too deeply into anyone's personnel, professional, or private business. It didn't put me at ease, this was the North after all, but it did relax me a little.

I had called Denny in Belfast and announced that the "eagle had landed" and would swoop by Monday evening. He said he'd have the "chicks cooped" before my anticipated arrival. That was a coded message to meet him at a certain pub owned by a Republican over in Andersonstown who raised his own chickens.

Monday morning after breakfast we were driven in university vans to the UU Coleraine campus. The buildings were of a distinct "British modern functional" architectural-type that were plainly "butt-ugly." We went to the Education Department and settled into a conference-seminar room. The windows at the front of the room caused problems with slide shows and overhead presentations. Too much light and glare tired our eyes and dulled the presentations that were actually quite interesting.

The first presenter (Sean Farren) from the SDLP gave us an overview of the Troubles and the search for peace, focusing on he Hume-Adams talks. Although clearly slanted toward a SDLP moderate position, it was palatable and certainly not overtly biased. Participants had read selections from the pre-conference reading list so everyone knew the gist of the Troubles. I had my own bias from actual experiences that I did not intend to share quite yet.

The second talk was about 'Integrated Schools' in the North from a UU professor. He had spent some time in South Africa and clearly understood the logistical problems of integrating schools: in the case of South Africa, racial bias, language difficulties, economic disparages, and fiscal and taxation problems. The speaker drew analogies with the North, and the questions from the seminar participants were decidedly pointed, since we had lived through our own integration of schools in the US.

Of more interest were the questions concerning the teaching of "political science-government," "history," and 'bible-study." Several of my colleagues had parochial school backgrounds and confirmed some differences in what and how periods of US history were covered between our 'public' schools and the 'Catholics' schools. There were differences for sure, but not to the extent that it caused a divide between US students. Parochial schools covered the same events, people, and chronology, but included some religious facets and content as well. Pilgrims and Puritans were covered on the east coast, while Jesuits and Franciscans and their 'missions' were covered in the west and southwest.

Everyone who attended a Catholic school attested to the 'romanticism' of the teaching 'sisters' and 'brothers' about certain aspects of US and North and South American history, but everyone also confirmed that there were no blatant distortions of the truth. The Catholic participants felt they got everything the 'public' school students got, and then some.

The question of 'trust' came up: could Protestants of a strong Loyalist leaning ever trust a 'Catholic' teacher, let alone a 'sister' or 'brother?' Could Republican Catholics ever accept a Protestant teacher? And if not, where would they get a neutral teacher?

Although I was prepared to keep quiet, I felt on education I could say a thing or two and not expose myself too much. I interjected that it was my experience from going to school here for several years, that there were

"Protestant neutrals and Catholic neutrals." Everyone laughed, but the UU staff said that it was by and large true, and they told a joke to that effect that I had heard years earlier.

I also said from my observation, that just as the church membership was a defiant association in all persecuted societies, like Poland, so the schools formed a similar role here. They taught the group's ideals, and those ideals were reflected in the church, school, athletic associations, teams, and sports. It was a symbiotic relationship. Until the institutionalized bias, discrimination, and prejudice were eliminated, at least one segment of the community couldn't and wouldn't support it. Almost everyone nodded agreement.

Everyone wished the Education Department at UU, who seemed to favor these integrated schools, 'good luck' in their endeavors, because they were going to need it.

At the lunch break several people came over to my table to continue the discussion of schools. I sat back and let them take over. I nodded agreement when I agreed and frowned, gritted my teeth and shook my head 'no,' when I seriously questioned something that was said. Only then did I get my two cents worth in.

In the afternoon we were taken to the Coleraine Town Hall, recently repaired from an IRA bombing in the city. We met local council representatives from the neutral Alliance Party, Sinn Fein and the SDLP representing the two wings of Republicanism and Nationalism, and the Ulster Unionist Party. The reception was very nice and the party reps were on their best behavior, friendly not only to us Americans, but as far as possible, to each other.

The group felt that the Alliance Party, largely unheard of prior to our visit, made the most favorable impression with its neutral stand on every issue. Furthermore, the council member was an elderly, well-dressed gentleman who clearly was at his best with the females in our delegation. I tried to speed things along since I was to meet Denny in a few hours and I had a fairly long drive ahead of me.

On the ride back to the motel, no one was interested in eating supper, and they were disappointed in the fact that I would not be able to drive a few round trips to a local pub about a mile and a half away from our lodging.

"Sorry. But I have made arrangements to call on some old friends from my school days here. Unless I get roped into something tomorrow night, maybe I can be of service then."

Some one from the rear of the van suggested, "We are willing to pay."

I retorted, "That goes without saying!" Everyone laughed. The UU Professor driving the van suggested a pub further out from town past our lodging and only about three quarters of a mile away.

"But you must take care. The road is narrow and it has several dips. You might check at the desk and see if they have a torch."

"A torch?"

"A flashlight," I explained.

"Oh, good idea," someone said.

Bad idea I thought. Most of these people couldn't find their ass if they used both hands in broad daylight.

"The people you encounter out there will be local farmers. Good sturdy Ulster stock," our driver said.

"Also remember, you are in the North and Coleraine is a Unionist town so most of the patrons tonight will be Loyalists or possible Orangemen. Be careful what you say. Let them talk. Say, 'Is that so,' and 'I didn't know that,' and 'How nice,' and 'How terrible,' or 'How awful.' Play dumb and live to fight another day," I warned.

The UU Professor driving simply looked over at me in the passenger seat and never said a word. I wondered if he was going to say anything, or warn the group. I hoped so, and thought, *Maybe I just stepped in too soon.*

But his hesitation was the first warning signal that went off in my head. I would pass his name on to Denny for some further scrutiny.

———————•·◆·•———————

It was so good to see Denny that I was beside myself. He was getting grey around the temples and was wearing prescription glasses for reading.

"Boy that's ironical. You wearing glasses. Why don't you grow a beard. Then you'll really look the part," I chided.

"Fuck off. You'll get here too Rudy. You used my stuff as I recall, but you'll have your own sooner that you think," Denny shot back.

"God its good to see you and hear your voice. I know why you never made it into the Kesh, you're too fucken pretty."

"What was it your mother used to say? 'Eat shit, drink gas, step on glass, and die in a fire.' Your mother is a saint, and she had to have adopted a wretch like you. Pretty? Pretty? I'll pretty you Rudy Castle," Denny said with a malicious grin.

"Enough of this sweet talking. What's the craic," I asked? "Can we talk in here?"

"Aye, its clean. Seamus say's his chickens check the place out every other day or so. Some years back the chickens found some listening devices. He swears by his fucken chickens to keep the place clean."

"I hope he goes beyond his chickens."

"Aye, the help take sweeping seriously and sweep the place regularly. If not, a lot of business ends up some where else. Profits are the name of the game. Like back home."

"Aye. I think Clinton is a capitalist and an American Republican at heart. Money, money, money. It's the American way, obsession, and dream."

"Don't get on Clinton, the hush-hush word is that something is in the works with Clinton and Adams. Something big. But its hush-hush."

"I'll believe it when I see it, and I'll be looking for it in the news."

"That's the crux of the problem facing us now Rudy. Some of the men are buying into Adam's initiatives, but others want to drive the Brits and their Loyalist allies into the sea. You know, a military victory.

"Hell, Rudy, I'd like that too, but many of the experienced men are in the Maze, and the new generation is wet behind the ears. So what Adams is doing is giving us time to weather these new boys, give them experience, test them.

"A new split is in the works, from the highest levels on the Army Council down to the local cells. I fear for the Army and the movement, Rudy, so I do."

"Don't they trust Adams?"

"Aye, they do. But it's like he's working on a different level. He's so involved with politics that when he plays it with us guys I don't know if he realizes what he's doing. I mean, he knows he has to play us a bit, but he gets so involved he gets zoned out. Its like he's above us, and no matter how hard he tries to explain things to us, he isn't dumb enough to talk down to us, he's just beyond us. Do you know what I mean Rudy? Am I making sense?"

"Aye, I think so."

"McGuinness from Derry, and he was a hard man, is now working cheek and jowl with him. They seem to be on the same page, and people respect and like McGuinness, and they trust him too, but its Adams who is in the driver's seat.

"Its like he has the map and he explains where we are going, but he just points to the new location. We see the straight way to the objective, but he says, 'no, not that way.' He seems to tell us what not to do instead of telling us precisely what to do. All he wants us to do is follow him. Its not enough.

"I understand some in the Army wouldn't take a command from him. Hell, they might not take a direct order they disagreed with from the Army Council either, but Adams wants to build 'consensus.' Consensus, most everybody on board, you know? But some of the boys are stubborn. They want victory through action.

"No matter how much Adams talks to them, explains things, spells things out for them, he's not telling all. You can feel it. What he says would and should convince most people, but some of the boys need more than convincing."

"So what you are saying is that you feel Adams is holding something back and some of the Army doesn't want to hold back," I offered.

"Exactly. Its not that they don't trust him, they want to, they really want do."

"Once again, they want more, and for whatever reason he can't give them more, and apparently he doesn't want more war. Maybe he doesn't know what's in store. Maybe he simply trusts in himself to be able to figure it all out when the time comes. So we are back to 'trust Adams,'" I offered.

"But they don't want a dictator, Rudy. If you are right, and he thinks he's the one to figure out what has to happen when it happens and no one else seems to be able or willing to see the whole picture or whatever, it makes him a dictator, doesn't it?"

"If we are on to something here, I'm sure he's very much aware of this predicament too. I'm sure this is part of what ails the man. He clearly is the leader and he isn't denying that others might see what he sees coming, but he's the leader. He can't simply wait for consensus and then proceed. Michael Collins didn't run the IRA that way. He was the leader, he had to answer to De Valera, the provisional government and later the Dail. And it killed him.

"I think Adams sees himself in the same sort of mess. Things happen so fast that he can't afford to let time pass for consensus. He needs flexibility, authority, and freedom of movement, because timing is important. He can't dilly dally. Time is of the essence.

"Some personalities couldn't let Collins rule with a free hand, let him become a dictator. It led to civil war. I think Adams is trying to avoid the same thing. His plan rests on his ability and talents to resolve problems quickly and correctly, authoratively, not dictatorially. He doesn't want to be a dictator. But he is the authority. That's not pride, it's honesty. He knows it's not the best way according to modern convention, but it's the only way now and in the foreseeable future."

I had no intention to go off on such a tangent, but there it was, strictly my point of view. "Denny, let's not publicize my views, OK?"

He nodded consent. Denny and I just sat there for a while and neither of said anything. What more could we say. We ordered another round of sparkling water.

———◆•◆•◆———

Denny said what was in store for me was to visit people in Chicago, Milwaukee, St. Louis, Detroit and Cleveland. "We need to get a read on them, and to try to convince them if necessary to stay with Sinn Fein and the present IRA. No splits, no divisions, no civil war," Denny explained.

"The CIEE group is coming over to Belfast to visit Carrickfergus, Belfast City Hall, and Stormont on Wednesday." I said that I would drive separately and I would meet up with him after the days work.

The next day, Tuesday, we went to the Magee Campus of UU in Derry. Derry was like a fortified British Army camp. Down along the River Foyle as you turned once over the bridge and circled in back of the Guild Hall, a vacant lot with a fence around the parameter contained a small army of men dressed to kill and armored vehicles set to go. I just caught a glimpse of them as we rode by and the gate opened to let a Saracen armored troop carrier out.

The highlight of the day was meeting and listening to John Hume. His presence radiated a busy but tired confidence. Everyone felt exhausted after his talk. Not that he was tedious or overwhelming, but you could tell that he had spent his life trying to end the Troubles and work out from under the Troubles, and he was carrying everyone he could with him. Amid all his commitment and confidence, he simply looked worn out.

Everyone had great respect for him and the Herculean effort he had expended over the years. But deep down you had the feeling that it wasn't so much events that were passing him by, but rather a new personality was making his way to center stage. It wasn't jealousy that was settling in, rather realization that he was moving off center stage. After all the years he had given to ending the Troubles and establishing a real democratic state in the North of Ireland, he was no longer 'the' man. He was one of the key players, and although his prestige was still there, a new player was forging an identity that borrowed the best of what John Hume's stood for. Adams packaged it in a new political form that was eroding the political expression Hume had developed over the years.

Whereas Hume had been the genuine voice and face of moderate Nationalism for years, now he had given of late the mantel of legitimacy to a rival in the Nationalist community. And this rival benefited from Hume's association with him and clearly he was becoming the popular expression of Nationalism, Republicanism, and legitimacy in the North.

Gerry Adams was not so much a rival as a replacement, although politically, the SDLP that Hume had helped create would be replaced by Sinn Fein as the Nationalist party in the North. Politics made for rivalry, but the personal contact between the two men ruled out rivalry in the usual sense.

Hume's time was passed and Adams' time was not only present, but he anticipated what was to come. Just as Hume knew how to present the civilized face of the civil rights movement, an achievement that was monumental, so Adams now personified the next step of fighting the system and, at the same time, of participating in the system that had for so long excluded Nationalists and persecuted them, and at the same time promising to transform it into a New Ireland.

John Hume was not bitter or jealous, maybe disappointed, but certainly he was aware that he was being edged off to the side. He was man enough to realize that it was not Adams' intent to have this done to him, but the British, the Republic to the south, the Americans, and last but not least, the electorate in the North had unconsciously and without malice done it to him.

The times had caught up with him and passed him by. He now spoke to his fading party, his dwindling friends in America, and groups visiting the North. He collected honorary degrees and reaped praise for what he stood for during the dark days of the early modern Troubles. But a new dawn had broken and he was the respected man of the past. But as John Hume knew, the future harkened another.

I don't recall whom the other speakers were that day, John Hume and the presence of the British Army in the City loomed so large. As we drove back to Coleraine there was little conversation. A hush of respect permeated the van. We had been in the presence of greatness; our esteem for Hume had drained us of energy, even to talk.

That evening we were taken up to Port Rush for a meal at a very good restaurant. It was there that the banter, laughter, and humor returned. It was a light evening after a ponderous day.

———•◦◆◦•———

MAKING NEW FRIENDS

The next day, after a relatively early departure, we visited Carrickfergus Castle and the bank across the road from the entrance. In Belfast we had a tour of the City Hall. We saw the 'Table' where the 'Solemn Covenant' was signed by Loyal Unionists in 1912 to defy the Home Rule legislation pending in Parliament. We also met the Lord Mayor and the group received a plaque of the city Coat of Arms.

Then we made for Stormont. I was in my rented auto so I missed any talk, questions, and answers during the drive. That was too bad because I enjoyed listening to the informal banter in the van on occasions I was along.

After the security formalities we were given a brief tour of certain sections of the building. We were ushered into a conference room and were addressed by two Ulster Unionists. They identified three key issues their party faced: how difficult it was for them to deal with "murderers and criminals" of Sinn Fein who wanted access to the political arena, the pressure from the British government that always seemed to make deals with the Republicans behind the Loyalists' back, and how they had to face the expectations of their Unionist constituents. No one in our seminar group felt much sympathy for the men.

The question that received the greatest rise from the Unionists was, "Is it really that you are disgusted at having to deal with former 'rebels,' or is it that you will have to deal with Sinn Fein as a legitimate political party?"

One of the Unionists said, "They are one and the same. The IRA and Sinn Fein are two sides of the same coin. When IRA men get too old to reek havoc, murder and mayhem, they become Sinners."

One of my colleagues responded, "But the question remains, are you prepared to deal with Sinn Fein as a legitimate Nationalist party?"

Making a pun on the nickname of members of Sinn Fein, Sinners, pronounced "Schiners," one Unionist answered, "Hardly. Sinners are sinners, why would we deal with them?"

I couldn't contain myself. "But in South Africa and else where, former rebels sat down with the men they opposed to begin a peaceful transition to a new state. Many of our Founding Fathers were active rebels and they forged a peace with Britain at Paris and established a leading power in the world today. Yesterday's rebels often become today's statesmen and political leaders. I suspect that some Sinners feel that some Unionists have blood on the conscience if not hands. But they are ready to sit down and do business."

"I think you are naïve and simplistic," one countered.

"You may think so, but that is how the rest of the world works, and I suspect your future will work that way also," I responded with a grin. "So get ready."

After a lunch in the basement cafeteria, we returned and met with the SDLP leader, Seamus Mallon, who was much easier to listen to and, at times, much more realistic.

In the late afternoon I left Stormont, driving past the "grotesque statue" of Edward Carson, the "intransigent advocate of the continuance of Union," according to the *Blue Guide Ireland*. His statue has him standing there defiantly, legs apart, looking down the mile long avenue to the official guard hut at the entry off Newtownards Road. His right arm is stretched out, and his hand is gesturing as if beckoning his fellow Unionists to come, for this is their place, their building, their government.

If he was making a signal of triumph to his Loyalist followers, the index and middle fingers are extended somewhat, seeming to indicate at the same time the sign in the North of Ireland for "fuck you;" no doubt clearly directed at Nationalists and Republicans. Could the editor of the *Blue Guide* have had the same thought, he described the statue as "grotesque?" I would like to think so.

As I passed in front of the statue I raised my middle finger to return his salute, in the American tradition, for "fuck you Carson and all you stand for," before I headed down the "The Prince of Wales Avenue," that broad avenue that had to be such an unwelcoming approach for non-Unionists!

When I caught up with Denny he was waiting for me outside the "Felon's Club," and he had invited a guest along. I recognized Danny Morrison immediately. We had met years earlier and I had always admired his work.

"Danny, how are you doing?"

"Well enough. And how are you doing? Denny here tells me you have been busy back home with the family. Two girls is it? Nice."

Lowering his voice to a whisper he said, "Our regards to your brother-in-law. Give Danny our best. Rumor has it someone like yourself rescued him from some Orangies in Canada. Good on you, if it was you who done it Rudy."

The smile on his face and twinkle in his eye left no doubt in my mind he knew perfectly well who had done it. But he was the information manager of Sinn Fein for good reason. He could keep secrets.

"Well, credit for that sort of thing brings laurels on your head and a bullet between your eyes," I said with a smirk. "I'm just glad it was done and that he is safe and sound as we speak."

"True enough. That's why it's only you and a very few who know that rumor about you two, if indeed it was you. We certainly do not want anything to happen to you, or Danny Conlon."

At this point Denny put his two pence in and said, "Jaysus, I have my hands full trying to keep these two out of trouble on both sides of the pond. It's a full time job."

"I haven't been here for more than a dozen years and look how old he looks now. I'll have to stir up some trouble to get him active again, loosen him up, get the cobwebs out. But it will take coloring to get the gray out of his hair," I teased.

"Fuck the coloring, I hear they're watering down the Guinness here. The Felon's Club is chiseling felons. What's the world coming to," Denny barked.

"On a more serious note," Morrison said, "you will make the rounds for us there in the mid-west to get a read and to stick up for what we are doing?"

"Aye, I will. The last thing we need is a division getting out of control. I remember the split back in the '70s. Bad shit all around," I offered.

"Amen to that. I've got some literature for you to read before you call on the supporters. I've some other material here you can look at and then leave with the groups you see.

"Denny here told me about your analysis of Adam's role in the fracas. I think you were spot on, and you put it all very well," Danny said as I gave Denny a cold stare and exhaled in disgust.

"Rudy, now before you get upset with me, what you said about Adams and the obvious problems was brilliant. No one could have put it better. When I saw Danny here, I told him some of what you said. He thought maybe you were spot on. We need all the help we can muster to get us by this mess in tact. So I told Danny here."

"Rudy, don't be sore at Denny. What he just said is the truth. You seem to have a better insight into the problem than those of us within arms length of the mess. And personalities bruise easily, as you know.

"Obviously I won't be able to come out and say a lot of what you said, but I can pass it along to Gerry and a few others who can use it, and I'll spin some of it to help the cause."

"Look, I'm no mind reader. All I'm saying is that it seems to me that Adams seemed way ahead of almost most everyone else, even in the party. And those who could keep up, often find it difficult to sort out the wealth of ideas, impressions, objectives, obstacles, tactics and strategies.

"Adams, it seems to me, can articulate and pursue what others sense at best. He is the leader. He can distill the essential from the dispensable and he can then formulate the essence of what will become a new policy, tactic, or plan more accurately and precisely than almost anyone else. It's almost a curse to have that talent or gift. We sure as hell don't want him to stop using his natural talents. He proves time and again to be the natural born leader."

Danny and Denny looked at each other again; they both gave a wee laugh before Danny said, "How long can you stay here. I've got a job for you."

"I'm going home Saturday as Denny knows full well."

"I know, I'm kidding you. But we do need your help over there, in mid-America."

"You've got it as I said."

Danny left shortly thereafter. Denny sat nursing a soft drink.

"What's with the Guinness joke, we all know you only drink soft drinks or water?"

"Smoke and mirrors, Rudy, never let anyone except the closest see the real you," Denny said cryptically.

"Are you trying to tell me something?"

"Nooo, no. Nothing at all. Just making light, that's all."

"I liked it better when you wore that fake beard and fake glasses to make light," I said.

"When I wore my disguise I was not making light. That was serious business. It was all business," Denny said, but then broke out in a laugh. "How do you put it Rudy, 'serious shit?'"

"That's it, Denny, 'serious shit.' No shite about it," I said the last bit in my best Belfast accent. We both laughed and spent the next hour talking.

Denny said in a very low voice, "Hopefully, Rudy, you won't have to kill anybody this time."

"I didn't plan on it the last time."

"Danny Conlon filled me in on what happened in Canada. He says you saved his life. Aye, its all hush—hush, but some know Rudy. They know a lot of what you've done. You are a legend."

"Fuck that legend shit. You nip that talk in the bud, Denny. It could get me killed and make more trouble for my family. I don't relish having to hunt down dip-fucks because they have threatened me and my family and friends. 'Loose lips,' and all that crap."

"Rudy, I've told two at the most. They promised to protect you by keeping quiet. But others have heard things. Added up the cards and came up aces. They aren't blind, Rudy."

"Aye, and if they aren't blind neither are the Brits. That means I'm in trouble then."

<hr />

Thursday morning we had two speakers at the UU Coleraine campus. The first was a sociologist from the university presenting the social chaos related to he Troubles. Obviously, deaths and maiming headed the list. But teenage delinquency, the rise in drugs, often sold by Loyalist paramilitaries to finance the war, in Unionist neighborhoods, punishment shootings and killings by the IRA for drug dealing in Nationalist communities, domestic violence, psychological problems because of paramilitary involvement, including destruction of autos, houses, Orange Halls, Catholic Churches, and businesses.

The second speaker was a Methodist minister who addressed the spiritual crises caused by the Troubles.

Clergy had to bury and counsel church members, comfort survivors and try to caution against obvious sectarian slurs and outbursts.

After lunch the participants were taken up to the Giants Causeway. We made a stop at Dunluce Castle, and I had all I could do not to follow a path down to the waters edge, to look at the cave I knew so well from years before. We ate that evening in Portrush up on the coast. A couple of participants were leaving on Friday so it was their swansong.

The farewells continued at the motel bar. I called it a night about midnight, but I heard the party lasted a couple of hours later.

Friday saw a RUC publicity officer address us. He sang the praise of the police in the North. He cited the number of those murdered, wounded, injured and threatened. During "Questions and Answers," I waited for someone to bring up some of the embarrassing points associated with the RUC.

When they were not forthcoming, I cautiously put my hand up. "Yes sir," he called.

"I have friends back home that are police officers, and I have nothing but respect for them. They enforce the laws evenly. They also obey the laws that are clearly defined by procedural rules.

"The European Court has been pretty consistent in its condemnation of investigation procedures, interrogation procedures, incarceration procedures, let alone the practices directed against prisoners, especially

Republican prisoners incarcerated here, especially in Armagh Goal and Long Kesh Prison. Could you address these charges fairly?

"Second, could you say something about the use of rubber bullets? Something besides the fact that they are made in the US. We also make cigarettes, guns and nuclear weapons. We know we make some bad stuff, but why do you buy them and then use them on citizens? Many victims seem to be children."

My colleagues held their collective breathes. The UU professors and staff sat perfectly still. The RUC man was uncomfortable, but professional.

"Well, actually, some of the cases before the European court were everturned."

"Would that be an example of big country versus no country?" I asked. "Britain against 'rebels?'"

He was clearly rattled. My philosophy since eighth grade football was, if he's down, keep him there.

"Do you really think the five interrogation techniques that are applied by the security folks here in the North are legal? Do you think they are moral? When this thing finally comes to an end do you think some people will have a list of people to get even with?"

The UU senior professor stepped in at this point and said, "This seems to be getting too personal and beyond the scope of Officer Mac George's brief."

I interrupted, "I don't see how my question is any more personal than the torture the RUC and others subject Republicans to while under incarceration. Hell, torture is torture is torture, to borrow a theme from the Iron Lady. When a person from a neighboring street, neighborhood, or a cross-town neighbor is doing the nasty to you, that's personal.

I for one would want to confront the son of a bitch the first chance I got.

"In the former Soviet Union, there are reports of just this sort of thing happening between gulag survivors and KGB and prison guard personal. The latter are being killed pretty regularly. Because the RUC is British, not Russian, do you think that will make a difference? I don't think so. I suspect a day of reckoning is coming. Even if you move, I suspect they will find you. This is a small place."

Officer Mac George was clearly upset. Professor Rich from UU Coleraine was pissed, but he didn't know what to do about it. He announced it was lunchtime, thus ending the question session. I held back to talk to Mac George.

Neither Rich nor Mac George was pleased to see me loiter after the end of the session, but they were at a loss at how to avoid me. I positioned myself at the door of the room, and they had to go through me to exit.

"Officer Mac George, I didn't intend to insult you, but the comments and questions I raised are the same that are mentioned in American news media, Irish organizations, and by common citizens.

"When I was a student here, at Queen's, nearly twenty years ago, students from both Unionist and Nationalist communities were concerned about violations of civil liberties and civil rights. Further, many from Protestant backgrounds acknowledged the sectarian nature of Northern Irelands governments, economics (hiring practices in particular), trials and arrests. They admitted wrongs and they were more than embarrassed, they were ashamed.

"I have acquaintances here in the North, from both communities, and I know they continue to be concerned over these issues and the potential backlash by Republicans when the inevitable change comes in government, society and the police force. It has slowly been changing dramatically over the past twenty years, and there is no reason to expect that to change. Gerry Adams has been consistent and adamant in his insistence that no reprisals are on Sinn Fein's and the IRA's agenda, but it will be difficult to restrain rogue individuals, don't you agree?

"What has happened in the former Soviet Union, Eastern Bloc, even South Africa, are examples of this and a warning. It is said that admission of such offences is the first step in reconciliation. Both individuals and institutions will be expected to come forth and offer acknowledgement followed by some form of apology. Don't you agree?"

I kept firing my observations in quick order, ending with short answer questions. Both men were uncomfortable. They both squirmed at having to answer.

"Back home, we are still wrestling with the discrimination directed at 'Black Americans' for generations. The divisions between the races unfortunately continues, in part because of refusal to acknowledge many injustices committed, and the expectations of acknowledgement and compensation.

'Affirmative action' has been one way to address our problems, but it has raised issues of its own. Overcoming past injustice is not easy. I just wanted your take on it, perhaps personally and speaking for the RUC," I said in a sympathetic and contrite tone.

Both men seemed relieved, and Mac George finally said hesitatingly, "My colleagues in the RUC are concerned about revenge killings of both prison guards and police. Some just call for harsh retaliation, others are reconciled to follow what you described as happening in the States. Their personal safety and that of their families is paramount. Admission of guilt will be difficult."

I responded, "Exactly. In a state like Northern Ireland, like that of South Africa, a certain culture existed that put the stick in the hands of the authority and condoned the use of force to maintain the status quo. Might meant right. When I first came here the RUC uniforms were virtually the same as those of police in South Africa. The use of violence on unarmed civilians looked the same too.

"The color of your skin made the 'enemy' obvious in South Africa. The color of your skin in the North of Ireland was your religion. Racially it was a bit more difficult to spot the 'enemy,' but there were those who claimed you could tell a 'taig' by certain physical traits. But there were other ways: names and schools attended, right?"

"I would like to think those days are behind us. Loyalist communities and mobs are as violent to us as Nationalist ones now. We are on our own, mutually despised by all sides," Mac George explained.

"Aye, and the British, the news media, and the Nationalist politicians of the SDLP and now Sinn Fein have made that a reality. You are caught in the middle. Do you see a way out?" I asked.

"No," was his answer. "The IRA have not gone away as Adams said. And we in the Loyalist community do not feel we can take his word of no reprisals as Gospel. There are too many guns out there and Adams cannot control the individual with a grudge. He can't guarantee 'no revenge'."

"Well, he is preaching that message, and the IRA has policed its community and organization pretty harshly for 'breaking the law,' so maybe he is willing to enforce it. Granted, it will be reactionary; it will kick in after a reprisal. But if the punishment is severe enough, maybe it will serve as a deterrent.

"Of course, turning over to the courts, now, individuals who exceeded their legal brief in mishandling prisoners would go a long way to defuse the issue. But that probably isn't going to happen. But it would be the correct thing to do, legally and morally, and it would help calm the waters," I added.

Mac George responded weakly, "I can only hope that both sides decommission their weapons and reign in their members."

"The IRA have committed to that scenario, but it remains to be seen if the Loyalist paramilitaries do too. I doubt if the British Military will abide by the legal and moral imperative. They never have in the past. As Churchill said, 'The victors write the histories.' Although they are not the victors they tell themselves they are. They believe they are. Their politicians tell them they won. When you live on an island, so insulated, isolated, so ignorant of reality, anything is possible, even 'victory' when there is none.

"I am encouraged that you didn't deny the wrongdoings to prisoners. Nor did you say that you were just following orders. That is a step in the right direction, as far as it goes. I also noticed you didn't agree or commit to having the RUC and its members face charges, stand trial, and go to prison. That is a shame. So I'll say it on behalf of the Irish, American, and other people, 'Shame on the RUC, and you Officer Mac George as their spokesman'."

In the back of my mind I thought, *You didn't deny it; you didn't say you were just following orders, but I wouldn't be surprised if you documented some of it by filming it like the Nazis.*

Again Rich was upset. He broke in and with disgust said, "Mac George has to get back to work. I wish to thank you Mr. Castle for your insights."

At that he led Mac George past me and down the hall. I followed them to Rich's office. They had entered and closed the door. I suspected Rich was turning over to officer Mac George my application and curriculum files as I passed by the office.

Leaving the country could be interesting, I thought. *If I come home with bumps and bruises the way I did the last time, Barbrie won't let me come back. I just couldn't let any interrogation come to that.*

I would pass on Mac George's name to Denny. He already had Rich's name and now he would have some homework to do while I was back home.

I was satisfied with the encounter. Mac George heard from an American, without an Irish sounding name, bring up some very uncomfortable issues that I hoped he talked to his associates about. I also hoped these same issues would keep him and his buddies up at night.

———•◦•◦•———

The Friday afternoon session featured a well-known professor of Politics from Queen's University who went over the possible forms a new government could look like in the North once all the issues were settled, like cessation of military action, decommissioning of arms, and prisoner releases.

He was interesting, but it was a waste of time. That sort of speculation was worthless, at a time when the British were demanding decommissioning as a precondition to inclusion on talks, when that had never been demanded before by any peace negotiators in other conflicts in the 20th century. Nor had it been a precondition in the current talks in Ireland. That was THE issue, and discussions on that issue needed to be held. But, the well-known professor of Politics, as well as the British ignored it. They seemed to live in la-la-land.

———•◦•———

Mac George called Special Branch when he returned to his office. He hadn't stopped for lunch. The American, Castle, Rudy Castle, certainly was an obnoxious inquisitor. He deserved a dose of his own medicine. If he had been here before, and had been as big an arse then as he was today, Special Branch was sure to have a file on him and just might be interested in raking him over the coals.

"Mac George from Coleraine RUC here. Could I speak to someone about an old suspect?"

"A suspect in what case?"

"No case in particular. I had a run-in with an American at a conference at UU Coleraine. He really went off on me about how the IRA was up to revenge killings, etc. He was here about twenty years ago and at least once or twice since then. I suspect a real agitator. Just want to pass this latest incident along to the right party, that's all."

"Hold on, I'll see."

After a pause some one came on the line and said, "OK, you have some information about an old case?"

"Hello. My name is Mac George, Coleraine RUC. I had a confrontation with an American this morning who referred to revenge killings by the IRA on security personnel. He spoke as if he knew something. I was not in a position to question him thoroughly. He was at a conference in Coleraine and possibly leaves for home this weekend. We can check.

"I thought Special Branch should be informed about him and his comments. His name is Rudy Castle. He has been coming here to Northern Ireland, off and on, for about twenty years. He has obviously gotten to know some Republicans in that time. He seemed pretty informed about the situation here."

"Castle, huh. Rudy Castle. I'll pass it along, thanks for the information, Mac George, right?"

"Yes, that's it."

"Give me your number in the event we need some more information. We will also let you know if we intend to pursue this matter of Castle."

The section chief smiled. *Castle*, he thought. *Right back to his old tricks and he's back in Northern Ireland.* He didn't need to pass this information along to someone higher up. He was higher and further up the chain of command than most in the North. The call was his.

ACTING UP AND ACTING OUT

On Saturday the UU staff had arranged for a visit to Bushmills Distillery for anyone sticking around until Sunday before flying out. I had a Saturday flight, but I left early Saturday morning to pick up Denny in Belfast and to head for South Armagh. There was a new youth center in Mullaghbane, which might be perfect for my college group to stay at when our program was up and running.

We met up with some old friends from Crossmaglen and Camlough. They showed us the location of the Ti Cuchulainn Center. It was going to be perfect when we arrived. I took pictures, met some of the board members of the center, and checked the location as to ease of traveling here and there. I was told it would be a pleasure to host foreign guests. I said we would be ready in about a year or two.

The drive back to Belfast afforded some time for Denny and I to talk shop. "Rich is the professor and Mac George is the RUC Public Relations Liaison. Anything about them would be interesting. Rich spent time in Africa, South Africa I think. He's interested in 'integrated schools' and the 'Peace Process' down there. He's trying to implement what he observed there up here. Mac George nothing."

"You know they are going to be waiting for you? So what is the plan, Rudy?"

"I'm not going to cooperate with them. They'll want to know who I consorted with and where on my free time. I'll not tell them. I suspect they'll threaten me with all kinds of things. I'm not due back to teach

until next Wednesday, so I have some time, and for what I have planned
I'll need it.

"You've got the name of a good lawyer for me, because police brutality
must be reported and prosecuted."

"Aye, a lawyer friend of the late Pat Finucane. He'll serve you well. Just
don't get too carried away, Rudy."

"Me? Carried away. Never. But after the circus, it will be the greatest show
on earth. I'm also thinking of Barbrie and the children. They come first."

I dropped off Denny on the outskirts of Belfast where a friend in a taxi
was waiting for him. We said our 'good-byes' and he said, "Safe home
Rudy. My best to everyone."

———————◆•◆•◆———————

On Friday afternoon Mc Gregor sat in his office and mulled over the
notes his man had taken from the Coleraine RUC. He also flipped
through the folder, the official confidential folder, on one Rudy Castle.

He slowly read the information and analysis collected over the years. Then
he put the folder down, tilted back in his chair and began to process the
information.

*Castle first came here in the late sixties and eventually got into Queen's,
sticking around for a degree, and a doctorate at that. He studied myth,
legends, history and literature.*

*More importantly, he married Barbrie Conlon, a school teacher and sister of
Danny Conlon, wanted IRA sniper extra ordinare.*

*An agent kept notes on him at the time, feeling at the time that he was up
to no good. Nothing specific. Before anything was established, the agent was
killed.*

*Castle returned to the US with his wife. Nothing in the notes linking him
specifically to Danny Conlon.*

But a few years later, Castle returns with his family in tow for a visit to Belfast. Made contact at Queen's with an old mentor now colleague, Professor Smyth, a some-time practicing Roman Catholic. Came to the religion through his wife, "a somewhat" devout Roman Catholic.

I wonder who wrote this report on Smyth? What the hell does "somewhat devout" mean? Dedicated? Excessively pious? Fanatical? An enthusiastic supporter of Nationalistic causes? A fervent supporter of Republicanism? A zealot IRA supporter?

I doubt that Castle's Smyth is any relation to Reverend Martin Smyth, the Grand Master of the Orange Order. Wouldn't it be ironic if the two Smyths were related?

Smyth and Castle made arrangements to do some archeological work up along the coast again related to his studies somehow. All the equipment he sent over was stolen from Queen's, not once but twice. SP contacted him about his brother-in-law and he tells the boys to 'fuck off.'

He comes back to Ulster, has a run in with one of our 'eyes' in the field he remembered from his first stay, and accuses him of being a 'tout.' Our people arrest Castle, rough him up a bit, but he is saved by an active British Army Colonel by the name of Summerville. Castle had somehow worked with and for him early on. British military, but not us. Hmmm.

After Castle leaves in 1981, or about the time he leaves, the three SB people involved in Castle's arrest and case are killed. Professionally shot. The report says that Castle could not have been the shooter.

It sounds to me more like Danny Conlon; he certainly could have been the shooter.

As interesting, our agent provocateur is run over by a bus here in Belfast. He is run over by a bus! So everyone involved with Castle's arrest are killed. Coincidence? My asrse!

Castle has been home for fifteen years or so and now he is back. Again he is stirring the pot.

I'll call UU at Coleraine and see if they have information on Mr. Castle's departure from Ulster. He deserves a special send-off, so he does.

Mc Gregor telephoned Mac George and informed him that they decided to have a go at Castle at the airport before he left for the US Saturday at 13:05.

"We will have some local RUC people there. If you want to join us you are welcome."

"No thank you. I would enjoy seeing the look on Castle's face seeing me, but I don't want to compromise my position as Public Relations liaisons with visitors to Ulster. I also enjoy my work with the University of Ulster. I don't want to jeopardize it. But thanks for the invitation. Maybe you could let me know what happens."

"Yes, we'll see."

———————◆◆◆———————

I got to Belfast's airport with some time to spare. I turned in the car, headed over to the ticket counter. I presented everything, turned in my luggage, and headed for security. I saw them waiting for me.

The Airport security checked my ticket, boarding pass, and passport, and then the fun began. They had an hour to fuck with me before my flight. Two RUC men joined us, and then two Special Branch men. I had six goons all total. They took me into a side room where they frisked me. They discussed, for my benefit, the possibility of a strip search, including a cavity probe. It was meant to intimidate me I was sure. "Sounds like a gang date," I said flippantly.

"Mr. Castle, you were at a conference up in Coleraine, correct?"

"Correct."

"But you rented a car, why?"

"Why not?"

"Why did you rent the car?"

"I needed to do some personal travel."

"Going where? Doing what?"

"Nothing illegal, meeting no fugitives either."

"Where?"

"Belfast."

"Who did you meet?"

"Just people that I knew from the time I was a student here years ago."

"Who?"

"I'll not tell you. You will hassle them, probably intimidate them, falsely accuse them of subversive activities, and God knows what else."

"Names, Mr. Castle."

"No."

"This lack of cooperation is in violation of the Prevention of Terrorism Act. This is serious."

"For meeting old friends? Your accusations are a violation of my rights, for your accusations are groundless."

"Your lack of cooperation suggests subversive activity."

"Charge me."

"Look, Mr. Castle, we don't want this to be any more of a an inconvenience that it has to be. Just cooperate."

"I cooperated with your system since I landed here. I bought items, like gas, and paid the taxes. I rented a car and paid the taxes. I bought food and paid the taxes. I drove the speed limit, obeyed the traffic laws, and stayed on the wrong side of the road, cooperating all the time. I've cooperated. Now you are hassling me for some unknown or personnel reason."

"We want you to identify whom it was that you met in Belfast. That's all."

"No."

"You are making this difficult, Mr. Castle."

"When I was here the last time I was wrongly accused of wrongdoing. I had to call on a certain British Army Colonel. He said if need be I could call on him again. May I make a call?"

"Why won't you cooperate?"

"I told you, I have cooperated with your laws for a week. Now can I call my Colonel friend?"

"Give us one name. Just one name."

"Besides Colonel Summerville, no."

"What you are doing is illegal."

"Look, why don't you beat me up. Then you can say you won. You beat up a tourist. You pounded a foreign conference member. You will have appeared to have won."

"It's not winning, it's a name that we want. Just one name."

"No. Beat me. You'll appear to have won. Pretend I'm Irish. Beat me like I'm Irish, pretend you are winning. That will help your image, it will help your self-esteem, and you'll probably get a promotion. That's how it works here in the North of Ireland, right?"

He smiled and sighed, "Just cooperate, one name, Mr. Castle. One name."

"Turn off the camera and the microphones and have the rest of the posse leave us alone. I promise I won't hurt you," I said with a wolfish grin.

After some hesitation, the headman told the rest of them to leave and to have the camera turned off. About thirty seconds later the red light went off on the camera up in the corner of the room.

In an aggravated voice, just in case the mikes were still on, I yelled, "Don't! Don't do it. Stop."

I immediately smashed my face into the table, nearly knocking myself out. Before he could stop me I threw myself backward into the door handle cutting the back of my head. I was bleeding from my face down the front of my shirt. I was crumpled in front of the door so his buddies had trouble getting back in the room. I faked being unconscious.

"What did you do?" one of them asked their boss.

"I didn't do anything. He did it to himself."

After several seconds of silence, another one said, "He's really bleeding bad. We need to get him help."

"This isn't going to look good," another one said.

"He did this to himself?" another asked incredulously.

"I told you he did. He just slammed himself into the table and then back into the door."

"He's bleeding from the back of his head," someone said.

I "came to" in the hands of a couple of paramedics. They said I had a couple of nasty cuts and bruises, but that I would live.

"I've got to catch my plane back home."

"Not today you won't. Where is home Mr. Castle?"

"The US."

"Can you be more specific?"

"Aye, I can, but why do you want to know. The police did this to me because I wouldn't be more specific. They accused me of not cooperating because I wouldn't tell them who I talked with.

"I was at a conference up at Coleraine, and I'd come to Belfast to contact a few old mates from student days fifteen or twenty years ago. And this is my souvenir. What the hell is going on up here in the North of Ireland?"

"Stay calm Mr. Castle."

Turning to the RUC men standing nearby, the paramedic said, "He probably needs a stitch or two in the back of his head. We'll have to take him in."

One of the goons rode in the back of the emergency vehicle with the paramedic and myself. Back in Belfast, I was stitched up while a crowd of RUC and Special Branch men stood about mumbling to one another.

I asked if I could use the phone. An RUC officer came over and asked whom I was going to call.

"First my wife to tell her I've been delayed by your people. Next a local lawyer."

He turned to the rest of his colleagues while motioning for the hospital orderly to keep me where I was and **not** to provide me with a phone.

After some time passed an older plain-clothes man came over to me. In true Hollywood style I flinched, winced, and held up both hands as if to ward off an assault.

"Please Mr. Castle, no more dramatics. There has been a gross misunderstanding here. We will see that you call you wife to explain that you will be a day late. We will put you up for the night at the Europa Hotel and we will see that you are brought back out to the airport for your flight tomorrow."

With that he turned to leave. I said, "Hold it. I want to talk to a lawyer."

Returning to me he said curtly, "That won't be necessary."

"Like hell it won't," I shot back. "I can wait until I'm at the hotel, or will you block my calls? What kind of country are you running here? I thought the Iron Curtain folded some years ago. I was wrong. It simply moved to the police state in the North of Ireland."

He walked away with out responding. He huddled with his subordinates, then the party broke up and two of them bundled me up along with my suitcase and carry-on, and hustled me off to the Europa.

I called the attorney who showed up in the morning with an assistant to film a deposition on what happened. They took several close-ups of my face and stitched head, before my ride took me to the airport.

"They'll offer a monetary compensation but deny culpability," the attorney explained. "They might also try to get you to sign a confidentiality or disclosure document at the airport before you leave. They'll say its necessary or they will not compensate you for your injuries.

"I'll come with you to the airport to witness any transactions of this sort and offer legal advice. The decision will be yours about money for a cover-up."

"Will they prevent me from coming back?" I asked.

"I suppose it will depend on what you do about the incident. If you have news friends who can make a big deal of this in the media and the police can prove you associate with paramilitaries and criminal sorts, they might bar you from returning to the UK, which includes the Six Counties."

"OK."

At the airport I was indeed approached by several officials and informed that a monetary compensation would be offered for my "inconvenience."

I immediately interrupted, "Being bashed and getting stitches is more than an 'inconvenience.' I wouldn't expect an apology, after all this is technically the UK and I'm just a 'wild colonial boy.' But make no mistake, what happened was no inconvenience, you understand?"

I felt all of the officials got my nuance and understood that what happened "was in fact no inconvenience . . . ."

"I'll take the money and I agree that I won't sue and I won't tell a juicy story to the press. Give the check to my attorney here who will take his remuneration out of it and keep the rest in safe keeping for me.

"And that brings up a last point: I intend to return here, to conferences and to bring American students here to study the Troubles and the peace process. I don't want any problems returning. OK?

"My attorney will draw up a memorandum of understanding concerning this matter. I hope that one of you will be willing to speak to my students about the police . . . you thought I was going to say 'brutality,' but I'd like you to address police **hospitality** in the North of Ireland."

All the G-men had turned and were starting to walk away. But I needed to get the last word in. I had to think of something fast.

"Maybe a talk about policing in the North. I'll bet my students could see a definite parallel with policing in Birmingham, Alabama some years back, or East Germany, Soviet Russia, or North Korea."

I shook hands with my lawyer, turned to the officers who were walking away and simply said, "Thanks."

HOMECOMING

The trip home was long and uncomfortable. I flew via London and JFK to Chicago. Barbrie and my mother were there to meet and greet me. With a gash on the bridge of my nose, a split lip, and stitches in the back of my head, two slightly black eyes, I looked a sight.

Barbrie just hugged me and cried. My mother was not so sentimental.

"What the hell did you do to deserve this? I sure hope you got the better of who ever did this to you. He, they, must be hospitalized. Good thing they have socialized medicine over there, right Rudy?"

"Exactly right mom."

There was no small talk about the weather, the flight, or Denny. We just collected my bags and we headed for the car. I said I wanted to drive to keep myself busy and my mind off the hurt.

My mother was more disgusted than concerned. Barbarie just sat next to me in the front seat while mom scowled from the back.

"All right Rudy. What the hell happened? Was it Special Branch again? What's with you and those boys?" mom demanded.

"I behaved myself until the last day when an RUC public relations thug came to talk. No one asked any questions that were worthwhile, so I stepped up. I talked about rubber bullets, arrests, interrogation techniques and all the other shite that goes on to Republican prisoners. That rattled him."

"Rudy, I've noticed over the years that many of your questions are in fact statements." Mom observed.

I continued undeterred, "What really got to him and this one Professor from the University of Ulster was my reference to decommissioning and the threat of revenge killings of the police and guards by former prisoners, like what is happening in the former USSR.

"I suggested if the RUC, British Military, and other security folks stepped up, stopped doing it, and admitted wrongdoing and criminal action, and then prosecuted the offenders, that such action would bode well with the Nationalist community and the IRA in particular. Indeed, it might deter revenge killings.

"I said that Gerry Adam's has made it clear that the IRA and Sinn Fein does not endorse, nor will it condone, revenge of any sort, but that no one can control individuals who go rogue."

Barbrie said, "Well Rudy, I'm proud of you for restating the position of the Republicans on revenge. Your suggestions were reasonable too, don't you think so mom?"

I didn't give my mom a chance to respond. "My honesty got me in trouble. They were waiting for me at the airport. They said my information suggested a familiarity with terrorists, or something to that effect, so they wanted names of people I had met with in Belfast. When I refused, they said they would settle for one name. Just one.

"I was going to miss my plane at that point, so I got the head boy to dismiss the other five goons from the interrogation room and had him turn off the camera. When they complied with my requests, then I smashed my face into the table and threw myself back into the door cracking my head. The goon squad waiting outside had a hell of a time getting back into the room because I was jammed against the door.

"I suspect they thought I was killing their man. When they got in and saw me their suspicion fell on their man. I feigned to be passed out. It was a great performance. At the hospital I got sutured up, Denny had an attorney waiting for my call, and the rest is history."

"So you and Denny had this all worked out? You give yourself a concussion and a mug that looks like you were hit by a bus—you think it was worth it," my mother said in disgust?

'I got a monetary settlement and a document that says I can come back without hassle."

"Oh, they'll let you in all right Rudy, they just beat you up on the way out. You need an exit guarantee not to be maimed for God's sake."

"They didn't, it just looked like they had. I also had to agree not to tell the press what happened."

"And you are OK with that," mom said in a decidedly disgusted tone.

"The RUC guy from Coleraine and his buddies are up at night worried about revenge. The Special Branch guy was embarrassed and somewhat discredited. They gave me a monetary settlement that will be used by Denny to help Nationalists. I get to return with students. What's not to like?"

"When we get home you look in the mirror," mom said with spite.

———◆———

A week after returning home, I receiver a special delivery from my attorney in Ireland with a copy of the signed Memo of Understanding, the "No Disclosure" document, a statement of his charges, and my compensation balance which he set up in a bank account.

I called Denny about a week later and reported that I was doing fine. He said several of my Republican friends heard about my run in with the law at the airport. "They all send their regards."

I asked if any info had been gathered on Rich or Mac George. He basically said, "Nothing that you didn't already know about the two." Everything was very guarded. "But we'll get something," he ended. I thanked him for trying.

I gave Denny the bank account number, telling him if he or anyone else he could vouch for needed some financial help to dip into that account. He said he would monitor the situation and inform me of any decisions. He closed with, "All's well that ends well."

I thought, *Aye, like this is the end!*

AMERICAN SUPPORT

I had agreed to call on various clubs and organizations that had supported the Republican cause over the years. I was to feel them out on Gerry Adam's leadership position within Sinn Fein, especially as "politics" was taking a major role in the struggle for an acceptable peace in the North.

Second, I was to register how these groups felt about the slow but steady shift from armed struggle to non-violent political power sharing in the North. I explained that I was sent by Danny Morrison to gather this information and to share some literature he sent along with me.

Most of the groups were on board, but two in Chicago and one in the Cleveland area were clearly opposed to what was happening. An IRA splinter group called "Continuity IRA" was their champion. They had emerged shortly after I got home in June of 1996, and they promised to continue the 'Long War.'

I went back to the two groups in Chicago twice in 1996 and two more times in 1997. I figured, as they began to recognize me as representing the main stream IRA and Sinn Fein, they would feel more comfortable in approaching me and asking me any questions they may have.

The leadership of both groups told me privately that they suspected that Sinn Fein and the IRA were concerned about their defection because of the disruption of money going to those organizations. They also accused me of constantly showing up to register the names of people holding positions in the two renegade clubs for whatever reason.

I came right out and asked them, "And why would we do that?"

They both claimed some "retaliatory action."

"By whom?" I asked.

"A Provisional IRA agent," one man said. "An IRA assassin," another said.

My response to both men was the same, "There are no IRA hit men in the United States. I am here representing mainstream Sinn Fein in the hopes you will reconsider supporting their effort to adopt non-violent approaches to peace in the North. This 'Continuity IRA' is divisive and unrealistic in its effort to continue the struggle simply from the military angle."

"That's your opinion. We hold another opinion. We think it is possible to defeat the Brits and bring home a military victory," was how one fellow put it.

The other leader said, "We support the struggle, and Continuity IRA is the way. They represent the tradition of Collins, Hughes and Sands. The 'peaceniks' are a joke. We'll be on the winning side, and your people will be standing on the side lines."

Relegated to the dustbin of history, I thought, but did not say. Instead I said, "Like the time Collins signed the Treaty, the people were tired of war and the Army was so depleted any major operation would have been suicidal. He decided to give peace a chance and to rest up in the event another round was necessary. And remember, Sands stood for Parliament."

One man responded, "And look where that got both of them—dead."

And I shot back, "By another Republican in a fucking 'Civil War,' and by the leader of the Brit military. That's what we are trying to avoid, more useless deaths."

But logic, history, and facts were beyond these men. I just figured I'd keep showing up until I was barred from their meetings and events.

A year later, one of the original leaders of a Chicago group came up to me at a social event that I had brought Barbrie to, and he whispered in my ear, "You still making your list to pass on to the assassins?" He smiled a sinister smile and gave an audible "Humph."

I stood up and reached out and grabbed him by the nap of the neck and hissed, "Look shit-head, if they wanted you dead, you'd be dead. I'd do it myself, in front of your fucken family. Now go away and behave. I ain't killed anybody since Nam, but I was good at it and I had no regrets. Well, there were those guys in Mexico and Brazil, but they had it coming, and I needed the practice. Now get out of my face."

That took him aback. He avoided me like the plague the rest of the night. But before the night was over I approached his table and introduced myself to his wife, right in front of him. I said, "It is a pleasure to meet you. Your husband and I share a love of Ireland and support the struggle for peace and ultimate victory. Although we disagree on the means, he has always been gracious in letting me avail myself of his Irish hospitality to be present periodically to answer any questions he or his friends have for Sinn Fein and the Army. He's a real gentleman. On the other hand, I've been involved in things in the North and else ware that I'm not too proud of. But your husband is a good man and he indulges me. It is a pleasure to meet you."

At that point Barbrie came over and in her distinct Belfast accent asked me to introduce her to my friends. I did, with a Belfast accent of my own and putting emphasis on just the right words I adding that she was "one of **my spoils of war** from the North. After years spent in the North doing **what I could**, I eventually **had to leave**, but not before I took my prize. She's had me **on the run** ever since."

Barbrie blushed, but my man turned white. "Again, nice to meet you," I said to his wife. I turned to the ghost and said, "I'll be back in a couple of months to see if anyone has questions. I'm looking forward to seeing you again then, for now, safe home," I said as Barbrie and I walked away from the table. By the look on his face, message received and mission accomplished.

Working with he Cleveland people was easier. There was a core of "hard liners," but clearly the majority was open-minded and welcomed me graciously. After my first call on the group I knew the greater part would return to the Adams camp.

The second time I went to Cleveland I stopped by a club in Toledo whose members were solidly behind the mainstream Sinn Fein and IRA. They asked questions about the peace process and I answered those I could. I also promised them they would be hearing from Danny Morrison of Sinn Fein directly.

I contacted Danny and he sent the Toledo, Cleveland and Chicago groups a bevy of up to the minute information on what was and was not happening. The important point was that his contact brought them into the loop and up to date. They appreciated it greatly.

The anti-Adams rump in Cleveland was threatening to split off and take several key members of the local group with them. I gave them my best pitch, referred to Morrison's information, sat back and hoped for the best.

Unfortunately the split in the Cleveland association did take place, but at least the splinter group was small, only about nine or ten members. The problem was that several of them had deep pockets, and if money went back to Ireland, Continuity IRA was in for substantial contributions to keep the war going. My concern also centered around the fact that if Continuity pulled off some spectaculars of their own it might encourage more supporters to donate large sums and the war might just drag on and on.

I knew from history that sometimes wars just had enough momentum to carry them well beyond any practical reason to continue. They took on a life of their own. I sure didn't want that to happen in Ireland.

I thought Morrison's "Armalite and ballot box" approach was fine: the political initiative was slowly but gradually making progress and carrying the day. For the sake of the Irish in general I hoped it would eventually replace the gun altogether, and that was what Adams' program was putting into practice.

I only returned to Cleveland once more in the coming years because they were clearly on board with Adams' plan. Only one of the splitters eventually came back. The rest of the splinter group formed an association, but their recruiting did not bring in many new members. I wrote that faction off, and although I didn't go to Cleveland personally, I corresponded with the leadership of the main group quite often.

At the college, I had started a general survey course called "The History of Ireland." It proved to be very popular. So instead of offering it one a year, I offered it each semester, once during the day for traditional students and the next semester at night for mostly adult students. Both sections filled each semester.

I started contacting businesses in the area that had Irish owners, also the local Gaelic League and Ancient Order of Hibernians, to ask them if I could depend on them to make a modest contribution to an Irish Foreign Studies Program I planned on starting in the near future. Once I had a dozen commitments I felt I was in good shape. I continued over the years to add to this group of supporters.

Next I started to take courses that would help me set up online computer classes as a preface to actually taking students to Ireland. Students would have to enroll in the online classes in order to participate in the seminar in Ireland, and they had to complete the pre-departure classes prior to leaving for Ireland.

Learning how to set up the online classes posed no problem. Rather than set up fake or make believe courses for the instructor to evaluate, I knew what material I intended to cover in the Irish classes, so I set up the actual courses I planned to present to my Irish Foreign Studies students. None of the other six fellow instructors taking the online class thought of doing it that way. I wanted to get the ball running and didn't want to waste time with some generic exercise.

At first the techie teaching the class on how to develop and set up an on line class was upset that I was not following his protocol. But after a private talk I had with the man, he agreed to my agenda. I suggested he allow his "students, who were all faculty members," the option of the generic or their proposed courses to develop in his class. He agreed.

I bought him a gift card to a local restaurant, not for letting me do my course but for being open minded.

———————————•◦•◦•———————————

Since many of the students at my community college still lived at home and usually worked while taking classes, I decided to run my program during our calendar first summer session in May and June. The students would take the online classes during May, so they could still work, and then in June we would go to Ireland where they would see, smell, taste, touch, and hear what they had seen in pictures and video and read about in May.

I had gotten permission to videotape presentations during the CIEE seminar, and I had taped interviews of noteworthy people on my own. I incorporated these videos into my filmed lecture presentations. Students could log on to this material each day. They only had access if they were enrolled in this class, and they could only take this class if they were going to Ireland with our program in June.

According to the State of Michigan students had to attend class for so many minutes per credit hour to satisfy the college's requirement for attendance. The administration claimed this requirement was mandated by the State of Michigan for community colleges. The daily presentations were straight up: sixty minutes of lecture went as sixty minutes of required time, but any field work was a two to one ratio. Two hours of non-lecture equaled one hour of class time needed to satisfy the college and state mandate.

May was devoted to online presentations, lectures and interviews. Students would log on, watch the presentations at times they desired, for the presentations were available twenty-hour hours a day.

There were two hours of material per day for each class they were enrolled in. June, in Ireland was our field study or lab time.

The cost for the Irish Foreign Seminar was a package price including two three hour classes, all inclusive travel to the airport from the college, round trip air to and return from Ireland, identified and scheduled trips to various locations while in Ireland, two or three meals per day depending on the visitation schedule, and lodging (either in the youth center, Ti

Cuhulainn, or youth hostels, or hotels), and in some cases entry fees to historic sites, museums, and events. It was pretty much all-inclusive and rather inexpensive.

I actually offered four courses. They had to take the History of the North of Ireland, but then they had their choice of one of the following: "The Politics of the North," "Peace and Reconciliation in the North," and "Art As A Weapon: Murals."

Hence students got two courses automatically, but they could take either one of the other courses, or all four, if they had my permission and paid the extra tuition for the extra class or classes.

They watched the online presentations each day, and they had to participate in an online "discussion board," responding to my questions and react to each other's discussions and comments a minimum of three times a week. Everyone in the course saw these postings. I only intervened if what students wrote was incorrect or to keep them on task. I kept track of the times per week students participated.

They drew upon the online presentations and the textbooks they were assigned. They often fed on each other's comments, information from other classes they had taken, news information, books read, and information derived from having met Irish citizens. Then at the end of the week (on Saturday or Sunday) they had to submit a one page summary drawing from all the above-mentioned materials to the three questions I posed at the start of the week for that course. These summaries were sent to my "digital drop box" that only I had access to after they submitted their answers.

I kept track of these entrees (grades reflected their participation in the discussion board and summaries in the "digital drop box"). I sought brevity, accuracy and precision. I explained that students could not just go through the motions in either of these tasks. Their grade would also reflect: following directions, punctuality and accuracy. I periodically contacted a student reminding them to be punctual, truthful, and accurate. I knew BS when I saw and heard it. I wanted their comments to reflect analysis, problem solving, and logical assessments of topics for discussions. Their grade depended on all of these criteria.

There was a "chat-room" where students could communicate with each other electronically. I didn't want anything but academic and pertinent discussion on the subjects under consideration in the discussion board. Frankly, I never visited the "chat-room." Students met each other, made friends, discussed rooming with each other in Ireland and other 'non academic' subjects there from what I understand.

I made hard copies of their "digital drop box" summaries, and at the end of each week over in Ireland I distributed one of these assignments, had them read what they had written a month earlier, and had them edit this material in lieu of actually being in the North of Ireland for some time. Certainly their earlier impressions had changed now that they were in Ireland and had heard and seen for themselves, from the people themselves, the topics of importance in Irish history, politics, heritage and the quest for peace.

Final grades were based on the timely reflections students had regarding topics that were both timely and important to the areas of consideration. As we met people, some of whom I had interviewed on tape, students got a more personal, intimate, and dramatic insight on subjects, which cast a new light on topics. It was obvious from student reactions, I had told them the same things, "but I didn't have the accent."

While in Ireland for three weeks in June, we visited historical sites, like the 'Bogside' and the Apprentice Boys headquarters in Derry City, the Loyalist bastion of the Shankill Road and Tiger Bay, the Nationalist mainstays of the Clonard area, the Falls Road; Milltown Cemetery, the City Hall, and Stormont, in Belfast, and castles, Neolithic marvels, archeological and geological sites, murals, and people directly involved with each of these areas in turn. We met with politicians, participants, victims and perpetrators in events associated with the modern Troubles. All of these factors greatly influenced student experiences, knowledge, and understanding, and possibly changed their thoughts and attitudes toward conflict, peace and reconciliation.

I had everything set to go and students anticipated the enrollment for the Irish Foreign Studies Program. But there were still procedural and administrative hoops that I needed to jump through. I had to go before Department Heads Committees, Dean's Council, the President of the college's Executive Council, and finally before the Community College's Board of Trustees.

In all it looked like more than two years to get all of this behind me. I had a dean whose first name was Rick. Whenever I made proposals for anything they sat on his desk for not weeks, or months, but semesters. I nick named him "Rick a Mortis," a play on "Rigor Mortis," for obvious reasons.

I knew I would have to use some devious manipulation to get past him. What the Board, Executive Council and Deans Council all wanted was an Honors Program. The usual higher qualitative courses with more rigorous criterion and students with high grade points. Who could argue with this?

But what was also called for were two added components above and beyond those previously mentioned. The administration wanted a "service learning" component built into classes where pertinent. Some departments created some service learning projects that were far fetched, but the administration accepted them.

The other component was a permanent foreign studies program. I saw my Irish program as the perfect fit. So, I got myself appointed the "Faculty Advisor" of the new Honors program. Although I was committed to an Honors Program for purely academic reasons, my ulterior and immediate motive was to expedite my Irish Foreign Studies Program and to get it up and running.

The Honors program helped fast track my Irish Program and side stepped "Rick a Mortis." I had it all set to go within a year. Why an Irish Foreign Studies Program the various councils and committees asked?

"Twenty-five percent of all Americans claim Irish ancestry. There will be no language problem for students going to Ireland, 'They sort of speak English,' I would explain. Lastly, the Irish by and large still like Americans," I explained to their satisfaction.

But first, I had another CIEE seminar to attend and A family trip to the North to lead.

RETURNING TO IRELAND

My oldest daughter had been accepted and enrolled at the University of Notre Dame. It was difficult to believe that my little girl was at the university. She was interested in things Irish, such as literature, art, history and "Fighting Irish" football. I pointed out to her that Boston College and a few other colleges and universities seemed to offer as much in the area of Irish studies, and she might apply to them as well.

But no, she wanted Notre Dame, and ND was located only an hour south of Hartford, so she would be close to her mother, sister and aunt Eve. When she was accepted there it was final. Eoffa had grown up head strong, much like her namesake, aunt Eve. On the other hand Eve and Paul's daughter, Barbrie, named after my wife, was much more like her namesake: quiet, reserved, reflective.

Barbrie and I hadn't told either Eoffa or her sister Emma, still in high school, that we were planning to bring them to Ireland. We hoped that Paul and Eve could bring their two kids, Barbrie and Paulie, and that my mother would join us too.

Eoffa came home for the summer break after her first year at Notre Dame and was thoroughly enthusiastic and upset at the same time.

She informed us, "They offer some interesting classes through the Keough Naughton Institute of Irish Studies, but nothing on the current problems in the North of Ireland. Further, when the Modern Irish Troubles were touched upon in some courses, it was just brushed over for the most part.

"There is hardly any mention of the modern Troubles. There is virtually no talk at all of real substance. I've asked about specific event, topics, and people in some of my classes, and been politely told by one prof that 'that tragedy is better left alone.' Left alone! Good grief, how can they ignore it?"

I had explained to Eoffa that in all likelihood the topic of the current Troubles would probably be taboo. I had all I could do to refrain from saying, "Told you so." Barbrie's look directed at me during this discussion was enough to hold me back. She didn't give it often, but I knew she could back it up with hell-fire. My brother-in-law Paul and I referred to it as the "Conlon Cold stare." It was lethal.

Her second year was equally disappointing. "Not only don't they offer anything in the history department in the way of the Troubles, but in courses that touch upon it, such as English history," Eoffa said, "the profs are Anglophiles."

I simply responded, "Like your grandmother would say, 'Tis a shame.'"

"Aunt Eve says I should talk to some people," Eoffa said.

Good luck, I thought. *Taking advice from Aunt Eve was like getting advice from the Pentagon on a neighborhood dispute; I think they call it 'overkill.'* "That's the thing to do," I said hypocritically.

Barbrie said, "That was very diplomatically said, Rudy. You are learning."

I whispered, "I'll get an application for Boston College. Those Jesuits are hard core, but they are offering courses in current Irish subjects and they are more willing to listen to a lowly female student than the boys at ND, especially after she is getting advice from your sister."

———— •·•·• ————

At the next break when Eoffa came home, she was irate at the History Department chair, Father Martin McConnell. "He patronized me. He said, 'We have been at this pedagogical business a long time and we couldn't afford to give in to faddish causes.' Faddish causes!"

I responded, "Maybe he's trying to stay out of the fray because the university told him to."

"Irish-Americans like 'Tip' O'Neil and Edward Kennedy haven't ignored it. It is timely, immanent, and it is important. You'd think the university that calls itself the 'Fighting Irish' would be in the mainstream," she said sarcastically.

"Well, you've put the bug in his ear. Maybe he'll be stirred."

"It was as if he hadn't heard there was a war going on in the North. He didn't exactly deny it was happening, he is simply ignoring it."

"I'm sure he has his reasons."

"Well it was obvious, he was patronizing me and tolerating my questions because I was a female student. You can tell he likes looking over some of the females but yearns for the good old days when ND was an all boys' school. Some one said he went to school there when it was an all male institution. 'The good old days'."

"Now, now, let's not get too personal here. As I said, he must have his reasons."

"Rumor has it he had something going on with a female prof some years ago. I also heard she left and ran off with some wealthy student heir to a fortune or something."

"Eoffa, for God's sake, that is besides the point, it just fuels your dismay. Leave it alone. It's below you. Don't dignify such rumors with you comments. Deal with the issues, Irish History in general and the 'modern Troubles' in particular," I offered.

"As my grandmother would say, he's a 'highheejens,' so he is, so full of himself. I know I should at least respect the cloth and collar, and really, I do. I also know that grandma is a bit of an anti-cleric, and that I admit has rubbed off on me.

"But dad, he's ignorant. You taught me dad, the root of the word 'ignorance' is 'to ignore.' So he's ignorant. I've been winding up some students who plan to go over his head. We're going to the dean."

Good luck with that, I thought again, but I said, "Are you sure that's the thing to do? We called that sort of thing 'pulling rank' in the army, and it often came back to bite you in the ass. Aren't there any faculty that are inclined to offer any courses on the Troubles? Maybe a seminar, or an informal salon on the topic? Have you checked with the Political Science Department?"

"Why would I want an informal seminar on Ireland, especially of the North? You've taught me all I need to know from the Republican point of view. I want a good well rounded course from an objective point of view on the Troubles, sorry dad."

I couldn't argue with that. Being as involved as I was for so many years, I was certainly biased, and I'd probably forgotten more than most Americans, even profs at Notre Dame, would ever know about the Troubles from personal experience, I thought, but I said, "Well, you could probably hear the British point of view from them, right?" I said sarcastically.

"Precisely. They're all in love with England I guess. I'll have to rely on you and not get any credit for it."

"It's the knowledge that counts!"

Eoffa rolled her eyes, smiled the Conlon grin, and said, "Absolutely."

<hr />

The very next year Notre Dame announced an Irish Studies Program would offer study in Ireland, but it would be in the Republic and would not, it appeared, go to the North, nor address the "Troubles" per se.

"I'd like to go to Ireland, but I'd like to go to the North too. I think they only go there for a day or so."

"Well, check and see if they are to offer a year or semester in Ireland. Here is your mother, she has some news on the North."

Barbrie was listening to our conversation, but I covered the speaking end of the phone and said, "Tell about our surprise trip to Ireland. Maybe we can meet her after she completes a semester over there and we can then all go North."

"Are you sure?"

"Aye, it will excite her and calm her down some."

When her mother told her of the surprise trip we were planning for us all, her yell must have been heard all over campus. Even though I was off the phone and had gone into the kitchen to grab a snack, I was sure I heard it up here in Hartford.

"Will we meet some of dad's friends?"

"Aye, you surely will. It will be grand."

I thought, *It will be expensive, too.*

———— •◦•◦• ————

In April of 1998 the peace process and the "Talks" finally produced results. With some heroic patience, former US Senator George Mitchell, in conjunction with Herculean effort by many Republicans, Unionists, Nationalists and Loyalists, an agreement was made. The "Belfast Agreement," better known as the "Good Friday Agreement," was in the words of the SDLP leader, Seamus Mallon, "Sunningdale for slow learners."

The key element in the agreement centered around the idea that six-counties of the North would continue their Union with the UK as long as it was the will of the majority of the people in the North of Ireland.

In recognition of this relationship by the government of the Irish Republic, Nationalists there and in the North, Unionists and other Loyalist parties had to accept cross-border cooperation between the Republic and the North, and power sharing of all parties in the new government in the North.

In return for ending the IRA's active "armed struggle" for independence and the IRA's recognition of the North's present union with Britain, Unionists and Loyalist participating parties had to accept Sinn Fein's participation in the new government. By and large Nationalists and Republicans supported these arrangements, but Unionists and Loyalists were divided, just as they had been in 1973 with the Sunningdale Agreement. But now, the majority of Unionists, politicians and people, backed this new deal. Everyone was war weary and knew this was the best hope for peace.

In fact, leading up to the called for referendum in the Republic and the North, the mechanics of the political settlement was downplayed. Rather, especially in the North, the obvious "peace" was stressed after long years of war, along with elements the settlement contained, like release of prisoners, decommissioning of arms, and the long overdue reform of the RUC.

On May 22, 1998, the referendum proved beyond the shadow of a doubt that all of Ireland wanted peace. The largest turnout in the North since 1921 (81% of eligible voters) saw the agreement endorsed by 71% (early opinion polls predicted only 60% endorsement). In the Republic (56% turnout) the vote in favor (94%) of changing the Republic's Constitution (articles 2 and 3), dropping legal claims to legitimate governance of the North and changing the favorable position of the Catholic Church in controlling education, the status of females before the law, and dictating sex education and medical procedures.

There were some sectarian murders by the UVF, not only as intimidation against accepting the agreement, but also in reaction to the killing of their leader, Billy 'the Rat' Wright, in the Maze by the INLA in late December of 1997.

It was against these remarkable events that our plans of bringing the whole family to Ireland began to fall into place. Between saving money, making travel arrangements, coordinating Eoffa's seminar with our family trip, time seemed to fly by.

As I tried to synchronize all the pieces of the puzzle, I threw a monkey wrench into the mix myself. On a whim I applied for a CIEE seminar and a grant from my college. To my great surprise, I got both again.

The plan now was to have Eoffa come up to the CIEE conference, again at Coleraine, and stay with me to see a wide variety of people and topics all directly related to the Troubles. Then, after the conference, she and the rest of the family would meet my friends and acquaintances on the Republican side, people she had heard about from both uncle Danny and myself over the years.

We were hopeful that my daughter Emma and mother, Paul, Eve, and their children, Barb and Paulie, could come too. Since our "Irish cousin" Maya was taking summer classes she was staying in Hartford for the two weeks.

It turned out that Eoffa was to spend the second semester in Dublin, and she arranged to have her return flight delayed to coincide with our homecoming flight.

I told Eoffa that she should call Professor John Smyth at Queen's. She knew he was a former professor and confidant of mine and it would mean a lot to me if she called him while she was in Dublin. Just a social call, but he might have tidbits of interest for her. She said she would, and as it turned out she did, several times. "It was sort of like talking to you, dad," she confided later.

HISTORY: 1996-1999

*T*he British Prime Minister, John Major, dumped a 'Report' by the Mitchell Commission. The 'Mitchell Report' said that paramilitaries would not decommission before all party talks got started, but suggested that some decommissioning during the all-party negotiations would be appropriate, rather than after or before the talks.

After consulting Trimble, Major rejected the Report and called for elections to his "Forum." The elected members of this "Forum" would be the delegates for each party negotiating a peace; Sinn Fein was specifically denied participation. If Loyalists were overjoyed by this rejection, Nationalists were outraged. The IRA was more than outraged, and they ended their seventeen months of cessation of war with a huge bomb blast at Canary Wharf in London.

John Hume and Gerry Adams held a meeting with the IRA leadership. Amid further violence on the Garvaghy Road at Portadown, the RUC forced the way for the Orange parade.

In 1997, in both national general elections and local government elections, Sinn Fein made major advances, actually becoming the largest party in Belfast. Major and the Conservatives were defeated and Tony Blair of the Labor Party became Prime Minister. Both Gerry Adams and Martin McGuinness were elected to the British Parliament.

Some things did not change with a new administration though, because the new Secretary of State for the North, Mo Mowlam, agreed for the RUC to force through the Orange march down the Garvaghy Road in Portadown. Even so, the IRA announced another cessation of military action.

However, there was serious internal conflict within the IRA. Although Sinn Fein was now allowed to enter the Castle Building at Stormont to participate in 'Talks,' the IRA internal tensions led to a split and the emergence of "Real IRA" who opposed the peace negotiations.

A Sinn Fein delegation held an official meeting with the British Prime Minister at Downing Street for the first time in about eighty years. Closer to home, a notorious Loyalist prisoner at Long Kesh Prison, Billy Wright, was killed by the INLA.

In 1998 Mo Mowlam visited Loyalist prisoners at Long Kesh Prison, although the UDA had embarked on a series of sectarian killings against targeted and random Catholics.

After strenuous negotiations and the guidance of Senator Mitchell, the delegates arrived at an agreement called the "Good Friday Agreement" or the "Belfast Agreement," that paved the way forward for peace in the North. Democratic, peaceful, and respectful principles were accepted by all parties, and a popular vote of confidence in both the North and the Republic acclaimed acceptance of this new "Peace Accord."

A delegation of senior members of the African National Congress attended Sinn Fein meetings throughout Ireland, visited prisons and Republican prisoners. Two Sinn Fein general congresses (Ard Fheiseanna) discussed the Good Friday accord and overwhelmingly accepted and backed the Agreement.

In elections to the new Assembly called for in the Agreement, Sinn Fein won it's largest vote seating eighteen, and guaranteeing two ministerial positions in the power-sharing Executive.

It appeared that the armed struggle had by and large come to an end, and as some commentators said, now the long arduous struggle for peace began in earnest. As eighty years earlier, the war weary population sought peace, so the people of the North after forty years of the current Troubles yearned for peace. On the surface the "war" in the North of Ireland had stopped, and there were serious attempts through formal governmental institutions to manufacture an ongoing peace.

There were still rumblings of some factions of paramilitary groups that there had been "sell outs,"

"betrayals," and "desertions." The detractors of the Agreement were a small minority, but a dangerous one, and at times they were able to forcefully demonstrate their ire in public with demonstrations of violence.

There were some acts of violence that were throwbacks to sectarian and political hostility and brutality. But they were seen as reactionary and isolated acts of violence. They were, and were seen as, extreme, destructive, and desperate actions of a frustrated few, no matter how terrorizing. They were exceptions, no longer the rule it was hoped, in the North. To the majority of the citizens of the North, those days of perpetual violence were over and there was "hope" for a sustained peaceful tomorrow.

IRISH CONFERENCE: 1999

I t dawned on me while packing for the CIEE conference in the North of Ireland that it had been over two years since I had been in the North. This time I felt really out of touch since so much had changed.

The key transformation of course was the "Good Friday Agreement." It seemed that everything was hinged on that accord: the "peace," release of prisoners, all parties being included in the new government, eventual decommissioning of weapons and paramilitary organizations.

On the one hand everything had changed, and on the other I knew, deep down, that nothing had really changed. Real change would be a slow, gradual process, as it has proven to be. I was excited to get to the conference to observe the obvious academic and polite reaction and reflections on the 'peace," from the cleaned up participants in the conference.

I was also excited to meet my friends on the lower levels of society, those from the periphery of academic and polite society, from the Falls and Clonard neighborhoods, from the South of Armagh, and my family relations in Saintfield, County Down.

———◆◆◆———

My daughter Eoffa and her Notre Dame friends were experiencing both the academic and professional delights of Dublin, but also the social life as well. She was loving every minute of it, especially the nightlife and weekends, spent with friends, both American and Irish. Her mother and I were somewhat concerned, but her aunt Eve was "comfortable" with it all.

"Eve, what the hell does 'comfortable' mean?" I demanded.

My mother scolded, "Rudy. Your language."

"Jaysus mom, you are concerned about my f . . . language when my daughter's virtue is at stake."

"I doubt it. She had more likelihood of compromising her 'virtue' to those 'Fighting Irish' at Notre Dame than those boys in Dublin," mom shot back.

"Good on you mom. How does it feel to get a slagging from your own mom, Rudy?" Eve teased.

"Barbrie, help me," I pleaded.

"I trust my daughter, in both South Bend and in Dublin. Don't you, Rudy?' Barbrie teased.

"You are making light of my concern? You are as bad as the rest of the women in my life."

At this point my daughter Emma made her presence felt. "Dad, lighten up. Eoffa is neither naïve nor stupid. She can and will take care of herself."

"Well at least you didn't say she had already compromised her virtue."

There was a chorus of "Rudy!"

"Let me finish. What do you mean 'she can and will take care of herself'?"

Eve just shouted, "Wouldn't you like to know" to the glee and squeals of Barbrie, mom and Emma.

"It's a conspiracy of . . . I don't know what to call you," I conceded.

Barbrie came over to me, gave me a hug, and said, "Just call us some, if not all, of the most important women in your life. We do appreciate you fatherly concern. We are three generations of Castles. You are the 'Patriarch.' You are supposed to be concerned. And to your credit, you clearly are. We have all raised this youngest generation to be honorable, pure, and dedicated to what is right. She'll be fine, Rudy. She will take care of herself."

My mother came over and gave us both a hug. "My God Rudy, you chose such a wise, amazing, and wonderful wife. I couldn't have chosen better for you myself. I worried about you for a while, and then you showed up with this angelic woman, as your wife. And she had a sister. God knew what She was doing."

"She knew what She was doing? God's a She? What the hell does that mean?" I demanded.

There was a loud refrain with three "Rudy's" and one "Dad." Then there was a chorus of laughter.

Eoffa met me at the hotel in Coleraine. She was wound up over her semester in Dublin and excited to finally be in the North so as to get a taste of the Troubles and the Peace Process. All I had to do was pay for Eoffa's room and board, which was very considerate of the program leaders.

At this year's 1999 CIEE Conference, the two best presentations made were, first, one evening at the RUC Clubhouse at the RUC Sports Ground in Lagan Meadows on the edge of Lagan Regional Park, in the southeast suburb of Belfast, far from the Troubles. The Chief Constable of the RUC, Ronnie Flannigan, gave a heartfelt presentation on behalf of the police. His presentation made the RUC look like the most uncorrupt, altruistic, honest, professional and neutral police force in the world.

My old friend from my previous CIEE conference, Professor Rich, was there and he was just waiting for me to start asking embarrassing questions. I asked Flannigan how his men and women felt being pitched into the middle of this quandary between armed Republicans, armed Loyalists and the British Army?

He bit, and went off on a rant, "The Loyalists are as bad, if not worse, than the IRA. Since most of the police officers are Protestants and lived in staunchly Loyalist neighborhoods, they put up constantly with insults, shunning, threats and physical intimidation by neighbors.

"As to the British Army, they are a force and a law unto themselves. If they despise and fear the IRA they belittle and mock the Loyalists in the North as ignorant and provisional lowlifes. They feel both sides of the conflict deserved each other and what they hand out to each other. How can you work with these people? They don't respect you, your institution, or your efforts?" he asked rhetorically.

"Thank you for your candor," I said and smiled at Rich. He just gave me the fish-eye stare. I felt I had scored two points with one kick. Speaking of kicks, Eoffa kicked me in the leg after my exchange with Flannigan, for my loaded question.

The second outstanding presentation came the next day with our keynote speaker, Professor Brice Dickson. He is a well-known professor at the Law School at the University of Ulster and head of the Northern Ireland Human Rights Commission. He introduced himself, admitted his unpopularity with all the British, both domestic and foreign, that is, Loyalists and "Big Island British" (English).

I didn't bother to put my hand up, to Professor Rich's annoyance, but just blurted out, "Then how and why did you get the job?"

His answer was a prelude to what was to come. He said, "I am the resident Catholic and main target on the Northern Ireland Human Rights Commission. My experience in law, human rights, and comparative systems made me something of an obvious choice for the job. I had experience with the Equal Opportunities Commission here in Northern Ireland, and I had the opportunity to study the application and effects of various Bills of Rights in several southern African countries.

"I don't think the powers that be who decided to appoint me to the current Commission thought I would be a thorn in the side of the security forces, the government, and the courts here in the North. I was, more or less, an academic, not an activist.

"I actually do not see myself as an activist in the usual sense of the word. I just insist that everybody involved in the governmental systems at work here in the North of Ireland adhere to the law. No one is above the law, nor is anyone a law unto themselves.

"The police, the British Army, municipal and village councils, county government and officials, provincial government and officials, and the British government and their officials, have to obey the law. British law and European Union law must be observed.

"I know these laws and I speak out when they don't adhere to the law. That makes me very unpopular."

I pushed the envelope, "I'll bet. Last night we had a very civil and polite interview with Chief Constable Ronnie Flannigan. To hear him, the RUC here in the North of Ireland is unappreciated and unjustly criticized, assaulted and belittled, both here and abroad. The RUC is the most professional, unbiased, objective police department in the world. Their record is only tarnished by innuendo, unsubstantiated attacks and biased reporting in the press."

Professor Dickson barged right in, "Of course he'd say that, he's their boss." It was the only time he seemed to get exited and raise his voice slightly. He continued, "But look at the record of the RUC since 1921. You've been here for a few days, you've talked to people, or maybe they have talked to you. What is your impression? How do they stack up with your police back in the US?"

Some one offered, "They remind me of the police we see in the historical film footage of American southern states police during the civil rights years of the sixties and seventies. Hardly impartial!"

The professor smiled and said, "Not an entirely unwarranted comparison. As you know our Civil Rights movement of the sixties and seventies was modeled on yours, and the nonviolent civil disobedience of Reverend Martin Luther King. But as you also know, our 'professional and unbiased' police, (is that what Flannigan called them?), well they acted like your Alabama and Mississippi police. Unfortunately, not just back in the sixties and seventies, but there are still accusations of such behavior now.

"And what went on once in custody was reminiscent of Eastern Bloc interrogations, or Nazi prisons. This has all been established under oath and corroborated by doctors and even some prison officials themselves. Facts are facts, and the European Court has condemned these practices.

"Clearly they are no longer practiced so brazenly as before, but from what we hear it still goes on. So I still have a job to do, and so I am unpopular, and Ronnie Flannigan boasts that his force is the best."

Professor Dickson was forthright and answered all the questions put to him in a professional and unflinching fashion. He impressed everyone in the room, even if he made the obvious Unionist on the staff uncomfortable.

Eoffa liked Professor Dickson straight away, and approached him following his talk and after he had answered questions from the seminar participants. She introduced herself and what followed was very satisfying to me, obviously, for she carried herself very well in both her questions, observations, and comments.

At the end of their forty-five minute discussion, Dickson turned to me and said, "You've taught her well, you can be proud." Returning to her, he said, "Eoffa, if you want to pursue the study of Human Rights, Equal Rights, and International Law, I will find a place for you here at the University of Ulster. Or, if you stay at your American university you can intern for me here for a term or what ever."

"Thank you very much. I'll consult with my advisors and professors back at the University and will definitely consider your generous offer. I will contact you as soon as I can determine the best option. Thank you again for your presentation and your offer. I was privileged on both accounts."

"Professor Castle, Doctor Castle, you have a gem of a daughter."

"I know. She takes after her mother, a Belfast girl I met some years ago and brought home to America."

"But I hear you return here to Ireland every so often. You could visit this young lady if she returns to join us."

"I definitely would return then, and so would her mother, just to say 'hello,'" I said with a smile.

"I understand you are starting an Irish Studies Program for your college back home and plan to focus on the North, with a stay here as part of the schedule. That's wonderful. Down in South Armagh, that will help their economy."

"I would like to impose on you to come down there and make presentations for us, in the same vein as you did today," I said.

"Indeed I would like that. Here is my card, and if the calendar allows plan on me participating."

"Thank you for both of your offers, the one to my daughter and this one for my program. We truly appreciate them and your time talking to us."

The next day we made a trip to Belfast, visiting the seat of government in the North of Ireland at Stormont. We met with representatives of several parties who presented their official positions on the Good Friday Agreement.

A Reverend Coulter from the Ulster Unionist Party trashed Sinn Fein because the IRA had not begun decommissioning. A few in the group stated that it was their understanding that it was not a precondition to participation. A colleague of Coulters, I forget his name, alienated the majority of the group by stating, "You Americans come here with a 'green' sympathy," meaning that we are biased in favor of the Nationalists and Republicans.

One of our group, a young professor from California, shot back, "That's insulting. We've studied the issues and history of the Troubles and the Agreement. Why can't you give us credit for that? We've studied the facts, and base our sympathies on those facts."

The UUP man asked, "How could the Assembly allow former IRA men into that organization? Men with blood on their hands."

I quickly responded, "Excuse me, but we are Americans. Our Founding Fathers conducted the Paris Treaty ending our War of Independence from Britain, and they were 'rebels' with blood on their hands. Many American Presidents were former military men with blood on their consciences if not their hands. We've dealt with former enemies from Germany and Japan since World War II as leaders and officials of their governments and businesses. It's how it's done. You boys have got to get over it."

Several members of our group nodded in agreement. Someone said, "Look who represents Vietnam now, and Russia, China, several Asian, African, Moslem and South American nations, former 'rebels,' and enemies of the US and Britain. We may not like it, and we may not like them, but as Mr. Castle said, it is how it is done and how it has been down throughout history. Even the Brits sit down with former enemies."

We also met with a former paramilitary and prisoner from the UVF, David Ervine, representing the Progressive Unionist Party. He was very articulate and presented a vision of cooperation of all groups in developing peace and prosperity in the North of Ireland. He also had no problem with working with former IRA men.

Sean Farren who worked closely with CIEE at Coleraine, also represented the SDLP at our meeting at Stormont. He was very lucid and coherent in his presentation, and he also stressed the importance of cross-community inclusion in government and social and economic teamwork as the recipes for success.

Ian Paisley, Jr., who seemed confident and self-assured, represented the Democratic Unionist Party, or DUP. He projected an image based on a combination of President Clinton and Prime Minister John Major. He was relaxed and bold in his presentation that focused on two key points:

retaining the RUC in all its vestiges, from its uniform and symbols to its authority and name, and his insistence on everyone in the North being "British."

Several in the group expressed the ideas surrounding the decision to change the name, uniform and symbols of the RUC as necessary because of its past history of preferential, biased, and unlawful practices.

Paisley nearly came out of his chair, his suit, and his skin after these comments.

On the issue of being "British," I commented that "Englishmen call themselves 'English,' Welshmen 'Welsh,' Scotsmen 'Scots,' whereas only Loyalists and Unionists in the North of Ireland insist being called 'British.' Why is that?"

"Because, we are British," he responded.

"Can you define British?" I asked.

"British refers to being British," he said as if it were a matter of fact and not illogical.

"So a coin is a coin because it is a coin," I said.

"Precisely."

"Isn't that a circular argument? Or statement?"

"No. It is a fact."

"What is?"

"That being British is being British."

"But what is this thing called British? What is the "Britishness" of British? The essence of it?"

"Being loyal and respectful to the crown, the crown's heritage, traditions and government," he explained.

"That's the definition or description of a Loyalist, or being loyal to the English crown and its heritage and traditions and government. But I suspect that all Loyalists are indeed British, but being British includes some who are not loyal.

"Nationalists and Republicans, since they live here in the North of Ireland and are registered as citizens, are British, but hardly Loyal or Loyalists. Agreed?

"So British includes being loyal, but it seems to be more than merely being loyal. British and loyal are not mutually exclusive terms, nor are they synonyms.

So again, what is British?" I asked.

"As I have explained, being British is being British," he said by way of explanation.

"I'm still confused. You see, all U S citizens are Americans, but not all Americans are US citizens. America is bigger that the US. It can be defined geographically. Yet, Hawaiian are US citizens, but are they Americans?

"Is British bigger than England, Wales, Scotland and the North of Ireland, or is it synonymous with the four geographic locations? And if this is the case, if a section decided to pull out of the arrangement, it could still be British because of geography. But, this seceded portion would no longer be loyal. Hence they would be, and not be, at the same time, which is impossible, since you cannot be and not be at the same time, you know, the principle of contradiction. Do you see the confusion?" I asked.

"You are confused and are trying to confuse the issue. British means being British. It's that simple."

"For some simpletons it is," I said under my breath to the delight of my daughter and those sitting close by.

As we exited the building Eoffa laughed and said, "Whoa, da, did you get your shoe back? Sticking it that far up his asre jeopardized getting it back."

After the Stormont visit we stopped at Belfast City Hall, for a quick tour and to meet with the Lord Mayor. The Lord Mayor was not available, so we had his proxy instead, the stand-in deputy Lord Mayor, Sammy Wilson of the DUP. He had quite a reputation for haranguing, mocking and disrupting any Sinn Fein member of the city council. He consorted with Ian Paisley's daughter Rhonda, also a council member and thorn in the side of any and all Sinn Fein councilors.

He was wearing the chain of office and was polite and all smiles. We had tea with him (I didn't, because I don't drink tea and I wouldn't drink with his likes, ever). He consented to answer any questions we might have for him.

I spoke right up, "Mr. Wilson, you seem so gracious and polite, prim and proper. I am at a loss to understand why the international, and especially the American press, vilifies you so. You are constantly referred to, and I quote, "a royal horses' ass." But here you are, so pleasant to be with. How is that? Where do they get that image of you?" I asked and then repeated, "a royal horses' ass?"

All he could muster was a weak, "I, I don't know."

All the Americans were greatly amused, and even some of the UU staff, Catholics if not Nationalists, but Professor Rich and his loyal Unionist colleagues were not.

Rich immediately intervened. "Please, that is uncalled for. It is rude and insulting. An apology is warranted."

"Possibly, but I can't apologize for members of the American press and news media. I will bring this whole episode to their attention when I get home though," I said with a smirk.

"Jaysus, da, are you on a roll or what? Did your buddies in the RA give you a hunting license," Eoffa said with a grin. "I've never heard you like this. You are lethal. Your man Denny will be so proud when we tell him all of this shite."

We were given some free time to shop in the city center after the City Hall tour and tea. It was during this time we met up with John Smyth for a cup of coffee. He was pleased to finally meet Eoffa in person. He could only stay a short time because he had a seminar back at the Queen's.

We had also arranged to meet with Denny half an hour after Smyth headed back to the university. Denny watched Eoffa and me lose two G-men trying to tail us. He gave me the all clear and we met face to face in the second story seating area of a Mac Donald's Restaurant on the corner of Donegal Place and Castle Street.

"Denny, this is my daughter Eoffa. She already knows you like a long lost uncle."

"Jaysus it's a pleasure to finally meet you. You are lovely and thankfully resemble your mother."

"Aye, thank you for the compliment."

"We've got some great stories to tell you," I said.

"Wait until you hear this one Denny. Da just had fun with Sammy Wilson."

Eoffa proceeded to tell him of the City Hall tea and my insult. He was laughing so laud that I thought he might draw the wrong kind of attention to ourselves.

I confirmed when and where the family would be staying here in Belfast and our itinerary. He said everything was ready on his end. He was excited to meet the whole family.

"You rented a small bus?" he asked incredulously.

"Aye, actually a big van, we'll be a small army. There are nine of us, and we couldn't all fit in one car. With some help from Sinn Fein I got a good deal on the wheels and a driver. He's from the South, but he's spent time in the North and knows people in South Armagh and Derry."

We talked a bit longer, then we left separately, Denny first. He ducked into an arcade and returned with his fake beard, glasses, and a hat. He saw us laugh, and I read the expletive on his lips. He also gave us the all-clear sign as we passed down the opposite side of the street. We were not being tailed.

On the way back to Coleraine several of my colleagues said they thought my performance at city hall, and indeed all week, was outstanding. They enjoyed my antics, and thought I exposed several chinks in the Unionist and Loyalist armor and agenda.

I appreciated their comments, as did Eoffa. But little did I know that my behavior had been followed by an old foe from back in the early 1980s, one Peter Jeffries of Special Branch. Reports had been filed every day on my questions, comments, and demeanor since I had been at the conference. I was a person of interest and was a watched man.

———— •◆•• ————

THE FAMILY TOUR OF 1999

E offa and I traveled down to Dublin to meet the family early in the morning immediately after they landed. My plan was to save the Dublin and the meager portion of the Republic we were to visit for the end of the trip, so we headed North once we were all through the rigmarole at the airport.

The van was parked in the lot and the driver was in the terminal waiting for us. By nine that morning we were on the road for our hotel in Belfast. The Europa Hotel had been refurbished several times during the Troubles and was a great place to spend the night and from which to stage day trips. The location, staff, meals, and accommodations were excellent.

Later the family and college would spend a few nights in Crossmaglen for historical reasons, at the new Cross Square Hotel which was and still is an excellent spot from which to stage day trips.

On the way North we stopped at the historical city of Drogheda, the scene of Oliver Cromwell's massacre and the shrine of Oliver Plunkett, Catholic Archbishop of Armagh, and the religious site of Monasterbois, a fifth century monastery which has three exceptional high crosses.

After checking into the Europa Hotel and lunch we rested until about 15:30 and then treated the family to a walking tour of the city center.

The next day, following a very good Irish breakfast we headed for South Armagh and had a walking tour of Camlough, a visit to Hunger Striker

Raymond Mc Creesh's grave, followed by a talk from a local Sinn Fein Councilor, all arranged by Des Murphy.

That evening we had presentations by a Hunger Striker whose family requested that he get medical treatment after forty-seven days on the strike. Also by the sister of a young man killed by the security forces that were on a "shoot to kill" mission.

The following day we stayed in Belfast and met up with Denny. The children had heard so much about him they were thrilled to finally meet the "legend." My daughter Emma said she was disappointed that he did not bring along his disguises of fake beard, glasses, and duncher. He told her, "Your father absolutely forbad it," shifting attention to me. He joined us for a drive past Nationalist Murals and a walk along the lower Falls Road and up past Clonard Monastery. He was full of stories about the areas, the defenders, and explained the murals at length.

We finally left Denny to cross the "Peace Line," onto the Shankill Road, down towards the Shankill Leisure Center, crossing the road toward the Sports Ground and the large number of Loyalist Murals.

After stopping for lunch at a fast food place we were picked up by the van and whisked away to Stormont for pictures and a brief talk with Gerry Adams, Martin McGuinness and Connor Murphy from Sinn Fein; we happened to run into Reverend Ian Paisley (of the DUP) by chance and had a photo op; we met David Ervine of the PUP who spoke to our group.

We returned to Belfast city center for a look at city hall, spent some time shopping, and registered the still obvious security forces, security checkpoints, but the rather large throng of shoppers and somewhat relaxed atmosphere. It was refreshing.

I kidded my sister-in-law that she must be disappointed that there were no police or soldiers to badger, verbally assault, and inform in her decided Belfast accent that she was an "American." We had great fun explaining to the young one's how Eve took on the RUC and British Army in her youth and on the last trip North. They were proud and mortified of her at once.

Denny had made arrangements for us to meet with Brendan Hughes, "The Dark," my old friend now living in the Divis Street Apartments. It was an emotional reunion for me. We didn't stay long, but it was apparent that Darkie was not pleased how things were unfolding in the Republican Movement and the Peace Process. He was on the verge of, not disappointment, but bitterness.

"Fuck Rudy, everything and everyone has changed," Brendan said bitterly.

"Aye, events took over, then the politicians. I fear it's always that way," I said by way of commiseration.

"Aye, but some of the lads who became politicians I fear sold their souls. Now they're used to wearing suits, getting driven around, living the good life."

"Do you think nothing will come of the Agreement?" I asked.

"Nothing good. We accepted the status quo. All that shite for all those years. For what?"

"It happens," I offered.

"It happens every fucken time. Collins back then, now this lot. As Marx said, 'History repeats itself, the first time it's a tragedy, the second time it's a farce."

All my mother said as we climbed into the van was "Tis' a shame."

We drove by Barbrie and Eve's parents' house, and the house they shared when I met them. The kids were only mildly interested, but both places were nostalgic to the "Conlon sisters." Our last stop on the tour was at Milltown Cemetery for a visit to the Republican Plot and the many heroes of the recent Troubles.

We were back at the hotel for a late supper at the hotel and a jar or two at the bar. The pace was finally getting to us and we were all in the sack by 22:00.

The next day was bright and beautiful, a perfect day for our visit to the Boyne Valley and the Neolithic sites of New Grange and Knowth.

Our final day in South Armagh saw us on a ten-stop archaeology tour by a local schoolteacher, another Murphy. It was outstanding. Unfortunately we didn't have time to climb Slieve Gullion, the great mount of South Armagh with a tomb (partially wrecked by the Brits in the 80s and 90s).

That evening we went up to Saintfield and visited with our relatives. It was great to introduce one and all to everyone again, all the Eddies and Emmas. I got more confused as the night wore on with all the firsts, seconds and thirds. Emma, the young girl who had stayed with us in Hartford was especially anxious to introduce her "American cousins" to some friends who were spending the evening for the occasion.

Everyone asked about their Maya, who had stayed back in Hartford. She was taking summer classes and was house sitting for us. She planned to return home next summer. We said that although she was becoming more American than Americans, I wouldn't let her abandon her Ulster ways. Everyone appreciated my humor and respect for tradition.

Emma asked if she and a friend, Elizabeth, and maybe another friend could go back to the US with us for a month or so. Barbarie and I said of course, so arrangements were made to meet up with us in a week in Dublin and to fly back to America with us if it could be worked out. If there was no room on our flight, we knew they could get another easily enough, and we did plan to stay a day in Chicago on the way home so we could wait in the event it was needed.

The young girls were all making plans and getting whipped into a frenzy. We older folk caught up on all the gossip and hated to leave, but it was close to midnight.

The next day, after stopping at Ti Cuchulainn, the cultural-student center in Mullaghbane, South Armagh, and Navan Fort and Visitors center, we went up to the Giant's Causeway and then over to Derry. Many in the group missed the countryside since they were sleeping because of the late night at Saintfield.

We had a walking tour of the Derry City walls, had a friend arrange a tour of the Apprentice Boys Hall and Museum, and then were bused out to the (often rebuilt) great ring fort, the Grianan of Aileach. We finished the day by traveling along Lough Swilly, stopping at Buncranna where Theobald Wolff Tone landed and was arrested. We took a ferry across the lough to Rathmullen to see the Martello tower and visit the monastery from where the Flight of the Earls departed in 1607.

In the morning we headed south and just outside of Raphoe is a great Beltnay Stone Circle. From there, we lunched in Donegal City with its Plantation House Castle, the town's "Diamond," and the historic abbey, now in ruins, associated with the "Annals of the Four masters." I knew my mother would find this place intriguing because of this association.

After lunch we moved inland to Lough Erne to see the Janus Figures, but returned to the N 15 highway stopping at Creevykeel to see one of the finest Court Cairns in all of Ireland. Next we made a quick stop near the great mount of Benbulben, at Drumcliff, with W. B. Yeats grave, a damaged round tower and high cross. After spending the night in Sligo we continued on south, pulling into Galway in the afternoon. There was plenty of time for exploring the city and shopping.

The following morning was bright and unusually warm. We spent much of the day in the Burren and at the Cliffs of Moher, returning to Galway rather late in the evening. As we walked to the hotel after supper mom entertained us with a soft rendition of the song "Galway Bay."

I apologized to the group, and our driver who was from Cork, that we would not be able to go further south toward the old Province of Munster, but we'd catch those areas on the next trip, for sure.

"When dad?" was the chorus from my daughters.

"I don't know exactly, but we'll get back."

I noticed the melancholy look on my mother's face, for she knew that she would certainly not be making that trip. This one was her last, and both of us knew it. Although she kept up with the pace, she was looking tired and a bit ragged around the edges. She looked forward to Dublin and then home to Hartford.

As we headed east toward Dublin, we stopped at Clonfert Cathedral with its Hiberno-Romanesque west doorway caped by a pyramid of sculpted human heads. Then on to the vast monastic settlement of Clanmacnois on the banks of the Shannon River.

We entered Dublin at rush hour, so getting to the centrally located hotel on the south side of the Liffy River was slow and tedious.

We slept late and well. Mom led us on the pilgrimage to all the familiar sites, starting at the General Post Office, up to the Garden of Remembrance and Parnell Square. We took two taxis out to Glasnevin Cemetery to visit the graves of the heroes. On the way back to Dublin center we drove by the new Liberty Hall and the Classical Customs House.

In the afternoon we went to Dublin Castle, Christ Church and St. Patrick's Cathedrals, Four Courts, Robert Emmet's actual place of execution, and the work in progress at Kilmainham Goal and Museum. We used two or three taxicabs throughout the day, but we were still exhausted.

Again, after a late Irish breakfast, we visited Trinity College with its treasures, the National Museum, lunch at the Shelbourne Hotel, and a stroll through St. Stephen's Green. We returned to the hotel and young Emma and her friend Elizabeth were waiting for us in the lobby. They had not been able to check in yet, but had secured tickets on our flight for passage back to the US with us.

We made arrangements for the two girls to simply stay in our rooms with roll-a-ways brought in for them. Then we turned the younger crowd loose with the directive of sticking together and looking "right" before crossing the street.

"In the lobby at 19:00 Hrs. Everybody got it?" I asked. "I don't want to have to wait nor do I want to start looking for anyone. You all know the name and location of the hotel, right?"

After getting their nods of consent, I handed each of them, including young Emma and Elizabeth (who I dubbed "Beth"), Paul and Eve's children Barbrie and Paul, twenty Euros each and demanded, "I expect change if not the whole amount back at 19:00, 7 PM. Tonight."

I tried to be serious, but aunt Eve said, "Spend it, spend it all."

I looked with an exasperated expression at Eve and everyone broke out laughing, including me. Before I could say another word they were gone.

"Ok, mom, what do you want to do?"

"I'd like to wander down Dawson Street past Mansion House and poke around some of the book stores."

I said, "I'm game. When we hit Nassau Street we can loop around and hit the National Gallery. What about the rest of you?"

"I think we would like to go over to Grafton Street and do some shopping," Barbrie said.

"You've got two credit cards, right baby?"

"Aye. How much do we have on each, Rudy?"

"Five pounds, or eight Euros, or ten dollars!"

Everyone laughed. Paul said he could loan Barbrie some if she needed it.

"In that case give me back the credit cards," I said to Barbrie with a grin.

Eve grabbed Barbrie's hand and they ran down the street like a couple of schoolgirls. I hadn't seen them act so giddy for a long time. Paul shrugged his shoulders and tagged along after them. I smiled and nodded approval to him, and mom and I slowly headed for the bookstores.

———◆◈◆———

The flight home seemed long because everyone was excited to get home. Maya met us at O"Hare in Chicago with a fifteen passenger van. Sean Kelly, our friend and owner of Kelly's Auto Service, had gotten it for our use.

She was ecstatic to see Emma and Beth. It was a great surprise for her. We spent that night in Chicago and the young Irish girls were ga ga over everything, especially Chicago Style pizza.

Maya, in turn, had a surprise for us at home. Danny, Barbrie and Eve's brother and his wife Megan came up to Hartford from Atlanta to spend a week with us and to visit Megan's folks, the Kelly's. As the Irish say, it was "GRAND."

Amid the picnics at Lake Michigan and a day at Michigan Adventure Amusement Park north of Muskegon, Michigan, Danny and I had some "business" to discuss.

"So your Irish Studies Program in Ireland will be up and running next year?"

"Aye, if there are no glitches," I said.

"That's grand. There are some things we will need to button down regarding the cargo we discussed some time back," Danny suggested.

"I think I've got a plan, though it will take some careful tweaking to get it to work," I explained.

"What plan doesn't need tweaking?" Danny asked with a thick Belfast accent. "And then you just say 'Fuck it,' and improvise."

"Aye, coming from you, this sounds funny, for you are usually two or three moves ahead in every game like a chess master," I countered.

"You must be flexible. You have your plan, but you also have a couple of contingencies and fall back measures. It's not just what's up ahead of you, it's also what's happening beside you and behind you that you must be aware of, and prepared to deal with.

"Take it from an old 'fuck up,' Rudy. I haven't survived this long by straight up planning. It's been willingness to improvise, remembering old tricks of the trade, and pure luck. Zigging instead of zagging, walking instead of running, ducking instead of walking tall.

"We'll get it together. You'll figures it out. Denny say's you're the best. From our Canada experience, I know you are. And I hear you played some recent games on the security boys. That's why we are turning to you Rudy. You'll get it done."

"Aye. Put the pressure on by sweet-talking me. I know how you Conlon's work. Next you'll give me the Conlon grin, which I've come to learn, is like a hand shake to you people, sealing the deal."

"Aye, you're learning brother-in-law. So we have a deal then?" he grinned.

"Jaysus, what I don't do for love. If this was a religious request I was working on, I'd be assured a place in heaven," I theorized.

Danny smiled and said, "Bless you son, your faith and good works have saved you."

Not to be out done I countered, "The spirit is strong but the flesh is weak."

"I've noticed you are getting a little soft and pudgy Rudy. You've got to stay fit for my sister. She is speaking figuratively when she says she expects more of you."

How do you answer that, I thought? Best to just exhale, smile, and get down to business. But I couldn't let it alone. "I've been giving her more and she says it's getting better every day. Every day. Every day, in every way!"

"Really?"

"Really. Ask her."

"Maybe it will come up and I will."

"Oh, it comes up all right. On command. And she's loving every bit of it."

I was getting the heavy punches in now and I was loving it. Before it went any further, Megan interrupted us by asking, "What are you boys discussing so famously?"

Before Danny could answer I replied, "The American approach to life. And now that Danny is here, I have to give him some subtle instruction so he doesn't appear to be out of step."

"Oh, he's fitting in just fine. Really Rudy."

I raised my eyebrows, smiled, and nodded consent.

"That's what he claims."

Danny and I broke up laughing. Megan just frowned and walked away.

<hr />

Maya, Emma, Beth and Eve's daughter Barb had a grand month and a half. Our County Down girls, Emma and Beth, didn't want to leave. America was "so big" and they wanted to see more of it.

"Next time. Start saving your money and you can come back any time you want. Summer is best, for day trips and swimming," I explained.

"Do you mean it, uncle Rudy?" Emma asked.

"Absolutely."

"Plan on us next July and August then, if that is alright," Beth said.

Barbrie said, "We look forward to having you girls back next summer."

"We have a friend who will be so jealous when she hears about our stay with you. If she could manage, do you think she might be able to join us?" Emma asked.

"Of course she can. The more the merrier. With all of us in Hartford, the wee place will start sounding like Belfast and County Down with all of us about with our accents. It will be grand," Barbrie said.

I could hear the homesick tone of her voice.

"We'll be back in June and maybe you can come over a bit earlier if you wanted to. You'll have to check with your parents though," I suggested.

They were beside themselves. Seeing them to the plane in Chicago was sad. Goodbyes always are.

THE POST PARTUM PEACE

The plan was simple, but complex; it was straightforward, but full of deceptions; it was based on hope for peace, but it recognized threats of violence. It was as the BBC's Brian Rowan put it, a period of "The Armed Peace," for there was both "Life and Death after the Ceasefire."

My brother-in-law, Danny Conlon, representing the Army Council of the IRA had explained the danger facing many former Republican volunteers. The threats were made, they were real, and some of them had been acted upon. The Army Council wanted to protect all Republicans, but had a sense of urgency concerning many former IRA solders.

Danny Conlon found sanctuary, and after consultation, it was decided others could follow in his footsteps. He contacted me and, in so many words, he asked me to come up with a plan.

The plan was obvious. I had the means to pull it off with help from expert forgers. I proposed rescuing only two men the first year to test the procedure.

Two young men would be accepted into our Irish Studies Program, and their new passports sported pictures with beards and glasses that were generic enough that some one resembling them could pass as the original owners. Since the pre-trip classes were on line classes the students often never met each other. Even if students came to the face-to-face meetings, they didn't meet everyone because some students couldn't make those weekly meetings and they were not mandatory.

The plants, or "ringers" as they were called, were enrolled in two classes and did the work like everyone else. What they did with their credits was their business because I never planned on seeing them again after Dublin. In short, like some class members, they were total strangers to each other, and to me. The less I knew about them the better I felt.

At the end of the three weeks in Ireland, as we were assembling at the airport in Dublin I would explain to the rest of the students that the two young men were staying in Ireland and would return later, which was in fact an option for everyone on the trip. It had to be arranged with Aer Lingus before we departed for Ireland, and through the years about four to eight students took advantage of this opportunity each year.

The two ringers, that first year, would then return to the US through Canada and just drive in after a "vacation" or "fishing trip" (carrying their official passports just in case). No one would be the wiser. The two former IRA men would end up in Chicago after staying with us in Hartford for a day or two. They would thank me and head off for safety somewhere in the USA.

The Army Council accepted my plan, and I began to implement it in the fall semester as I began to recruit students for the Irish Foreign Studies Program.

———◆———

At the college there was a genuine interest in the Irish program, and I recruited the majority of students from my classes. I taught several sections of Western Civilization, a British History class, a Russian History course, an Irish History survey, an Introduction to Philosophy and Logic classes. I had access to a broad section of Liberal Arts students.

The balance of the thirty students accepted for the Irish Program, about ten, came by way of posters and word of mouth. But again, two of the thirty were the ringers for the IRA men. Since community colleges attract a wide variety of students, many in their twenties and thirties, after they had tried jobs and lost them or found them to be dead ends as far as income was concerned, they often return to school, and the community college was inexpensive and having an open door policy, accessible. So the two ringers did not stick out and were accepted as if they were real students, which, technically, they were.

During the three weeks we were in Ireland, we spent the majority of that time up at Ti Cuhulainn (Cuhulainn's House), Mullaghbane, in South Armagh. We hosted a variety of speakers, some local politicians, historians, social workers, political activists, clergymen and former paramilitaries.

Brice Dickson from the Human Rights Commission came down to talk to us, as did my friend Danny Morrison who spoke on the press and the media and the Troubles. I planned to add Mythology and Legends as a course, so my old friend and mentor John Smyth of Queen's was put on notice. We had at least two presentations per day, but sometimes as many as four in a day.

Other days we traveled as a group to Belfast for mural tours, walking tours, historical talks and political presentations out at Stormont from several political parties and their key personalities like Gerry Adams, Martin Mc Guinness, Ian Paisley, Sean Farren, and David Ervine, to mention a few and to indicate the quality of the speakers.

I always planned having weekends off including Friday. This plan helped students who wanted to travel around Ireland on their own or in groups to visit family, friends and/or places of interest not covered by the program. If we went over to Derry for a tour of the city, its walls, the Bogside, and the Guild Hall, and maybe a lecture or presentation with people affiliated with the University of Ulster at Derry, on a Thursday, students often did not return with the group that night. They spent the night in Derry and then had Friday, Saturday and part of Sunday to explore the Inishowen Peninsula or the southern part of Donegal.

I asked them to travel in pairs or groups, and to give me a brief outline of their plans. It always worked well. Adventurous students had a great opportunity to have a trip within the school trip. The students appreciated my flexibility on this opportunity, and I never had a problem with anyone abusing this privilege.

We usually spent two or three nights at the end of the program in Dublin before heading home or where ever. Students were given a quick "1916 Tour," as well as a ticket for the "Hop On Hop Off 24 Hour Sight Seeing Dublin Bus Tour." The rest of the time, with the exception of one hour for "editing" their last paper, was their own.

The morning of our plane departure for home we caught the special bus from Dublin to the airport. I never had one person miss a flight from tardiness. Everyone was excited to get home to family and friends.

During our time in South Armagh I had plenty of time to meet with old friends, make new contacts, and visit with my relatives in Saintfield, County Down. The format of the program made the opportunities for contacts endless. Sometimes they were integrated into the schedule and became part of the program.

From Nationalist speakers we heard of the ongoing violence perpetrated against the Nationalist community. Not as organized as in the past, but as brutal, vicious and deadly. Students were encouraged to read a variety of daily newspapers and to watch the nightly news on TV.

If the Irish Foreign Studies Program was an academic success, being a conduit for former IRA men to escape immanent danger in the North of Ireland was even more so. By the third year we expanded the study program to forty members and planned to evacuate four people per year.

The first real glitch came with the "9-11" attacks and the tightening of border crossings and reentry to the US. My concern with the retrieved personnel was their accents. I insisted that the candidates practice adapting American accents (American movies and TV programs where available and were indispensable for this purpose).

Second, that they had to know their "ringers" biography down pat, keep abreast of current affairs in the US, especially professional sports, like American football, basketball, baseball and hockey (being from Michigan at least the professional teams: like the Lions, Bears and Packers; Pistons and the nearby Chicago Bulls; the Tigers, Cubs, White Socks, and the infamous Yankees; the Red Wings and Black Hawks; and College teams like the Wolverines, Spartans, and The Fighting Irish).

When it came to the "ringers" we had to change location for reentry into the USA. For them, getting into Canada was a little tougher, but not impossible. But it was infinitely more difficult getting into the United States than it had been before.

I had a close friend who had a place in Detour, Michigan, up on the St. Mary's River coming out of Sault St. Marie in Michigan's Upper Peninsula. A ferry ran to Drummond Island every hour, and the island was a short distance from Canada. This would be the new entry point for the ringers.

After my Irish Program trip I would borrow my friend's cabin for part of a week for some family "R & R" and I would use a boat to extract the ringers from Canada, posing as fishing companions. Although there was a new Border Patrol station and personnel stationed on Drummond Island, it was possible to use the North Channel and the Canadian Cockburn Island to our advantage.

I purchased a big enough fishing boat (with donated funds), to hold my human cargo and to return to Detour without drawing too much attention. We had to be careful, always alert, taking no chances, and always assuming we were being watched.

But the constant coming and going of pleasure craft and fishing boats of various sizes in these waters facilitated our retrieval program greatly.

———— ◆•◆•◆ ————

A new wrinkle inserted itself in the fabric of my life when my daughter, in consultation with the Notre Dame Law School, where she had been accepted, was going to allow her to take some courses at Queen's University Law Department in Belfast, while working with Brice Dickson.

I had no hesitations about this opportunity, although I had some concerns. I called Brice and explained that my name was well known to the security forces in the North and that I did not want that to cause any embarrassment and complications for him or my daughter. I suggested that possibly Eoffa could use the Gaelic form of her last name, "Cashel," as an alias or "nom de guarre."

Brice laughed at my dark humor and related, "I am to believe that you have a history and reputation here in the North, and it is not solely in conjunction with the questions and comments you asked of certain people during your CIEE seminars.

"Professor John Smyth has filled me in on some of you exploits which he sanitized for me. He gave glowing recommendations for your daughter by the way."

"I didn't know she used him as a reference. They had met on our family tour, but I know she had been in contact with him while she did her semester abroad last Spring."

"Well, he was favorably impressed, and I quote, "in spite of her father's drawbacks," his words not mine, although he was smiling when he said them. He also asked me to mention that to you when I had a chance."

"I can't wait to see him next Spring. I'll also let you know the dates when I'll have a new group over in late May and June, and I hope you can grace us with your presence, sarcasm, and wit," I chided.

"Of course. I'll communicate with Eoffa about the name change."

"I will also have Eoffa stay close to Smyth. He knows my rules for her. Also I have a Republican friend named Denny who will be around, out of sight but vigilant, and in touch with her. If John will be her conscience, Denny will be her protector."

"Really?"

"Really and seriously. We go way back."

"All right."

"Oh, she also has relatives in Saintsfield, County Down. They would be able to help her in any way they can until I show up."

"You are serious aren't you?"

"She is my oldest. She is my daughter. She'll not pay for the sins of her father. It's just that simple."

"Rudy, you are scaring me."

"No worry. You are one of the good guys. I'd come over for you and yours too. So be careful. Or I'll have to come out of the closet and show my true colors."

"We'll all be careful Rudy. I'll keep her and advise her as if she were my daughter."

"I know you will, and that puts me at ease."

When I finally got a hold of Denny on a secure line I explained the situation, including the possible alias for Eoffa. He concurred that a change of names was warranted and a good idea.

"I don't think the Brits would cause her any grief or harm her physically. But if the Loyalists who were after me put two and two together and recognized her as my daughter, then I think there would be concern.

"We were thinking of keeping her first name, 'Eoffa,' but maybe changing her last name to 'Cashel.' We thought close enough so as not to trip her up but different enough to confuse the issue."

"I can see that clear enough," Denny said.

"Technically, Dickson, Smyth and you will be the only ones in the know. She'll have constant contact with Brice, and a little with John. I don't know how much she'll have with yourself, but the main job of protecting her will fall on you. If I can trouble you to watch her periodically, to check up on her once in a while, or physically protect her if need be."

"Rudy, she will be no trouble and she will not be in any trouble. Trust me."

"Jaysus, Denny, I wish you hadn't said that last part. 'Trust me,' is a phrase that I would never associate with your name. You got me in more damn 'Trouble' over the years by 'trusting you,' than I care to remember. Now I'm really concerned."

"Shite, anything that happened to youse was brought on by yourself. If you had used a disguise like I used to use you would have a clean record and a clean conscience," Denny mocked.

"Horse shit, cow shit, bull shit, sheep shit, pig shit. I was always a victim, usually of your making. I can't believe I'm entrusting my oldest to your care. And a daughter at that. God have mercy."

"It'll take more than arguing and begging for His mercy, Rudy. You, my friend, are a lost soul. But God's and your loss have been Ireland's gain, and on behalf of he Irish people, I thank you," Denny explained.

"But it profits a man nothing to gain the whole world, not just Ireland, but lose his soul," I countered.

"But I think you'll have your cake and eat it too," Denny volleyed.

"Where in the hell is that in Scripture?" I demanded.

Denny laughed and said, "You see, the good Lord didn't put everything down in the Scriptures. Some things he left unsaid. He left it to us wise men, us prophets, us holy men, to reveal the unsaid and hidden nuggets of gold, Rudy."

"In that case maybe I'll just have her stay with Reverend Paisley. He too claims all of those things to an even greater extent."

"Maybe so Rudy, but he doesn't claim to be Irish and Catholic. I do! I'm two hind-legs up on the old bigot. She'll be safer in my shadow."

"Indeed, I believe she will. Thanks Denny. I'll be in touch."

———— ◆•◆•◆ ————

A NEW CASTLE IN THE CASHEL

E veryone has their cross to bear, and Eoffa was no exception. Innocent as the driven snow from her home state of Michigan, she was about to be engulfed into a good old fashioned storm, more than a real Michigan twister or tornado.

She arrived in Belfast not exactly wide-eyed and bushy tailed, but close enough to being innocent as I could send her. For her own good I had explained some of my past and some of my concern for her.

She knew of her grandmother's involvement, and her great granda's exploits, but she had heard only whispers of her own da's experience. She knew uncle Danny was a hero, in the US illegally, and safe as long as silence was maintained. In short, she knew her family had secrets.

We had Irish kin from the North stay with us periodically, and niece Maya had taken up permanent residence with us for years now as another 'daughter' of mine and Barbrie's, a full time college student of late, and she was becoming more American than some Americans. She was even starting the naturalization process for US citizenship.

But my revelation of episodes in Ireland and the rescue of Danny in Canada a few years ago, though sanitized, were explicit enough to ensure she understood the gravity of her being careful in the North of Ireland because of her father's past.

"I knew, but didn't really know. Grandma had told me some things, very minor of course. But she was always so proud of 'every generation doing their bit,' and I saw the way she would look at you and smile. And Aunt Eve has told me a few things on the 'QT,' but made me promise to never say a thing to any body, especially you and mom. So I sort of knew.

"And I know I'm getting a cleaned up edited version now. But I understand better. You worked with Smyth a wee bit, but with Denny a ton. A slight concern, I turn to Smyth. Anything beyond a slight concern, it's Denny.

"I suppose he'll be spying on me too?"

I cautioned, "Spying is a term that needs to be used with care, Eoffa. He will certainly check up on you, some times with your knowledge and some times with out you knowing it. If it is any comfort to you, I didn't ask him to pry into your personal life there, but he will observe your coming and going and make sure you are not the object of interest to the wrong sorts of people.

"If need be he'll inform John who will assure Brice that you are safe, with relatives in Saintfield until I can join you there and the two of us decide what might be best.

"When you are involved in things that matter, you don't consider that your actions might come back and bite your kid and other family members in the arse," I confessed.

———————

When she flew out of Chicago for Ireland her mother and aunt Eve cried like babies. I must admit they brought moisture to my eyes as well. I was sure Eoffa was all right, but my God these two were a mess.

When Eoffa had gone to Ireland for the semester, she went with a group of students from Notre Dame. This time she was on her own. This only added to the drama that her mother and aunt were getting excited about.

"Of course, you arrange for the time off and we'll go over and check up on her. Oh, I mean, 'visit' her," I said to Barbrie by way of comfort.

"I'll come too, so it looks like a vacation," Eve offered.

"It's going to look like a fucken rescue mission any way we do it," I corrected with a smile.

On that note everything lightened up. We came straight home from Chicago, in the event Eoffa decided to change her mind in Dublin, and was going to return home and wanted us to return to Chicago to get her both Barbrie and Eve suggested.

I didn't say a word. Eve said, "OK, Rudy. What are you smiling about? Barbrie, he's quietly laughing at us. Look at his smirk."

"Rudy, are you mocking you child's mother and aunt?"

"God forbid. But she's not going off to war."

"Pull over so we real Irish can beat some sensitivity into you," Eve demanded.

"Only the Irish could envision 'beating some sensitivity' into someone," I observed to my regret.

"What is that supposed to mean?" Eve demanded.

"You beat someone senseless, not into sensitivity," I tried to explain.

"Says who?"

"Me and the rest of the human race."

"I'm sure the rest of humanity feels as I do if they stop and think about it," Eve reflected.

She was really getting wound up and I knew I had to stop for her to get some fresh air, some tea or coffee, and to go to the toilet.

"Rudy, we should stop for a break," Barbrie observed.

"My very thought."

"Aye, he's a mind reader now, taking credit for other's ideas," came from the back seat. I couldn't help but laugh. To my great relief, Barbrie started laughing too.

"Aye, the two of you up there. It's a conspiracy. He's turned a lovely Irish girl against her own kin," Eve said before breaking out with a laugh of her own.

"It happened a long time ago," Barbrie said.

"A **long** time ago," I reiterated.

"Jaysus, not all that long ago," Barbrie corrected.

"He thinks it's been a long, long, time Barbrie. What do you think makes him feel that way?" Eve asked.

"Sister-in-laws," I said quietly.

There was a pause, then the two of them started to laugh. When my Conlon girls laughed it was like angelic music. All was peaceful and good in the world. Well, at least their and my immediate world.

————◆•◆•◆————

It would be several months before I planned to return to Ireland with a Irish Studies group, and we didn't know what Eoffa had planned for Christmas break. First it was too far off. Second, she might make plans that didn't include us. She was after all over twenty-one years of age.

My Brother-in-law Paul and sister-in-law Eve's daughter Barbrie had graduated from college and was hired as the fulltime librarian in Hartford. Her mother Eve worked for her technically, but as everyone knew, Eve worked everybody as if she was in charge, as manager and owner.

I don't to this day know if Eve put young Barbrie up to it, but young Barb decided to visit her cousin over in Belfast. At first her mother and aunt talked of joining her, but I cautiously dissuade them from this intrusion. Eventually, they decided to abandon their joining young Barb on her holiday.

Eoffe would join her cousin down in Dublin for several days before the two of them came up to Belfast for a few days. They would shop, visit Trinity College's famous library, several old bookstores, and the old sights associated with my mother. I suspected this last bit was for my mother who gave young Barb a wad of money for her trip. She also gave Barb something to pass on to Eoffa.

"What the hell, I can't take it with me. I want to see it used for some good. These young ones are interested in Ireland and things Irish, and that's good. So there you have it," mom said.

"I'm not arguing or saying anything, mom. The more you give the less Paul and I have to fork over. I think its grand that you spread the wealth."

"If I didn't know better I'd say you boys were giving them wee girls some anyway. They are lovely girls, just like their Irish mothers," mom said with tears in her eyes. "You boys sure lucked out."

"What's this all about? You getting teary eyed and all."

"I'm not getting any younger, and all of these babies are growing up and moving on. I don't see them so much any more. I'm getting nostalgic and sentimental."

"Nostalgic, maybe, but sentimental, never. It doesn't become us, you or me. We are hardy stock, and know the hard facts. We are hard, not given to any sentimentality. Maybe sensitivity, but not any sentimentality," I argued.

"I'll accept that Rudy. I'm getting sensitive in my old age," mom agreed.

"Maybe next June at the end of the Irish Studies Program you and Barbrie can come over and we'll stay with Eoffa a while," I suggested.

"The truth is Rudy, the way I've been feeling lately you'll have to bring me in an urn."

"Jaysus, mom, what ails you?"

"The years and the miles. Put together, I'd say they would stretch to the moon and back. I'm feeling every bit of my age. I'll not be going back to Ireland. I'm ready for the long rest."

"Do you hurt? Feel sickly? What?"

"I feel old, Rudy. Old."

Before I could argue with her and make her angry, she was always at her best when she was angry (I used to say "pissed" but she'd correct me and say she "was angry, never pissed, after all I'm a lady!" She'd say with a grin. Furthermore, "pissed" meant "drunk" in Ireland and the UK. I never saw her drunk), she stood up. I waited and watched her for an instant.

With that she turned and walked into the kitchen.

She wasn't going back to Ireland. That would end a chapter in her life, my life, and for some few it would end a chapter in the life of Ireland.

I suddenly didn't feel so hard, and I felt nostalgic myself and maybe, just maybe, a touch of melancholy, but not sentimentality.

Eoffa was fitting in with Brice Dickson's staff at the Human Rights Commission and the classes he taught at the University of Ulster. Being the resident American was enough to attract admirers, but being beautiful, intelligent, and somewhat street smart, added to the magnetic pull.

She was able to apply many of the lessons of the American Civil Rights movements as suggested models for the North of Ireland. But she was neither doctrinaire nor a know it all, rather she cautiously offered suggestions. She offered examples that worked and failed; she offered insights from successes and failures; she listened and was never pushy or a know it all. There were other times she just listened and mulled it over, then privately passed on her thoughts to Professor Dickson.

Her dedication to her work at the Human Rights Commission was all consuming, and she lived her commitment every hour of every day, even on her weekends and days off. If she was consumed by her work, her youth did not allow her to be exhausted. Interestingly it was not weariness that came to the fore, but something more basic and personal.

As weeks turned to months she was so busy that she hardly noticed any homesickness, until her cousin young Barb said she would like to visit, and asked if Eoffa could put up with her for a week. Eoffa was so overcome with homesickness that she cried on the phone to Barb, and then her aunt Eve, and then to her mother.

"I'm so homesick. I need to see you," she said to one and all.

By the time I got to talk to her I asked, "I'll bet you have been so busy that you didn't notice until Barb asked if she could come and visit, right?"

"Aye, that's right da. How did you know?"

"I just know. We've all, well, many of us, have been there. So get busy again doing what you are doing and enjoy what you are doing. You might never get another chance to do it again. By the way how are Smyth and Denny?"

"Grand so they are. I see John at least once a week. I've had supper with he and his wife a couple of times. Denny just shows up out of nowhere periodically. I think he only reveals himself about half the time. I feel him watching over me, in a good way, like a guardian angel."

"That's right. That's what he is. He was like that to me sometimes. He was never nosy, never interfering, never bothersome, but covering you, just in case. Like being on point, or a rear guard."

"Da, I've got to get back to work. I love you all and miss you all. I'm looking forward to Barb coming over. It will be grand."

Peter Jeffries of Special Branch had been following my return to the North with my students over the past couple of years. Another year had passed and he had not observed or noticed me involved in obvious infractions of the law or suspicious activities. He didn't note any suspicious contacts with former paramilitaries, except where they were speakers to the studies group. And then, they came from both sides of the divide.

But still he wondered. *He's got to be up to something. He has an agenda, and although he might exhibit patience, I know he is a man of action. I wonder what the hell he's up to?*

And now he has a daughter over here working with Dickson at the Human Rights Commission and attending classes with him at the faculty of law at the University of Ulster. Castle's using his daughter for something. What kind of man would use his own daughter for some underhanded thing?

They all must be brainwashed. Her mother, aunt and uncle, especially Danny Conlon, must have turned the next generation into subversives.

I need to keep an eye on her. I know exactly how to do it too. A young, healthy, good-looking American woman in a foreign country. She may be subversive but if she is somewhat normal she won't be able to resist the friendship of a handsome administrator working for the RUC. He'll not be a policeman, rather just an adjunct for the RUC.

Let me think. Yes, in the public relations department of the RUC. Not a Peeler, just a bureaucrat. A bureaucrat who might have information she could use. She might feed both Dickson and her dad and thus compromise both of them. What a scandal!

He'll have to attract her first, and slowly. Then just bait her with a slight tip of the iceberg. In the mean time he might be able to play her and ply information from her. It would be sort of a lover's trade off. To seal their bond, their courtship.

This is just far fetched enough to work. Wouldn't that be something. Sink Castle and Dickson with one torpedo. If it works. Nothing waged, nothing gained. What's to lose? Nothing.

Going to the phone, Jeffries made two phone calls. The first was to the Public Relations Department of the RUC. The second was for Mark Prestin, a young, handsome eligible bachelor in the RUC whose career could be made in the next couple of months. Who knows, there might even be some extra perks for Prestin if young Eoffa Castle, known locally as Cashel, would fall for him.

———————————•·•◦•·•———————————

Although Eoffa was working day and night with Dickson at either the commission or classes and homework, she did notice the new RUC Public Relations man who had started stopping by the Human Rights Commission's office. He seemed friendly, but somewhat reserved.

He was polite with everyone, from Dickson down to the lowly staff. He smiled, was courteous, and tried to remember everyone's name. By the second week he seemed to be a fixture in the office. He ate biscuits that some one brought in, and true to his word, he brought some in to do his bit as well.

It was during a break of tea and biscuits he said to Eoffa, "So you are an American law student and intern of Brice's here at the commission? How do you like it?"

"Like what?"

"Your job, your classes, your home in Belfast?"

"I love it, I'm learning it, and I'm getting used to it, in that order."

"Very witty."

"Not really. Just answering accurately your questions in the order they were asked. I try to be precise," Eoffa said flatly.

"Americans never cease to amaze me. They can be charming one minute and brutally cold the next."

"Nice compliment. Which was I just now," Eoffa asked?

"I'm not sure."

"Thanks for bringing in the biscuits," Eoffa said coldly and she turned and walked away.

As she returned to her desk, she leaned over to a coworker and asked, "What do you know about your man over there? He's the one from the PR department of the RUC."

"Not a thing. He's been here and about for about two weeks, chatting up every one, being nice to one and all. Trying to fit in I suppose."

"He is RUC though, right," Eoffa asked?

"Aye, he is."

The next time she saw Brice Dickson, Eoffa inquired about the new, polite face of the RUC gracing their office on a regular basis.

"I got a call from the new director of PR at the RUC headquarters here in Belfast saying they were appointing a new man, with no long history as an active RUC man, to collect any inquiries we may have and to try and answer any questions we might have. Of course he has to check in with headquarters before he makes any noise to us. I suspect he's a watcher for them. So we all must take care with what we say and do.

"But you must be very careful, Eoffa, with your last name being what it is. We've tried to shield you, but these people know who you are and you just never know what they are up to," Brice warned.

That night Eoffa contacted Denny and passed on to him Mark Prestin's name, title, and description. She also passed on Dickson's description of him as a "watcher" for the RUC. "He also gave me a strong warning to take care around this man because of who he is."

"Sound advice, Eoffa. Keep your distance and let me know of any suspicious discussions or actions," Denny advised.

Denny thanked her, and said he would have the man checked out thoroughly. He also cautioned again, "Eoffa, be especially careful. When they are in uniform or identify themselves, you know what they want and what to expect. It's this type, posing as a nice boy that you have got to fear. Like a wee poisonous spider lurking in the corner, he is full of malice. I'm familiar with the type all too well.

"Keep me informed if he starts prying too much about the commission office and personnel. That goes without saying for yourself, especially. His boss may be an old acquaintance of your da's, from his past. He's too young, but his boss could be the daddy spider."

"Thanks Denny."

"As always young lady, I'll be in touch."

"I've no doubt you'll also be watching over me. Probably close enough to touch, if you know what I mean."

"Jaysus, you sound like your da. And yes, I am at times watching over you. Never to meddle in your affairs, mind you. Just to protect."

"I know Denny. I appreciate having you there whether I know you are or not. You make me feel safe," Eoffa said sincerely.

"Aye," Denny said as Eoffa rang off.

As the connection went dead, Denny thought to himself, *Safe. Who in God's creation is safe? Rudy has told her some of the past. He knows the danger of this sort of setup. I just hope she is as cool and detached as her da. She has recognized danger in this Prestin, I just hope she has the sense to avoid any and all contact.*

She's attractive so he'll use that as his approach to a nice American girl, away from home. Would she like to go for a drink sometime? Aye, Eoffa, be careful.

The immediate question is: when should I tell Rudy?

————•◆•————

A few days later Denny called me on a safe line at a colleague's office in the his department.

"Rudy? Nothing urgent, but I just want to keep you informed on a wee matter that Eoffa brought to my attention the other day."

"Aye Denny, she called me yesterday here at the college so as not to disturb her mother. She gave me the low down on this RUC dick, Mark Prestin. What have you got on him?"

"Not a thing. I don't think he's really with the RUC. Probably he's Special Branch. I'm not probing too hard. Don't want to spook them.

"He's supposedly a young functionary for the Public Relations Department of the RUC and has been assigned to the Human Rights Commission. He's officially a liaison but obviously he's a spy in their midst. Eoffa knows to be careful. If he tries to get close to her I'll let you know and you can tell me what do. I didn't have to warn her. She spotted him straight off. She's a good girl, Rudy.

"Don't worry, I'm watching her like a daughter."

"She is a daughter. My daughter. And this makes me nervous. Any thing that you see as dangerous, you let me know, PDQ."

"Okie dokie," Denny said reassuringly.

————•◆•————

DANGEROUS LAISIONS

Prestin reported directly to Jeffries. This was a special operation, and it was also a personnel operation as far as Jeffries was concerned. He would so like to get Castle. If his daughter was collateral damage so be it. Being a Castle, she was probably not collateral, but directly involved in what ever Rudy Castle was up to, so she was an accessory. She'd be burned along with the old man if it could be arranged.

"She's not only good looking, she's as sharp as a tack," Prestin reported.

"Is she approachable? Has she taken to you?" Jeffries asked his man.

"From what I've experienced, neither. She is wary. The 'RUC' does not bring out the best in her. Not exactly hostile, but cold and calculating. If I didn't know better, I'd say she is on to me, already."

"Keep playing nice, not too pushy. Be nice to every one. Do not show her any special attention. Keep building relations with the whole staff. We'll see if she doesn't come around when the rest of her colleagues start feeling comfortable with you."

"Yes sir. Is there anything in particular I should keep my eyes open for? Something Eoffa Cashel is working on, or involved with?"

"No, at this stage we just want you to get in with the Human Rights crowd, especially with Cashel. She is the key, and whether or not she is actively involved with any particular group or individual, she can lead us to people we need to take an interest in.

"She is related to a suspect, an American, who runs an Irish Foreign Studies program from a cultural center or something down in 'Bandit Country.' It's located at Mullaghbane, South Armagh. He is acquainted with a number of IRA people down there who help him with speakers, like the Murphys.

"He has a history that goes back to the late sixties and the beginning of this recent round of the 'Troubles.' Maybe she can help us get to him," Jeffries said cryptically.

"What's his name?"

"Castle. Rudy Castle."

Prestin screwed up his face and asked, "Isn't Cashel the Irish for Castle?"

"Look, I don't want you to know too much for fear that you might slip up and disclose something to her that would tip her off and blow this part of the operation. So actually, the less you know the better. By being naive and ignorant you will pose no threat to what we are up to.

"You know enough for now. Go slow, don't rush anything, get her trust and then we can proceed with phase two of our plan."

"Yes sir. Slow but steady."

"That's it Prestin. If she leaves her office and you have a chance to tail her that would be fine. Just don't get caught. In time maybe you can suggest that if she is heading somewhere in particular you might be able to give her a lift or accompany her since you have business in the neighborhood.

"But don't push it. Let it all happen naturally. We are on a schedule but not a time clock. Got it?"

"Yes sir."

"Now off with you."

It sounds like she is her daddy's girl. Well, we nearly had him the last time. He won't be so fortunate this time as to slip through our grasp, Jeffries thought. *Not this time.*

———◆◆◆———

The student came into the department office as I was discussing details for the upcoming Spring program in Ireland with my associate Tracy. The student just stood there for a second, not wishing to interrupt our conversation, when I spun around, holding my hands in an exaggerated Karate posture and said, "Don't ever sneak up on us that way. These hands are registered. They could slice and dice you six ways from Sunday."

Tracy quickly intervened and said, "Don't mind him, he is possessed. What can I do for you?"

Before the student could respond I interjected, "She wants information on the Irish Studies Program for this coming Spring in Ireland. Young lady, did you know for the all inclusive price of $3,200 you get round trip from the college to Ireland and back, all scheduled travel there (about 1500 kilometers), two meals a day, a lovely room at a rather new student cultural center located near the foot of Slieve Gullion, probably the highest point in South Armagh, which you will be able to climb for an all encompassing view for miles around, two three hour courses in history, political science, art, and or mythology.

"You can take the other two courses, thus having all four this early summer semester, you just have to pay the extra tuition costs. Since you'll be there and you will hear what I and others have to say on all the topics, why not take them. You'll do the class work on line in May and then we'll be in the North of Ireland for three weeks doing fieldwork and interviews. All you'll need is a passport and spending money. Here is the brochure, my colleague can answer any questions and help you with the application. Oh, yes, you may be eligible for financial aid. Nice to meet you. What did you say your name was?"

"Margaret. Margaret Mc Cormack."

"Jaysus, Tracy, get her an isle seat on the plane near the toilets and the pool. With a fine Irish name like that I want her treated like first class. Nice to meet you Margaret Mc Cormack. Tracy will fill in all the particulars. You can bring friends. The college has an open door policy, they don't have to be students here. When you get them to sign up they'll be college students, thanks to you. For recruiting I'll buy you a round periodically. Tracy help her, I'll catch you latter."

With that I headed for my own office and left Tracy standing there, with a smile on her face, with the student.

"I would like the brochure. Now I'm interested and I didn't even know the college had a foreign studies program."

"His is the best. He knows everybody whose anybody over in the North. As you can see he is a whirling banshee and he makes the program wonderful. Even rainy days when nothing is scheduled can be fun with him telling stories, and he claims to whistle in foreign languages, he says it's a gift. He rents a vehicle while we are there. Aye, I go too. He brings a handful of students to different places at night for a treat. Most say these little jaunts are the best part of the program."

"I came in to ask where my Western Civ. class was meeting. I forgot my tuition slip with the rooms listed on it. And here I am interested in going to Ireland next Spring. I want another brochure, my friend Ashley will want to come too."

"What time is the Western Civ class and who is the instructor?"

"Ten fifteen with Castle."

"Oh boy. You are in for a treat," Tracy smiled, motioning with her thumb over her shoulder down the hall where I had gone. "You just met your instructor. He'll have you laughing and spell bound at least once during each performance. He doesn't lecture, he talks to you. He tells stories, many historical, but some about his family. It's a performance, really."

As I came down the corridor into the open office area I said to Tracy and Ms. Mc Cormack, "I'm off to class. Is she signed up yet Tracy?"

"Almost. She's in your class so she's coming along with you."

"Aye, great."

But before we got out of the office a young man came in and I said to Ms Mc Cormack, "Go on down and tell them I'm on the way but I'll be late a couple of minutes. Young man, are you here for the information on the Irish Program? If not, why not? Let me explain it to you . . . ." With that I was off on my pitch once again.

Three minutes later I was off to class with the young man in tow, for he too was in my class. He now had two brochures and the promise for a drink or two in Ireland for recruiting a friend or two for the program.

At the end of the class I gave the pitch for the program and handed out about a dozen pamphlets. I also introduced the two students whom I had met in the office and were interested in going to Ireland. I said they might be able to talk to anyone before class who had questions about the program.

After class I had my two recruits stay a moment after I'd dismissed the rest of the class. I had them follow me back down to my office where I gave them desk copies of the text for our course.

"They are older editions than the one the bookstore has for sale, but you'll be able to sort out where we are in the thing for reading. It'll save you more than $75 for the course textbook. Just take care of it so I can let someone use it next semester. You can give it back the day of the final exam."

"Thanks professor Castle."

"Yes, thank you very much."

"Well look at it this way, here's your first $75 for Ireland."

"Ya, that's right. Thanks again."

"If the two of you are coming to Ireland with me, you need to get to know each other so I can depend on you for help. So get to know each other, sit by each other in class, just don't disturb my class. But before class you can talk up Ireland for me, another drink, see?"

"If you have any questions about Ireland and the Program, ask Tracy. She's the brains of the organization, I just know people. She runs it. She always come with us to make sure it all goes well. She is the best!"

As they walked past Tracy's desk I winked at Tracy and asked, what were we discussing earlier? But before she could identify the topic, a student came into the office, and I assaulted her in the name of the Irish Foreign Studies Program.

So it went for days, weeks, and months, until I had recruited our quota. By Christmas break we usually had thirty or more "live ones" as I identified them.

"Go to grandma and grandpa this year and be prepared to do without that butt ugly sweater, gloves or scarf they usually foist off on you, and say, 'This year, instead of a sweater, gloves or scarf, how about Ireland?' Thrust the brochure to them. Give them an enthusiastic pitch. Explain, 'It takes green to get to the green.' Play with them, play them."

Students would laugh, but those who tried it found it worked more often than not.

By the end of January we had our first meeting of students, family, friends and some "I'm not sure" types. After some power point pictures of Ireland and some of our speakers, many of whom were readily recognized from the media coverage of the "peace process," and some green cookies and punch, we were usually on our way. Friendships were being made, hesitant types succumbed to peer pressure, and some new people who just came to hear and see what it was all about, were on board.

We often had parents for students at four-year schools that had decided to take us up on our program. The word was out there that we had a fine program that delivered so much more that the others. And it was true.

This coming year's program was going to feature some one new, a young lady going to law school and interning in the North, and in the thick of the peace process. Ms Eoffa 'Cashel, from Hartford, Michigan. I was so proud and excited. Besides her father and his colleague Tracy from the college, her mother and her aunt were coming over for her presentation. The pressure was on.

The pressure was not only on Eoffa. I had been asked if I could make room for five ringers. Five! As this request came at the last minute I had to scramble to secure more airline seats. Fortunately, Aer Lingus was great to work with, and since it was in January that made the requests a reality.

But five! I wondered what was happening that was causing such an up swing in deportees. Then it dawned on me, the Good Friday Agreement called for the release of "political prisoners" who had been involved in the struggle. Some of these boys would need sanctuary. Northern Ireland was not that big, and hiding there was hardly an option for most of the ex-prisoners.

The shock came when my new student ringers included two female names. It was not a problem, I had just forgotten how active women had been in the struggle, while they were out of prison and while they were incarcerated as at Armagh Prison. Women had played a major role in the Movement and struggle, and some of them clearly needed protection as well.

I was more concerned with retrieving the ringers from Canada at the end of the line. Five new people could stand out and draw unwanted attention on a small boat along the borer with Canada and then staying in De Tour.

AN OLD FASHIONED DOUBLE CROSS

The Human Rights Commission was deeply involved with specific cases as well as overseeing the general involvement of the crown's forces in their dealings with the population of the North of Ireland. Clearly most of the cases involved infractions against the Nationalist community, but there were a handful of cases concerned with Loyalist claimants.

But the matter Eoffa was working on was one of the most notorious legal case in the North of Ireland. It involved the murder of Pat Finucane, a solicitor who often defended IRA suspects, who was shot to death in front of his family at his home in north Belfast by Loyalists in February of 1989.

In January of 1989, the Home Office Minister Douglas Hogg had singled out "a number of solicitors in Northern Ireland who are unduly sympathetic to the cause of the IRA," for special criticism. Coming just prior to the murder of Mr. Finucane, the statement seemed to be more than a simple coincidence. It also had the feel of more than a simple warning. It felt like a direct threat aimed specifically at Mr. Finucane.

In April of 1998, on the eve of the Good Friday Agreement, a UN investigator's report concluded that the RUC had intimidated, harassed, an hindered certain defence solicitors, and that an independent inquiry into Finucane's 1989 murder was warranted.

In 1999, on the tenth anniversary of the murder more than a thousand members of Amnesty International and legal figures signed a petition for an independent inquiry into his murder.

In March, even Ronnie Flannigan, the RUC Chief Constable, asked John Stevens, the Deputy Commissioner of the London Metropolitan Police to investigate new claims of collusion by the RUC in Finucan's murder.

The next month a UN reporter, named Param Cumaraswamy, criticized Flannigan for ignoring allegations of RUC harassment. He also claimed that evidence of collusion in solicitor Finucane's murder was evident, but Flannigan claimed these accusations were being addressed. Undeterred and dissatisfied, Cumaraswamy met with Dr. Mo Mowlam, Secreatry of State for Northern Ireland, and Chris Patten, chairman of the Commission on Policing.

In May Mowlam met with the Finucane family and heard that a confidential report by the Republic of Ireland had compelling evidence of collusion.

Eoffa was intellectually and legally involved in the case, and very emotionally involved because of the pain the family was still dealing with because of Patrick's murder and the intransigence of the crown's security forces, from top to bottom, and public officials, bureaucrats and functionaries at all levels.

Her involvement in this particular case made her a target for Mr. Prestin. He followed his boss's instructions and went slowly, but he was persistent. He never mentioned the case, nor did he mention the other main issue of the Bloody Sunday massacre in Derry that was begging to be objectively investigated.

He just chatted everyone up, made nice with every-body, and hinted at after hour get to gathers. A few staff members went out on Friday evenings, but Eoffa was not among them.

Then one evening she decided to tag along. She was instructed by Denny to sit back and watch and listen, not only to Mark Prestin, but also to her fellow workers at the Human Rights Commission. If some one was too talkative in public, one could only imagine what might be said in private.

Denny assured Eoffa that no harm would come to her co-workers, but the same could not be said for who was receiving the info. Also, possibly a word would be passed to Brice Dickson, that someone was leaking info to the RUC, the British security or military.

Maybe just a word of caution would be enough, if it was happening, Denny said so as to soften the comments. Eoffa agreed to do it. She didn't relish the idea of spying on her colleagues, but Eoffa knew that leaks were inexcusable; they would have to be stopped one way or another.

The mood in the pub was friendly and relaxed. There was a crowd of about ten, including Prestin. Eoffa took a stool as far away from him as possible. Deep down she knew this tactic was calculated not only to be coy with him, but also so she would not hear anything said by an associate that might be inappropriate and that she would need to report to Denny.

As the evening wore on people were moving about their group, changing seats to engage in various conversations. At just the moment she registered that Prestin came and sat on the stool next to her, she noticed a bearded man wearing glasses sitting on a stool at the bar but with his back to the bar taking in all the commotion of their group. He was smiling broadly as if enjoying the revelry and holding a jar and nursing it along. She knew at once who it was and also knew the drink contained no alcohol since Denny was on duty.

"Well Ms. Cashel, how nice to have you join our rowdy group. Have you been here the whole time, or have you just shown up?"

"I have been right here the whole time Mr. Prestin. You've been busy at the far end of our group and apparently didn't notice me down here," Eoffa suggested playing along with his obvious lie of not knowing she was present.

"You seem right at home in the public house. I suppose it is a little like a wet police station; there are the officers behind the bar, the foot pads hustling the tables, the regular drunks to be watched, and a fresh crowd of youngsters to be broken in to the routine of paying the fine, surrendering their innocence, and being handcuffed by the system that in name serves them. What do you think of that officer Prestin?" Eoffa asked.

"I didn't expect that. What an analogy. Have you dwelt on it long? Or did it just come to you?"

"Ouch, its obvious isn't it? When someone steps out of line after being served by the officers of the bar, they will rough them up, then lock them up. For what? Following the system, having what was served them. Isn't it obvious to you Mr. Prestin?"

"Please call me Mark. I think there might be some parallels, but I think the analogy falls flat."

"Speaking of the Falls, have you ever been down the road? Seen the wages of bigotry, or lack of real wages?"

"Actually, no I've never been down the Falls," Prestin lied. "You remember, I'm not really in the RUC uniformed division. I'm a police administrator in public relations. I don't patrol the streets. I try to develop trust, cooperation, and harmony between the RUC and the citizenry. Also with various groups, legitimate groups, too."

"And how does that appear to be working for you?" Eoffa asked, and her smile appeared to be more of a mocking grin to Prestin.

"The Nationalist community certainly is difficult to please. It's very slow going with them," Prestin admitted. Before he could broaden his answer, Eoffa cut him off.

"Gee, I wonder why that is? After hundreds of years of being here, does the Loyalist dominated security people and police have any inkling as to why Nationalists don't express trust, cooperation, or harmony with you? Or are you all blind, deaf, and dumb to what you and your kind have served up to the Irish for hundreds of years?

"No one else is listening to our conversation, their flirting with one another and their drinks, so we can be candid with each other. Tell me honestly, what is your take on the present, the past, and the future of the North?" Eoffa asked with a sincere look of wonder.

"Even if I were honest with you I don't think you'd believe me or appreciate what I had to say. My experience, limited as it is, is that foreigners, and especially Americans, are not at all in tune to what Loyalists and the British have done, are trying to do, and hope to accomplish, with the native Irish on this island," Prestin suggested.

"Maybe it's because, as my grandma says, we who left in most cases had no choice. We were thrown out of our own homes, off our own lands, from our own country. We were bitter. We Irish had no tradition of unity. We were parochial, fragmented, local, and united by family. We could not stand up to united, synchronized, coordinated assaults. So we scattered and became easy prey to centralized invaders. We were easily rounded up and shipped off.

"We were not always accepted too kindly into our new countries, or in our adopted accommodations, or comfortable with our forced exile; so it was all a bittersweet experience. Being forced out of what was ours into an often unfriendly, if not hostile, existence took stamina, courage, and stubbornness. It took time for us exiles to reconcile ourselves to the fact that we had to acclimate ourselves to new conditions, adjust to new climates and environments, and accept and be accepted by our new neighbors.

"We had been treated as strangers back home in Ireland and were treated often times the same way in our new land. We were bitter, but never lost sight of who caused our misery. The alternative to emigration, whether voluntary or forced, was famine, disease, and misery. To watch one's loved ones, the elderly, the young, babies, spouses, all manner of relatives, suffer and probably die.

"For the exiles, it took tremendous sacrifices, time and effort to finally fit in to our new homes. But our memory wouldn't let us forget how this all happened. Why it had happened. Who had caused this tragedy.

"Those of us who survived this tragedy, this veil of tears, this forced exodus, couldn't and wouldn't accommodate ourselves to what the Brits and Loyalists did to us, nor could we reconcile ourselves to what the Loyalists and Brits doled out to those of us who stayed. We knew that it wasn't that the remnant of Irish who stayed in Ireland all sold out, though some did, but they resigned themselves to their fate. They were tired, hungry, and willing to get peace at nearly any price.

"It happens all the time. My da points out that the Jews who were dispersed from Judea and were forced to live in exile experienced this bittersweet condition also. Many of the exiled Jews held Jerusalem and their religion in higher esteem than those few who had remained or returned to Palestine. The exiles, at least some of them, were all the more fervent, pious, and dedicated than the small remnant who were in the Holy Land. The ordeal of exile, culminating in the holocaust for many European Jews, made the generation of 1948 militant. Look at Israel today. Some would argue that they have become not just militant, but imperialistic. Look at their record with the Palestinians. Yet, the slogan, 'Never again,' is understandable. It was based on two thousand years of exile and all the pain that went with it, not just the recent holocaust.

"Many Jews in the United States often support the state of Israel fanatically. Israel is the culmination of all those centuries of pain, suffering, and sacrifice.

They may live in the US, but their heart and soul is in Israel.

"My da also explains that most of Eastern Europe for over forty years accommodated themselves to the Soviet domination. They were alone, had every thing to lose and were quite certain they were not going to gain much if anything if they rebelled. Resignation meant survival in their very own country. They wouldn't have to be strangers in a new land, nomads looking for a new land, exiles from their land in a new land.

"My da helped me understand it. My family, like thousands of others, simply didn't agree with resignation, accommodation and the saying 'better red than dead.' And when a few back here in Ireland raised their heads and tried to lead the masses out of the back of the cave to a 'real' world, a new world, and ideal world, hundreds, thousands, millions of us who left sought to aid them in their struggle to be free, to have dignity, to have their own country back.

"So if we sound skeptical, critical and hostile to the Loyalists and British here in Ireland, it is born of experience. It is born of memory. It is born of history. It is based on faith. It is based on hope. It is based on love; love of family, love of history, love of nation. Is any of this sinking in Mr. Prestin? Any of it?" Eoffa demanded.

Eoffa didn't wait for an answer. Neither did she know how long all noise from conversation, movement, and drinking had ceased. The public house was as quiet as a church. All eyes were on her. She noticed all her colleagues were spellbound. The other patrons were mesmerized. Even Denny was sitting there, his hands folded in front of his mouth as if he were praying and tears were welling up in his big eyes.

Prestin finally broke the ice and said, "Well Ms. Castle, why don't you tell us what you really feel?"

A couple of people laughed, but the silence, the dead serious silence, prevailed. Finally Eoffa said, "Enough of this serious talk, all of you get back to the partying and sooth over this veil of tears."

Still no one moved or spoke. Everyone waited for Eoffa to take the next step, and she did. She got up to leave.

"Sorry I put a damper on the festivities, but our RUC PR liaison pushed me a little too hard and far. I apologize for spoiling the party. I'll leave and you can get back to the good times."

With that she left. Four of her colleagues joined her in leaving. Once outside they each in turn hugged her and said, each in their own way, "Well said," or "Well done."

Eoffa said, "I didn't intend to do this."

Fiona, one of Eoffa's coworkers and friends in Belfast, said, "its all right Eoffa. It's been building for weeks. Prestin is the RUC, right to his core. In spite of his congenial façade, he reeks of the RUC. Your comments were spot on. You put him and some others in there right in their place. Good on you."

"I agree," Deirdre, another coworker said. "You explained things so even I could understand them. Thanks Eoffa."

Yet another commented, "That's correct Eoffa. It took an American to explain what all of us Irish, well some of us anyway, have felt but couldn't articulate. It was brilliant, so it was. I'll never forget what you said here tonight. Never."

———•◆•———

Denny followed Eoffa, and the group of young women who joined her. He stayed at a respectful distance, not wishing to draw attention to the fact that he was tailing them. He wanted to say something to Eoffa, he wanted to congratulate her, commend her, and tell her she was her da's girl all right. But this was not the right time. She glanced back once in notice of his presence, but did not draw attention to his shadow.

Three of the girls split off at a junction down the road, but one stayed with Eoffa. They walked along talking soberly, not paying much attention to passersby. They were as innocent as the day was long. Denny kept his distance, just in case he was needed.

Out of nowhere he came, running a good pace, in the shadows. He grabbed the other girl's purse and ran even faster. The purse-nabber had made a critical error. He came from the shadows in front of the unsuspecting girls and ran past them in the opposite direction.

Obviously he thought the road behind the girls was free of any pedestrian traffic, which it was. But lurking in the shadows was the old defender of defenseless women, children, and men. Denny knocked him ass over apple cart.

As Denny retrieved the handbag he leaned down over the thief and hissed, "Look you dumb fuck, this is Provisional turf. You not only broke the law just now, but you violated IRA community rules. I should knee cap you or shoot you in each of your elbows. But I'm in a good mood. So fuck off."

The youth was bleeding from his forehead where it had bounced off the sidewalk. He also limped as he headed off.

The two girls came over as this was unfolding and just stood there for an instant. Neither Denny nor Eoffa let on to knowing each other.

Denny said to Eoffa's companion, "I believe this is yours. He didn't have time to open from what I saw, so everything should be in there."

"Aye so it is. My cash, cards and keys. The essentials. Thank you so much."

Eoffa piped up, "Yes, thank you very much."

"I was in the pub, up at the bar when you gave your speech. By God it was the best thing I've ever heard explaining the foreign support of the Troubles. Brilliant it was. Brilliant," Denny exclaimed, happy for the opportunity to express his congratulations.

"Are you an American? Aye, I thought so by your accent. You referred to your grand mammy and your da; by God they would have been so proud of you back there. It was brilliant, so it was."

"Many of us thought so too," Eoffa's friend Deirdre said. "It was brilliant."

"I heard you say that this is Provie turf. Is that true?" Eoffa asked. Before Denny could answer, she asked, in a hushed voice, "Are you a Provisional?"

Before Denny could decide how to answer, Eoffa put on the most impish smile and said, "I hope so, and I am so pleased to meet you. I don't know any Provisionals, and I probably should. The two of us work for the Human Rights Commission. I think the Provisional IRA have gotten a lot of bad press over the years, especially from the British News Service.

"Clearly you are a protector of the defenseless. Thank you for protecting us, and those others you have helped."

Eoffa's friend chimed in and said, "I agree. Thank you so much."

Denny walked off not knowing what to think of this exchange.

Eoffa said to her friend, "I think we should report the attempted snatching, and also credit the Provies for helping us, don't you?"

"Aye, that's the thing to do."

"We'll not describe the IRA man though. He obviously patrols this area. No sense in making life difficult for him. He seems to be a decent man."

After Eoffa got to her apartment, and was alone, she called Denny and explained the last part of her conversation with him.

"My friend Deirdre has friends who are writers and editors for a couple of newspapers here in the North. I put the bug in her ear to pass on what happened tonight and thus cast PIRA in a favorable light. As defenders. Not blood thirsty villains. And still around."

"Aye, Eoffa, I was wondering what you were about there, but now it makes sense. There will be people on both sides of the divide who will be perplexed and probably upset by it. But fu . . . er, to hell with 'em, it will do them some good.

"You are all right though?" Denny inquired.

"Aye, thanks to you."

———————•◦•◆•◦•———————

Prestin was quite reserved on Monday morning when he arrived at the Human Rights Commission offices. He wandered around conversing with several of the members who had been at the pub on Friday. Several of them exchanged pleasantries with him. It was as if he were wary of encountering Eoffa, he kept glancing toward her desk expecting her to appear magically and cast a poison spell upon him.

When she emerge from Brice Dickson's office, she totally ignored him. She settled into her chair behind her desk and struck up a conversation with her friend Deirdre at the next desk.

He hesitated for an instant, but then he approached her desk and stood by the side waiting for her to acknowledge his presence. She sensed his presence and dragged out the long awaited recognition of Mr. Mark Prestin.

"Yes."

"Are you still angry with me? I hope not. I didn't mean to agitate you Friday night. I was only expressing an opinion based on observations I've made over the years," Prestin pleaded. Then he changed the topic while still trying to continue the contact.

"I hear you had an altercation with a robber. I hope he didn't cause you any lack of sleep or concern."

"Believe me, I lost no sleep over either of Friday nights unfortunate occurrences. How about you, did you lose any sleep over your apparent ignorance of Irish history, both here in Ireland or to where we Irish were forced to emigrate?

"Tell me you are not adamant in your ignorance, or just plain stubborn, realizing the truth but not willing to admit it," Eoffa commented.

"Look, I'm trying to make peace here. Take pity on a fellow human being. You are working for the Human Rights Commission, so treat me like a human, please," Prestin pleaded with a slight grin.

"It's a pity that the RUC representative pleads his case simply based on pity. It's pathetic, I guess if that's all you've got, I'll have to show some pity," Eoffa said mockingly, but then grinned.

"Let's go back to that bar, I'll buy you a drink, and if you give me a chance, I'll tell you my background. Not to try to convince you, but simply explain who I am and why I am the way I am. Would you?"

"When?"

"Any night. After work or on the weekend, it will be up to you. You can name it."

"Let me think about it. First about the offer, I have my reputation to consider. If I consent to sell my soul by meeting with you, then I have to decide which night? I'll let you know."

"I'll be anxiously awaiting your answer."

"It may be a while, I'm working on a new thread to the 1972 Bloody Sunday Inquiry. You wouldn't know anything about a cover up would you? Would you have access to info deep in the RUC? That would change everything."

"Change everything concerning our meeting?"

"Yes silly. We know the RUC acquiesced in a cover up and we hear a couple of Paras have consciences that are starting to bother them. We've plenty of surface material. We could use some help identifying who knew what and when and why it's been covered up by the RUC. We know one head RUC man tried to keep the army, especially the Paras, out of Derry. So he represents a good side of the RUC. But why the reluctance to talk publicly? It smacks of cover up? If you can enlighten me, on the QT, who knows, maybe we will get on famously."

"I'll have to think about that," Prestin confessed.

"Don't waste time, you are not the only copper on the table or under it for that matter," Eoffa said suggestively. "And don't go reporting this to your boss. I'll find out if you are playing me and playing with me. As I said, it's not just you we are in contact with. There are a lot of willing young men in Belfast, many within the security and police system. Don't try and double cross me, I know some people, so I'll let it go at that," Eoffa smiled threateningly.

Prestin just looked at her.

"I also know from my sources that you know exactly who I am, whose daughter I am, whose family my mammy comes from. So don't play innocent or coy with me. I'm not innocent, and my relatives are less so. Don't fuck with me," Eoffa said sweetly, then ignored him and returned to her work.

Eoffa had guessed on much of her accusations made to Prestin, but by his expression she had hit the nail on the head. He was perplexed, full of doubts, and unsure of what he should do. He knew one thing for sure. He was not going to talk to Jeffries for a while. Someone close to the boss was passing on information concerning him, and Eoffa Cashel had deadly relatives.

Eoffa called Denny and indicated through code that she needed to meet with him.

They met two hours later and she filled him in on her attempt to intimidate, seduce, and elicit information from Mark Prestin.

"But I need some dark secret to blow his mind. Can you get one for me? I need to have some information not of a public nature to share with him to lead him along. I think I can get things from him. If I was willing to sell my soul, I think I could turn him."

"I don't think he wants to buy your soul. Your body is a completely different matter," Denny said as a matter of fact while nodding his head.

"Neither my soul nor my body are for sale. But I still think I can get some tidbits from him," Eoffa offered.

"I'll check with some people. In the mean time be careful Eoffa. This is not a game. Surely your da has stressed that enough to you. You've seen him after he's played with the RUC and Special Branch. It's serious enough. So again, be careful Eoffa. Not only for yourself, but for my sake. I told your da I'd watch over you. I don't want something to go wrong and have to answer to your da."

"Denny, please. Da and I both know the limits. We calculate how far we can go. Neither of us is reckless. It may seem that way, but neither of us has a death wish. I find doing something for Human Rights and the Movement is satisfying; doing something covertly is exciting. Doing something for Ireland is important and sacred. How can you beat that: sacred, satisfying, exciting. It's the best of both worlds. It's the best," Eoffa confessed.

"Jaysus, you look like your mammy, but you sound like your da. God help you."

———————————•:•••:•———————————

I had been expecting Denny's call all day. "Thanks for calling me Denny and filling me in. Eoffa called last night. She talked to her mother first. Then she talked to me. I told her to be careful on the phone. She assured me it was secure. I told her nothing is secure.

"She was using a friend's cell phone. I asked how much she knew of her friend? She's from a strong Republican family from South Armagh. I quickly advised her not to mention the friend's name. You can't be too careful Denny. Even with this new technology.

"She did explain what she was up to. She also explained who this RUC man was again to me. She said you were not only going to watch over her but help her some."

"Rudy, she's your daughter. She's independent as a curse. I warn her to be careful. I watch over her. But I sure as hell can't control that daughter of yours. The best I can do is work with her, point her in certain directions, and try to keep her clear of others."

"Denny, I'm not criticizing you or your efforts. I'm just stating my concerns about her. What the hell put the bee in her bonnet? Why has she got such a hard on for this RUC dick?" I asked.

"I think, now mind you this is me and just me reflecting Rudy, that she's heard some stuff about her da over the years. Maybe from her aunt and uncle, who knows? Then she gets here and it's all academic, even though she's working on Finucane's case. Then she met the family.

"It affected her Rudy. She talked to me about it. Tears welled up in her eyes. She even cried some. It was beginning to become more real. She said she knew I couldn't or wouldn't tell her about you and uncle Danny and what you boys did. But she wanted to hear something of how and why you got involved.

"So I told her a cleaned up version. She said she could see that. She was nodding her head 'yes.' But it was still pretty academic, yet it was getting more real if you know what I mean? It stayed that way until she had contact with this RUC securocrat. He made it all real to her Rudy. From what I saw of him he is a Brit Loyalist to the bone.

"So he helped convert her. She won't be satisfied till she humiliates him and all he stands for. She is excited because . . . her words Rudy, 'it's my generations turn, before it's too late.'

"She's living her great granda's, her grand mammy's and her da's and uncle's tradition. It's in her genes and blood Rudy. I told her, she looks like her mother, but she's got your mind, attitude, and drive.

She's blessed and cursed at once Rudy, so she is."

"Watch her until I get there in the Spring, Denny."

———————◆———————

Eoffa had another meeting with Denny before she consented to meet with Prestin on a Friday night after work. She reported to Denny, who'd asked her to watch and listen to the Human Rights crowd, that she felt all of her co-workers were sound and not passing on info to the security folks. "With the possible exception of one I'm still watching, Deirdre."

"Your da gave me instructions to 'watch you like a hawk,' so he did. But equally important he wants you to impress your RUC boy with questions about the killing of Pat Finucane."

"I know. But I want to lead into Finucane by asking him about 'Bloody Sunday' first. We know a couple of 'Paras' from the Parachute Regiment are having qualms of conscience and have talked to some media people on guarantees of anonymity. That we know.

"What I want to hear from Prestin is this: when General Frank Kitson came to Ireland as Brigadier Commander of the 39th Brigade in Belfast in 1970, was he directly involved in Bloody Sunday?"

Denny piped in, "Well we know his book, *Low Intensity Operations: Subversion, Insurgency and Peace-keeping,* became the how to do it book for the Brits in the North of Ireland. He based it on fighting in Kenya, Malaya, Cyprus and Aden.

"The gist of it was to undermine the native community support of guerrillas by reforming the government, people and structures, the courts and the law, the police and the news media. They had to become weapons in your arsenal. Any and all of their policies—political, economic, religious, social, intellectual, and cultural—had one purpose: to defeat the enemy," Denny explained.

"We know he brought in at least three dozen SAS special forces for special 'shoot to kill' operations and to intimidate the Nationalist community," Eoffa added.

"We also know he started the 'Military Reaction Force,' the infamous 'MRF' as the Military Reconnaissance Force was now called. They killed Catholics and Protestants alike hoping to create a real sectarian war. The IRA would divert its attention away from the real enemy, the Brits themselves, and the Brits could claim the 'Troubles' was a religious war with no political basis, goal, or rationale. We knew what they were up to so we didn't bite. But a lot of innocent people were killed by the lovely peace abiding Brits, the two faced bastards.

"At the same time Brit intelligence agencies, with the help of the RUC and Special Branch, infiltrated Loyalist paramilitary organizations like the UDA and the UVF. Hell they helped set up the Ulster Defence Association and their cover group, the Ulster Freedom Fighters. The UFF was really the UDA's hit squad, thus the UDA avoided bad press.

"They killed and bombed at will, getting info on targets from British intell. In 1982 the Brits set up the Force Research Unit, FRU, within the British Army Intelligence Corp. Its secret role was to get intell from moles who'd secretly penetrated paramilitary groups and recruited informers and agents," Denny added.

"But lets not get ahead of ourselves. The question I intend for Prestin is what role did Kitson play in Bloody Sunday, if any? I mean, clearly it was supportive, no one thinks he was there, but was there more to it than his suggestions from his book? Did he give advice in real time, by phone or what ever?" Eoffa interjected.

"Okie dokie. We'll focus on Kitson in Derry, on Bloody Sunday. But you keep me informed as to when you plan to meet with Prestin. I plan to be there and after, just in case," Denny confirmed.

"I'll try for a week from Friday night. The same pub we were in the last time. It will put him on edge a little, I hope."

"In the mean time I'll start inquiring about your man Kitson. First with regard to January 30, 1972, then to February 12, 1989. Aye, the dates are emblazoned in my mind. I'll be thinking of them till the day I die.

"Keep in touch Eoffa. Talk to your da, too."

"Aye Denny, I will on both requests."

"They are not requests, Eoffa. 'Uncle' Denny here can make life miserable if his instructions are not fulfilled. A simple call to your da; a report that you are not cooperating, just a hint that you are putting yourself in the way of trouble, or that you cannot be located. Can you imagine the response?"

"This is unwarranted bribery, Denny. I thought we were beyond that," Eoffa pleaded.

"I'm sure we are, But it's not just you who are answerable to you da, I am too, and I've seen his handy work, and I do not want to be on the receiving end of his work. Seriously. Anything ever happen to you or any of his, and there will be hell to pay. You certainly know that," Denny concluded.

"I know Denny, you are right. I do not want to concern or involve me da. Were good., right?"

"Aye, as long as we're good, we're good!"

Eoffa mulled over Denny's last statement, smiled, and thought *I think that means we are good, maybe very good.*

"Denny, how much should I tell Professor Dickson? Technically I work for him at the Human Rights Commission, and technically I suppose I should clear my playing Mark Prestin for information with him, don't you think?"

"What if he says no to your little operation? Then what?"

"I hadn't thought of that," Eoffa said.

"Talk to your da about what you are up to and ask him about telling Dickson," Denny suggested.

Sound advice, Eoffa thought. *Not just sound, but good advice. Getting advice from da is good, and as long as we are good, we are good,* she thought to herself in a mocking tone.

———————◆———————

WARNING SIGNS

"**W**ell Eoffa, sounds like you are going to be busy. Besides your studies and Human Rights work, you are going to do some covert work," I commented.

"Now listen to your dad. This is not a kid's game. These people are dangerous. Maybe not your 'mark,' no pun intended, but the people he reports to are dangerous. If they pass any of this concerning you on to the Brits, they are not fooling around. They are dead serious and damn dangerous.

"I have no doubt the Brits are eves dropping on their RUC friends. Deep down MI 5 and Brit military intelligence has never respected their 'hick' friends in the North. It goes way back to 1916. When the Brits don't respect you, you are classified by them, just above known enemies.

"As to Prestin, according to Denny, the RUC knows full well who you are. The daughter of a known, but as yet unproven, enemy of the British empire, even though I have a Brit medal for supposedly working for the Brit army back in the early 70s. They know who I am, suspect things I may have done, but have yet to prove it.

"I keep bringing students over there hoping to wind them up. They think I don't suspect that they are watching, sniffing, digging around trying to nab me. I know what they are up to. But they don't think I think they are up to anything. But I know. I don't suspect, I know. They haven't kept their lousy empire by being lax and trusting. They keep files, they check those files, they add to those files, and those files keep hundreds of imperialists busy all the time.

"They are dead serious about those files. Their bloody empire depends on it. You and I are the lifeblood of those people. They exist because we exist. They justify their positions, their record keeping, their surveillance, and their whole apparatus, because of the likes of us. On the one hand we are expendable to them. But, on the other hand, we are necessary for them.

"For them it is the new 'Great Game.' It has replaced the old 'Great Game' over in the Near East. Two world wars, national liberation, and anti-imperialism officially closed down that theater of operation known as the 'Great Game.' They moved it to Ireland, after World War I. Some of Ireland's patriots flirting with the Germans during two twentieth century world wars sealed it. Add calls for national liberation and anti-imperialism, well these added insult to injury as far as the Brits were concerned.

"The Brits practiced anti-insurgency policies and tactics in their colonies during the fifties and sixties, but they applied their techniques in Ireland. Hence your man General, former Brigadier, Kitson, put these practices down on paper so his protegees could practice them in Ireland on the 'colonials' there. So again, Eoffa, be careful, damn careful.

"Your man is probably Special Branch of the RUC. I have special friends in the Branch, and that means you have special friends there too. You've got to be careful."

"How much should I tell Dickson?" Eoffa asked.

"Very little. Tell him Prestin has offered to talk to you on the QT about Bloody Sunday and the Finucane affair, since there may be a link between the two. Tell him Prestin wants the conversation confidential, off the record, and with anonymity. I suspect he will advise you to follow the Commission's rules and the law.

"If he says 'no,' threaten to quit (with a smile on your face), so you can pursue the 'truth.' Tell him you will return home here to the US and disclose what you've learned to the press with an explanation that the

Northern Ireland Human Rights Commission divorced itself from your research and findings. That will merit a call to me, and I'll confirm that you are pig headed and do not make idle threats. But I'm sure it will not come to that," I said, and thought, *I hope.*

"Good luck. Oh, one more thing, Denny is with you every step of the way. Every bloody step. You with me? If one misstep, I'll be over there within 24 hours and I'll be with you every bloody step from then on."

"Got it, da. I don't want to hear your footsteps until the end of May. Love you da."

When Eoffa talked to Dickson about Prestin's offer, he said to follow procedure and to professionally protect his confidentiality. Da was spot on with Brice.

———•◆•———

I called Denny again and reported my conversation with Eoffa.

"When she's out with her friends, with Prestin or just sniffing and snooping around, you are with her every step of the way."

"Aye, I know Rudy, I know. All those long years ago when we first started our friendship and partnership in this foolishness, had you any idea it would come down to this? Us two old guys, looking at armchairs fondly, but worrying over our children's involvement in this same old shite. What is the world coming to?"

"I know I could use a holiday from it all. At least most of the clubs have come around to the Adam's camp for Danny Morrison. I don't have to keep checking on them every so often.

"I often took Barbrie, told her it was a vacation. It was getting expensive to drive to these places, and the distances were frightful. But she knows Iowa and northern Ohio are not vacation destinations. She knew something was amiss, but she went along with it. But those days are finally winding down.

"She and Eve want to come over at the end of my Program in June and visit Eoffa for a week or so. I want that kid of mine to be healthy, cheerful, and safe when they get there. Sorry on you Denny, but we Castles are your burden in life, good friend.

"I do want you and Mary to come over here for a couple of weeks. Maybe this next summer. Summer time is good in Michigan. We can go to the beach, do some fishing, go to Chicago. It will be great. I'm working on Morrison to raise a few quid for you. You know, checking on me here, and my work with the clubs and all. He says 'maybe.' He said he would let me or you know in a few weeks. Wouldn't that be great?"

"Aye it would. Mary would be beside herself. So would I Rudy."

"Maybe we could fix it so you could come over when we were coming back, next summer. We'll probably be coming back with some of the Saintfield girls."

"Speaking of that, that's were Eoffa is off to this Saturday and Sunday. Visiting your relatives in Saintfield. I don't think I'll have to follow her there. She'll behave there all right," Denny said without conviction.

"By God I hope so."

The following weekend on Friday evening, Mark Prestin was waiting anxiously for Eoffa Castle at the pub for their non-date. She made it very clear that this meeting was not a date. Her family would disown her for dating a RUC man.

Prestin had pleaded his case to no avail: "I'm not a RUC man. I am a man who works for the RUC. I am a state bureaucrat who is attached to and working through the local RUC headquarters, but assigned to the Human Rights Commission."

Denny had done his homework and found that Mark Prestin had completed his course work at the RUC academy just outside of Belfast.

His family lived in a loyalist stronghold in County Antrim, and he was the only son of a staunch Presbyterian farming couple.

"I warned you not to try to deceive me," Eoffa threatened. "It is not a date," she said with conviction.

That exchange had been on Tuesday when she consented to "meeting" with him for Friday at the pub. "See if you can establish any contact between Brigadier, later General, Frank Kitson, and the troop involved in the Bloody Sunday massacre in 1972, especially the Paras. It's important to me."

On Friday he waited for her anxiously. He was scanning everyone who came through the pub door. He was beginning to loose heart when in she came like she was all business.

Approaching her, Prestin was relieved and pleased to greet her and steer her to the booth he had reserved for them.

"I am happy we can finally have our conversation without fear of distractions," he smiled.

Eoffa just teased with the slightest of a smile.

"I think we got off on a wrong foot over the past weeks, especially the last time we were here," he continued as if he was reading a script, or possibly he had taken to memorizing it.

"Tonight I think I can set things straight between us and dispel any wrong impressions you may have of me," he said with confidence. She hadn't interrupted him once with a witty or surly quip. Thus, self-assured he droned on.

"I am confident you will find me refreshingly honest, down to earth, and pleasing to be with, especially now that I am in your company.

"I know why everyone from Dickson to your co-workers admire you so. You are honest to a fault. You are quick, bright, and thoroughly educated. You are a credit to the American higher educational system. You are attractive, hold yourself proud, and are an example of health, in mind and body. I am so pleased to be here with you," he said earnestly.

"Are you finished flattering me?"

"Oh, believe me there is nothing dishonest in my portrayal of you. I am not trying to flatter you in a discourteous manner or with unvirtuous intent. I assure you.

"I only mean to portray you as I and others see you, and recognizing that, I am trying to assure you that I am honored by your presence," Prestin said solemnly.

"Good God, what bull shit. Listen to me, Prestin, you broke our agreement. You have tried to deceive me, my colleagues, and Brice. I know who you are, where you come from in Antrim, who your parents are, and that you **are** a RUC member, having come out of the academy a short time ago.

"If this were a different time, say a few years ago, lets say May 1977, I'd have you handled like Captain Robert Nairac was handled. Like him, you sought to deceive certain people. Notice, I did not say you sought to deceive '**us**,' but **certain people**. Let your fucking report show that distinction.

"I have contacts with '**them**' and they warned me about '**you**.' You know who I am, don't ever think for one minute I wouldn't turn you over to '**them**' if I or anyone in my family, or close friends, felt threatened by the likes of '**you**.'

"I told you not to lie to me and not to report everything to your superior. You fucked up" Eoffa said coldly.

"Listen, I didn't tell you who I am because it is my cover. The RUC manufactured it. I didn't lie because I didn't make it up, they did. I just didn't tell you the truth. That's different," Prestin pleaded in a whisper.

"Not to me and my friends. They are the same thing. Nairac pleaded the same way. I've yet to hear about your report to your boss," Eoffa hissed.

"I didn't say a word to my boss. He doesn't know we are meeting or having this conversation. He's out of it," Prestin said with real fear in his voice and eyes.

"You are being watched by **people**. Every minute of every day. They even nicknamed you 'Nairac.' I am your only friend to these **people**. They, well some of them, want to make an example of you. I pleaded your case. Now my credibility with them is shot all to hell. I suppose I could get it back if I told them to go ahead and do it because you lie, lie, lie to me."

"No, no, no. Eoffa, please listen to me. Give me a chance."

"There are some hard men who want to whack you, you understand. I got them to stand down. Some of them think an American, and American girl, is soft. I can only see one way to dispel that impression. I can give the signal to the two of them in here tonight and within three minutes you'll be taken out and 'Nairaced,' as they like to say. These are hard men. They have been through it all. They want vengeance, then justice. I can't blame them, they talk about Bloody Sunday and Tim Finucane's murder, in front of his wife and kids, like it was yesterday and they were related to all the victims. You are a dead man."

"Eoffa, I said I could talk to you about some things and I will, just give me a chance: about Kitson, Bloody Sunday and the Parachute Regiment. What I can tell you now is that RUC records show that there was military radio traffic between Belfast and Londonderry during the day of January 30, 1972.

"It seemed to be strictly informative. There were no orders given from Belfast or Lisburn, the army's main headquarters, to or for any one in Londonderry.

"What is not substantiated is who exactly was in Belfast doing the talking. It seems rather moot considering the lack of specifics and importance in the communication."

"So you have nothing for me. Why do I suspect that all of this is probably more deception? I think this meeting is over," Eoffa said in disgust.

She made an obvious gesture towards the bar, in quite the opposite direction of Denny who was at a small table near the door. But Prestin, who could not ascertain who exactly got the sign from Eoffa, was sent into a panic. Her message was load and clear: this prick is another deceitful Nairac.

Grabbing her arm gently but surely, Prestin pleaded, "Eoffa, no. I'll get more information. It will be good, I swear, it will be good."

Eoffa just glared at him, dropping her gaze to his hand on her arm. As he removed it she looked into his eyes and said, "It will not only be good, but it will also be true. Don't make something up to impress me. I'm going to check everything very thoroughly. I want accuracy, because my friends are very accurate at what they do. Do you understand?"

He shook his head in the affirmative as Eoffa walked out of the bar smiling and throwing a wink at Denny as she did so.

Prestin just sat back down and seemed to be waiting for something terrible to happen to him.

Using her friend Deirdre's phone, Eoffa called me and reported what happened. I smiled with satisfaction. I had to admit, she was a natural. She was a player and could bluff, threaten, and deceive with the best of them.

Changing gears only slightly, I thought to myself, *there is some guy out there who is going to fall for this woman, and he has no idea of what he is in for, and I don't know who he is and I already feel sorry for him.*

"So what's my next move?" she was asking.

"It sounds like you have him right where you want him. Treat him like a dog. Use him up. Get the info you want, then throw him back in the cesspool."

I heard her laugh.

"Ok. I've got to catch up with Denny and see what he has to offer. He stuck around the pub to see what Prestin would do. He also wanted to see if any one approached him after I left and it was obvious no one was going to haul his ass out to a car for a one way ride to hell.

"By the way, thanks for the info on the Brit Nairac. He nearly went white when I used that on him. He picked up on it straight a way and he nearly died."

"I knew he would. It's an old case but it would have significance for Prestin considering the circumstances. He probably feels pretty vulnerable. Good going kido. Talk to you later. Say 'Hello' to Denny," I ended.

———————◆◆◆———————

Twenty minutes later Eoffa met up with Denny who was all smiles. He had the grin and smirk of an accomplice.

"That man nearly soiled himself. I couldn't quite hear what you said to him, but his expressions and body language said he was in agony. Did he have any thing for you?"

"No. Well, nothing of substance. Hence the threats."

"He was scared."

"I called da, and he said to squeeze him dry."

"That's it."

"Did he see any one after I left?"

"No. He left after about ten minutes. He kept looking around the place trying to identify any threats. It was kind of funny, but a couple of minutes after you left a couple of guys left the place. He followed them out with his eyes.

"Just about the time he was ready to leave, two more characters got up, sort of stopped at the door and looked around as if they thought they were being tailed, and they walked out. Prestin sat back down for a bit and was clearly agitated and rattled.

"It was a thing of beauty. I followed him out with a crowd of four people. He hurried along but no one followed him or met him from what I could see. I followed him all the way to his car," Denny reported.

"It should be fun Monday at work," Eoffa offered.

———————•—•—•————————

Prestin did not come to the Human Rights Commission on Monday, Tuesday or Wednesday.

When he finally showed up on Thursday, Deidre poked fun at him by asking if the RUC only worked two days a week now with the peace and all.

Several people broke out laughing. Eoffa just smiled broadly. Prestin exhaled loudly as if in exasperation, and said, "How many times do I have to say it? I work for the RUC, I am not a policeman."

He was looking past Deidre directly at Eoffa as if waiting for her to contradict this statement. Instead, Eoffa looked back at the papers on her desk as if she were bored by this conversation.

Prestin made his usual rounds of the office, stopping to get a cup of tea. He engaged a few people in polite conversation. But he kept his eyes glancing toward Eoffa's desk. She sensed his attention. She purposely ignored him.

Finally she stood, gathered up a few sheets, brushed past him as she entered Dickson's office, pulling the door nearly, but not entirely shut. She and Dickson engaged in private conversation for about five minutes. Eoffa came out of his office, stopped by the kitchenette for some coffee, and returned to her desk.

Eoffa could sense Preston was nearly beside himself with her careful avoidance of him. Finally he approached her desk. He just stood there without saying a thing as she ignored his presence.

"Don't you know it's rude to hover over some one and their private research and papers?"

Before he could give an answer, she continued, "I think that would be especially so for a non-RUC man," she said loud enough for Deidre at the next desk to hear, but not loud enough for the rest of the office to hear.

"What do you think, Deirdre?"

"Aye, rude. Imposing, nosy, close to stealing information," Deidre said.

Another of Eoffa's friends at another close desk added, "Aye, Mr. Prestin, bad form."

"I can't get a break here. I've been gone for half a week, and I come around to say 'Hello,' and I'm accused of all sorts of things, none of which are accurate," Prestin said with a sheepish grin.

"Be careful on your denials, Mr. Prestin," Eoffa whispered at him. "Very careful. You might be found out, then exposed, embarrassed, and punished, severely," she said deadpan.

He held up both hands as if surrendering and started to back away when Eoffa said in a conciliatory voice, "It is good to have you back. You liven things up. When you are not here we are too serious and we accomplish so much. You disrupt all of that. How does it feel to be a disruption, Mr. Prestin?" Eoffa's tone was soft and innocent. And again, she whispered this last bit so only Prestin and her two friends heard.

She tilted her head, gave him a wink, and totally confused Prestin. His astonishment was complete.

This woman is getting to me. If I didn't know better I'd say she owns me. She plays me like a fiddle. I love it and despise it all at once. My God, what shall I do?

It took two hours for Prestin to get a moment with Eoffa at the coffee station in the kitchenette. He chose his words carefully.

"Can we meet? I have something of 'substance' for you. Maybe another place Friday after work?"

"I'll meet you after 18:00 Friday at the same place you have disappointed me the last two times. Let me warn you again about telling your RUC and Special Branch people about our meetings or the topics we are pursuing.

"My da says you are actually Special Branch, not just RUC. He was quite emphatic about that. His sources are impeccable. He is correct, right?"

"Yes," Prestin said in a defeated voice, drooping his head.

"We will see you then."

"We? Are you bringing someone," Prestin said looking at Deirdre.

"I am usually accompanied by **them**, not necessarily any one from here. The nature of our conversation excludes people from here. **They** will be there again, watching you and over me. They are friends of my da. They owe him for things in the past," Eoffa warned cryptically.

Prestin blanched and swallowed hard. "Of course."

"I thought you'd know by now. So now you know for sure. Behave Mr. Prestin. You are being observed, and my da's friends are not just on the outside of the law. He has sources inside also. That's how we'll know if you are going behind our agreement," Eoffa warned, as she walked back to her desk.

She neither looked for him nor saw him the rest of the day. The next day, Friday, their paths did not cross and he did not seek her out at her desk or the kitchenette. Although it was difficult not checking on him, to see if he was watching her, she ignored the temptation. The last thing she wanted to happen was to have him catching her watching or checking up on him. Her plan was one of indifference. She played at purposely ignoring him. She also knew her game annoyed him.

TRUE FRIENDS

"**Y**oung Prestin, you have not had much to report lately. What's with that?" Jeffries asked.

"She has not only kept to herself as of late, she has taken to totally ignoring me. I try to be friendly, neither excessively nor exclusively toward her, but she is decidedly unfriendly. Not hostile, but frosty.

God, a typical woman I suppose," Prestin said irritably.

"Does she suspect you are more than you appear? Does she suppose you are spying on her specifically?"

"No, I don't think so. I have given her no reason to suspect me of anything, or being anything other than a PR person for the RUC," Prestin explained.

"How are you getting along with the others at the Commission?" Jeffries inquired.

"Fine. I am hoping that my relationship with the others eventually brings her around to a more approachable relationship with me and I can begin to see what she is up to."

"Yes, that the thing to do. I have no doubt that the daughter of Rudy Castle is up to something above and beyond the Human Rights Commission. Although the IRA is in the process of disbanding, there will always be a core of them who will keep the light burning, even though shaded and camouflaged."

"She is a hard nut to crack. She goes into Dickson's office and partially shuts the door. They talk for a bit, then she comes out and goes to her desk and works for hours. I'll give her that, she is hard working," Prestin said admiringly.

"She doesn't run errands or go out side the office during work time?"

"I've not seen her do so."

"No chance of getting close to her desk to snoop about either, I suppose?" Jeffries asked.

"I approached her desk once and as she ignored me, I am sure she knew I was standing there, one of her colleagues accused me of snooping, actually spying on her work. It was quite embarrassing. I of course denied it, but I feel they would all be watching me if I even approached her desk now."

"What did Miss Castle say or do?" Jeffries inquired.

"She just looked up at me, gathered up the papers and covered them and mumbled something about being impolite, if I'm not mistaken."

Jeffries hesitated in thought for a moment, then offered, "Yes, we don't want to spook her or have her think you are singling her out for surveillance. Play it coy, Prestin. Keep me informed. That's all."

So it's all been a waste. But, nothing ventured, nothing gained I suppose. She'll come around. They all do. Women are fickle. Especially American women. What might she be susceptible to? Clothes? High-class parties? A trip to Paris? What might she be willing to sell her soul for? Jeffries mused.

———◆◦◆———

Denny was there an hour before Prestin was to meet Eoffa. He was wearing a duncher and glasses, and chose a table closer to the spot he reckoned the two of them would park. It was between what he assumed would be their spot and the door. He could survey virtually the whole pub with the help of the mirror in back of the bar, as his stool was taller than most chairs.

He had some pub grub and was nursing a non-alcoholic drink; he was on duty. At two separate times he was approached by locals and engaged in conversation. He stayed pleasant, revealing nothing of his home, neighborhood, or affiliations. He was just in for a bite to eat before he moved on. He'd said he had business in the city center. He commented on how this establishment seemed "warm and friendly." He said he'd been here before after he'd been in the city center. He always found the patrons welcoming and pleasant, not too nosy nor opinionated. 'Belfast friendly,'" he observed.

"Aye, that's it all right," one of his new companions said. "Spot on."

"Now enough about me. How about you? Local or outlander," Denny kidded? *Two can play this game* Denny thought. *Maybe this guy is one of Prestin's mates from Special Branch.*

"I think I recognize you from Stormont, right?"

"Stormont? You must be daft. I'm no politician," the man said with a laugh.

"Not a politician. Security division," Denny said very quietly. Nodding as he said it.

"No, I'm not with any security department. I used to work for the fire department. I was with my mates up at Stormont getting recognized for service some years ago. Maybe that's when you saw me there."

"That's probably it. You still look familiar though."

"I've a neighbor who works out towards Stormont. I can't remember exactly where their station is located though."

"Probably the one on Upper Newtownards Road near Strandtown."

"Aye, I do believe that is the one. Say, what are you lifting, I'll be handing you another." And with that offer to buy a round for the man, the subject switched to drinks, specifically beer. But Denny secured the knowledge that his companion was a Loyalist but not an employ of the RUC.

"Just a quick one, then I'm home to the Misses for tea, up at Ballyhackamore. I now work for the Post Office there. Near enough to retiring, so I am. Not soon enough. Paper work! I'm drowning in it."

"Surely you've not enough years to retire? You're still a young man."

"I wish."

The beer arrived, and they exchanged "Cheers."

The man drank up amid small talk, shook Denny's hand, said "Thanks. Next time on me," and left.

Denny was confidant that if anyone was watching he could now pass as a local, chatting up a regular like a long lost friend. He also knew intuition was no proof, so he'd stay vigilant. Yet he was pretty sure no one was watching.

There was just half an hour until Eoffa should be here and Denny was carefully scrutinizing everybody. Not staring, but studying. A nod, a smile, a head twist, but registering every face. The Brits had their files, but Denny had his memory. None of the faces in the pub registered with his memory, but they were now recorded there for the future.

The after work crowd was picking up and so was the noise level. Denny wiped his fake eyeglasses with the inside of his coat pocket, nothing else being available. Irish pubs use beer mats not napkins, so ingenuity was the only option. His glasses seemed to be steaming up. With all the people, talk and drink, the humidity was rising in the place. He had just replaced his specs when Mark Prestin came in, alone.

Fortunately, the table Denny hoped would be available for his rondaveau with Eoffa was available. It was perfectly located. He could listen to the meeting conversation and still scrutinize the clientele. "Brilliant," he said to himself, "and lucky."

Denny was nursing his drink and covertly scanning the crowd. He was looking for some one, any one, who might be working with, or on, Prestin, and ultimately, Eoffa.

Again he saw no one suspicious, and no one acting unsuspicious either. He would bet his reputation and life on the fact that Prestin was on his own.

Eoffa came into the pub looking like a rock star. Denny had to stifle a smile at how she came in, unpretentious yet begging attention. She was a looker, she carried herself with confidence, not false pride. She was wholesome, healthy squeaky clean and clearly the most attractive woman in the establishment and probably within several square miles.

Prestin was awestruck, and proud to be standing at the table she approached. He didn't dare hug her, and he offered his hand hesitantly. She just looked at him, but then took his hand in a limp handshake and sat down.

Clearly half the people in the pub were still looking at her when Prestin finally said, "Eoffa, I'm so glad you came tonight. I think you'll want to hear what I have to tell you. Do you want a drink before we begin?"

"Before **you** begin," she corrected him.

Again Denny had to suppress a smile at her comment. *She is relentless,* he thought. *Prestin just puts up with it.* Denny rolled this over in his mind. Then he went pale. *He not only likes it,* Denny thought. *He's not blackmailed, he's in love. Jaysus, he's in love with her!*

Denny swallowed hard and couldn't help looking at the two of them. Prestin was retrieving drinks for Eoffa and himself. *She's just watching him, studying him, sizing him up,* Denny thought. *Or was she watching him, considering him as more that an agent of Special Branch, more in tune with a potentially close confidant, or potentially a friend, a close friend?*

Denny's mouth went dry, his shoulders slumped, and his eyes kept drifting to them more than he should have let them. If he was right, this was serious, damn serious. It was just a hunch at this point. But he'd have to watch the two of them differently from now on.

Denny was shaken out of his state of reflection when he heard Prestin say, "This is all off the record, and said in confidence, right Eoffa?" He did not wait for an answer, he had to trust her because he had to tell her secrets for her to stay. He wanted her to stay more than he cared for his own safety, Denny thought.

"The Parachute Regiment was something of a reserve unit, a fire brigade, to douse spots that were too hot for the squadies on the ground. They were deployed in Belfast. It was understood that they would be used there and only there, to keep the lid on both communities. Brigadier Kitson was familiar with their work in Aden among other spots.

"He knew them to be, in his words, 'battle hardened,' and 'trained to move foreword and seek out the enemy.' They were aggressive by nature, they saw their role as offensive in nature, that is, to attack, to go on the offensive. Kitson advocated just such tactics and the First Battalion of the Parachute Regiment was shaped by this philosophy."

Eoffa didn't let him continue. She hit him with a critical question, "Did he instruct the Paras who were sent to Derry to be aggressive and to go on the offensive?"

"There is no evidence that he directed any such orders **directly**. He certainly did not radio any such orders or instruction to them once they were in Londonderry. The British Army did not feel the telephones were secure. Kitson would never use the phone for such an order or suggestion. He was army wise and far too careful" Prestin answered.

"I should think from what you describe as Para credo, that Kitson would not have to tell them. They followed his instructions detailed in his book to the letter, like the SAS. In fact, the MP Ivan Cooper, has said for some time that the Paras' conducted a 'high powered campaign of provocation' against the whole Catholic community.

"A good case could be made that the officer, whose operation manual was the bible for handling insurgencies, who was present here in the North of Ireland, his mere presence was enough to encourage his principles to be acted on and acted out.

"The Paras, his kind of men, came to Derry to aggressively provoke the Catholic, Nationalist community. Just before Bloody Sunday the Army had dealt with protesters and trespassers out at Magilligan Prison, and they put up with stones and insults within Derry. Kitson must have felt the regular army, the Royal Green Jackets, were unprepared to handle urban confrontations.

"Sorry, but their name, 'Royal Green Jackets,' come on! Even a Brit military vet could see some humor in just the name. Oh, I know, they have a distinguished history and all that, but their name doesn't inspire toughness or indicate a tough outfit. Sorry. Derry still had 'no go' areas where the Crowns' forces were not allowed, those Royal Green Jackets. That must have frosted Kitson's ass."

Prestin hesitated as if mulling over in his own mind if he should tell her, and he was considering what words to use as well. But he did want to impress this woman. He wanted to look good to her. He wanted to make her beholding to him, so she would be indebted to him. Not so he could impress Jeffries, but for his own personal pleasure and hopes.

Eoffa was just looking at him. She looked stunning. It was as if she had a twinkling halo of various colored lights made from the liquor bottles shelved at the back of the bar that served as a backdrop to this beautiful woman. He was smitten and damned near speechless. He had to say something or she would think him daft and she would leave.

"General Ford, an 'observer' for the Brigade Commander of the Royal Green Jackets, Brigadier Robert Mac Lellan, has said privately on several occasions, that Kitson used to chide him by asking, 'Why can't you sort out Londonderry?'

"Major General Ford, the Army Commander of Land Forces in the Province of Northern Ireland, chaffed at this jab. Whether he would ever come out and testify to this statement in public the Special Branch sources do not know. Once again, he was simply an 'observer,' and when 'One Para' were ordered to carry out a 'scoop up' operation during the march in Londonderry, their commanding officer, Lieutenant Colonel Derek Wilford, not only went in with his men but is on record as saying (again off the record at this point), that One Para would 'teach them a lesson.'"

Eoffa immediately broke in, "Teach who a lesson, the Catholics as Ivan Cooper suggested, or the bloody Royal Green Jackets?"

Prestin did not hesitate, "The Catholics."

"During World War II when the German Wehrmacht would bog down, the Waffen SS would be sent in to break through any obstacles. They were ruthless. They were aggressive. They were offensively oriented. Sound familiar? Your SAS and Paras sound like these boys. Kitson seems to have taken a few pages out of the Nazi SS manual, don't you think?" Eoffa asked.

Ignoring her question, Prestin continued, "The 'scoop up' operation by the Paras was simply to grab the bad actors that were throwing stones, also possibly nail bombs. They were under orders to wait for orders from Brigade Command. Brigade Command was Mac Millan, not Colonel Wilford of One Para.

Remember, the Paras were described as 'battle hardened' by Wilford, in Aden."

Eoffa continued the analysis, "You also said Wilford said these men were 'trained to move forward and seek out the enemy,' right? They were 'trained' using Kitson's book. They were just looking for an excuse to 'sort out Londonderry.' The Royal Green Jackets couldn't or wouldn't, so the Paras would. Wilford was the officer on the scene, but Kitson was the driving force."

"You make a convincing argument, Eoffa. You understand that much of this info, especially the quotes I identified as being given in private, are just that, **private**. You won't blow my cover and expose me will you? I am at your mercy," he said sincerely with soft eyes and a convincing voice.

"Please. Don't play that 'Eoffa, I'm in your debt, card.' This was a calculated risk you took to see me. Let's stop kidding around. You want to be with me, right?

"Now listen to me. You gave me a boatload of stuff here and it will take me some time to sort it all out. I don't want to make this meeting seem like we met just so you could tell me stuff. So we are going to smile, we'll have another drink, you can take your hand and put it along my face and lean over and kiss me lightly (no fucking tongue or I'll bit it off and spit it at you and put a cows tongue on your grave in that cemetery your family has plots in near that Presbyterian church in Newtown Crommalin where you and your parents are members). After a bit we'll leave together, hand and hand, like lovers.

"A block from here the charade will end. Got it?" Eoffa not so much asked as demanded.

Denny was taking it all in and was fighting off laughter. She is a master. Her da would be so proud of her. She's playing him like a tin whistle.

Then Denny heard Prestin say, to his credit, "God Eoffa, I love it when women throw themselves at me like you do. I take it this also means you'll not sell me out to your boss, Dickson, your da, or his friends both in and out of the law?"

Denny thought, *Good on you lad. This will wind her up. She'll be fit to be tied. She'll be ready for you the next time, so she will.*

Half, three quarters of an hour later, the two love birds left, hand in hand. Denny preceded them and was waiting for Eoffa two blocks away. He saw their departure and their separation. He did not hear any of the conversation after he left the pub, but he figured it was for public consumption in the event any one was taking notice.

Eoffa was clearly recognized by a few people in the pub, especially young men who notice beautiful young women. No police or military spotters, just horney young men.

Eoffa explained to Prestin that she would wait on the corner for her escort. She warned him not to double back and to try and get a look at her companions. They would know and would not take kindly to that activity.

Denny watched Prestin walk away at a normal clip and never once did he look around. At least he followed directions. That was good.

"Aye, he's gone. You've got him wrapped around your finger like a claddagh ring. You'll have him jumping through hoops before long."

"Aye. Back home we'd say he was 'whipped.' You know, 'pussy whipped.' He's just a boy in a man's body, playing with stone hearted Irish woman bent on revenge."

"Jaysus, Eoffa. I knew his comments about being at your mercy, and not blowing his cover, would wind you up. Sounds like it did. Good on you," Denny praised her.

"Some times he sounds like a pussy, or as you say, a cunt. I can see through it though. He's good for more info. I'll play him until he's dry."

"Eoffa, I couldn't help but notice that when he looks at you and puts up with your guff, he . . . well, it looks like . . . I think he's . . . ."

Eoffa cut Denny short. "He's fallen head over heels for me. Hasn't he? He's in love with me. All I've ever done is abuse him and use him. How does he repay me? He falls in love with me. Jaysus."

"More important, how do youse feel about him?" Denny asked.

Eoffa just stood there for a second in silence, then burst out laughing. She stopped walking and was clearly on the verge of crying. Denny hugged her and they started to walk in the direction of her apartment. The walk and the cool air would do her good he knew. He certainly needed to clear his head.

Denny could afford to be calm and understanding, this was not his daughter. This was the daughter of his friend though, an American poster boy for the Republican cause and militant wing of that cause. This situation would not set well with him.

"I'm starting to feel funny toward him, Denny. I think the feeling is . . . I think I'm starting to like him. I'm afraid that I'm starting to like him a lot. I can't explain it. I didn't want to, it is just happening. I can't help it. What should I do?

"Denny, for God's sake, don't tell my da. Let me sort this out. I need time," Eoffa pleaded.

———————•═•═•———————

My niece young Barb, Eve's daughter, flew into Dublin and was met by her cousin Eoffa, who was over joyed to see her. She needed to see someone from home and needed time away from Belfast, the Human Rights Commission, and Mark Prestin.

The two girls had no definite agenda, but they planned to stay in Dublin for a couple of days.

They took a bus to Galway and from there up to Derry. Denny put them in contact with some friends who could show them around Derry City and the area, and get them to the train station for the Belfast train. One day here in Belfast, then the bus for Barb back to the airport north of Dublin Saturday morning.

It was in Galway after a day's tour-bus trip to the Cliffs of Moher and the Burren, that Eoffa opened up to her cousin about her love life. They were in a cozy pub enjoying a wine, when she opened up about Mark Prestin.

Eoffa explained who he was, how it was that their paths crossed, what he was doing for her, and how badly she had treated him. Still, he was in love with her, and Rudy's friend and an acquaintance of uncle Danny's, Denny in Belfast, generally a hard man from the IRA, recognized that Prestin was in love with her.

Denny had checked Mark out, and Denny was afraid it was true love. It was Denny who, while discussing the situation with Eoffa, heard her first admissions of feeling something for Prestin.

Denny had promised not to mention any of it to "da," and agreed that a vacation out of Belfast was in order.

"Please don't get me wrong, you are not an excuse to get away. I am so glad you are here. I've been so busy that when I'm tired, so tired I can't sleep, I realize just how homesick I am.

"I am also so happy it is you who are here. I can talk to you and tell you things I can't tell others. Denny discovered the situation at about the same time I did. Although he knows the secret, I can't just talk to him about my feelings, really. He's a good listener, but . . . ."

"He's a man! He knows but doesn't understand. On the other hand, my mom would not understand either, and she's a woman. But she is in a class all her own, as you know. Jaysus, I'm just glad it's not me. Sorry. But I know what you mean, we need to talk girl to girl," Barb said.

"I had him kiss me, just once for show in this pub. It was for effect, to throw off any watchers, like we were a thing, which we are not! But I felt it. The kiss was the real deal. Shit. I'm fucked. Between my da and your mammy, I'm screwed, screwed all to hell," Eoffa said in despair.

"Well, maybe at face value, you are. But, you haven't done anything with him yet. You aren't pregnant, you are not carrying his child, and you haven't committed anything to him. You are OK.

"But you have to be careful. If your man Denny is with you when you meet your Mr. Preston on your clandestine rendezvous that may be good. Denny can continue to monitor and check up on him too. You can be reading him as a cop and a boyfriend," Barb offered.

"He's not a boy friend. I fear we are just star-crossed lovers. Well, not lovers, people in love. He's only touched my face and kissed me once."

"But you felt it."

"I did."

Barb leaned over the corner of the table and hugged her cousin, and said, "Keep your head, but don't deny your heart. Use your head, but listen to your ticker."

"Jaysus, you should have your own late evening and night radio program where you play sappy music, take requests, and offer advise to jilted lovers," Eoffa kidded.

Both girls laughed and giggled, ending the night on a happy note.

On the bus ride up to Derry, Eoffa said, "I am inclined to end this before it really begins. That would be best, don't you think?"

"Maybe. But won't you see him at work? That will not only be awkward, but painful. I wouldn't make any decision at this point. When you get back to work he may have more information for you. That will mean more meetings. Cutting him off cold could affect your work, your research, as well as your mental well being.

"Play it cool. Don't flirt or encourage him in the romantic realm. Keep it all business, business as usual. Don't let on how you feel. He doesn't know, does he?" Barb asked.

"No. I don't think so. I was as cool as a cucumber at the last meeting. I'm sure he thinks I hold his RUC membership against him. He knows my whole family is staunchly Republican and that we have people associated with the Provies. He's helping me because he likes me. I suggested that his help might melt the ice in my veins. However, I made no promises. I just don't know how long I can play the dead fish to him."

"Knowing Denny is watching will help, won't it?"

"It should. But what if Denny isn't there some time and I have a weak moment and say or do something foolish. I won't be able to redo it. There would be no turning back the clock then," Eoffa said in exasperation.

"It would be worse if Denny witnessed it. Even if you think you are alone, maybe you think you've slipped past Denny, or gave him the slip, and meet Mark on the QT, Denny could be there in the shadows. If he's as seasoned and good as you say he is, you can't try any sort of private meetings. He could catch you. Boy, that would be embarrassing," Barb ventured.

"Embarrassing? I'd have to kill myself," Eoffa proclaimed.

The two of them broke up laughing and totally disturbed the back half of the coach as it approached Sligo and a toilet break.

———————————•·•·•·•———————————

Back in Michigan I was having a meeting with most of the thirty-six Irish Foreign Studies students who planned and paid for the "experience of a life time."

Five of the students were 'ringers,' three males and two females. I had met them all weeks before and three of them were at this meeting. Two of the males couldn't attend because of work schedules. Tracy videotaped these 'Orientation Meetings,' so any absentees could view the sessions and not miss any information.

Every one introduced themselves to the group and were encouraged to say a little something about themselves and their interest in Ireland, Irish Studies, and participation in the program and trip. Family heritage was the major ingredient.

Tracy and I spoke about the need to have already started on their passport applications (everyone already had their passports which was a favorable sign for this group: they followed directions!); clothes they could layer and purchase in Ireland to wear; the amount of money they might want to bring (travelers checks were a thing of the past and debit cards and credit cards were in), we also identified local banks were they could buy Euros and Pound Sterling (we also explained that in the Republic they would need Euros and in the 'Six Counties' they'd need Pounds).

Then we began to describe the importance of symbols like the 'harp,' and the 'red hand,' the 'tricolor' and the 'Union Jack,' the flag of 'Ulster' Province, and the flag of 'St. Andrew.'

We explained that Nationalists, Republicans and many Catholics supported a United Ireland, whereas Unionists, Loyalists, and most Protestants wanted union with Britain. For many, the term 'Irish' meant Nationalist, Republican and Catholic, but 'British' was associated with Unionist, Loyalist, and Protestant.

Referring to the 'North of Ireland,' the "six counties,' the 'occupied six counties,' said you were a Republican, but if one heard 'Northern Ireland,' or 'Ulster,' you were in the presence of a Unionist, etc.

Names could tip one off as to a person's background and affiliations. Not so much the last or family name as the first name. A Nationalist, Republican, and Catholic might have their first name as Seamus, Sean, Mick, or Liam, Siobhan, Niala, or Bridie. But they probably would not use the Loyalist names William, Willy, Billy, George, Victoria or Elizabeth.

Schools were also a give away to one's background. Catholics usually attended Catholic schools on all levels (elementary, secondary [sometimes called 'colleges'], and college), and Protestants attended 'Public' schools.

County areas, villages and city neighborhoods were usually inhabited by one group or the other: in Derry the Bogside and the Creggan areas were Nationalist strongholds, while the Waterside of Londonderry was Loyalist (note, Derry to Nationalists, Londonderry to Loyalists); in Belfast the Falls and Andersonstown were Nationalist, Republican and Catholic, but the Shankill and Tiger Bay were staunchly Unionist, Loyalist and Protestant.

A Nationalist, Republican, Catholic might refer to a Protestant as a 'Prod,' with no slur connotation intended, whereas a Unionist/Loyalist/Protestant might refer to a Catholic as a 'taig,' with a derogatory meaning intended.

We also explained the importance of clothing and colors: sports teams jerseys, pendants and color combinations could cause trouble in some areas and neighborhoods. Wearing a shirt printed with the British Union Jack, popular in the US as a 'Beatles' allegiance, would have a completely different connotation in a Nationalist area in the North. A shirt, blouse, scarf or pin extorting a Nationalist theme of Irish dance, a high cross, a religious center like Croagh Patrick and the pilgrimage center of Knock, or a popular place in the Republic like Cork or Galway, might cause one grief in the Loyalist parts of the North.

The students were not so much confused as horrified.

"How are we going to remember all this stuff?" was a common refrain.

"Tracy and I will remind you daily of certain thing. If we are going into a Loyalist area we might ask you to change you shirt or scarf. That sort of thing."

"One last point. In a pub, restaurant, or public place, don't start talking about the 'Troubles' and mouthing your opinions. You will be asking for trouble. These people have lived this stuff and have endured the 'troubles,' they sure as hell don't want to hear a snot nosed American shoot off their mouth about the 'Troubles.'

"Be polite and respectful. If the subject comes up, let them talk. If they ask your opinion, say something like, 'its very troubling and I'm here to hear about it. What can you tell me? Can you tell me your take on it? Can you share any experiences you had?

"Let them talk. Do not come off too opinionated, you don't know who you are talking to or who might over hear you talking. Say things like, 'very interesting,' and 'I didn't know that,' or 'That puts a different slant on it,' and 'I'll have to think about that.'

"Remember, you are here to learn. I will have a certain slant, as many of you already know, but you are encouraged to temper what I say with your experiences. I would like to think you would agree with me in the end, but Tracy can testify to this, I have had people who have moderated my views considerable and not only survived the ordeal, gotten a good grade, but I've even brought them home at the end of the program."

That last bit usually got some laughs and smiles.

"I am a firm believer that there are two criteria for academic integrity, grades, and success. They are 'validity' and 'truth.' Is your conclusion drawn from proper and correct thinking and does it follow scholarly criteria? In short, are you using critical thinking? Critical does not mean its argumentative and pickiness, rather that it follows the criteria of logical assessment.

"Second, is it 'true.' Truth doesn't mean that I agree with it: rather does it correspond to facts, does it cohere to recognized principles held by scholars to be accurate, and does it hold practical value? If what you hold to be true is not true, what are the consequences? These are the tests for 'truth.'

"So again, there are no substitutes for validity and truth. I had instructors at the university who did not always hold to these criteria. They judged my papers on whether they agreed with my conclusions or not. That was bogus. One guy wrote on my paper, 'I don't agree with your conclusions.'

"I thought 'so what?' I went to his office with the paper and said, 'My conclusions are drawn from a series of arguments. Each section is a syllogism, validly argued, and connected to the next in a series of chain syllogistic arguments.'

"Then I explained, 'I quoted my subject through out the paper. I used my subject's quotes. My conclusions were simply drawn from those quotes. They were not my ideas, and I did not necessarily agree with them, but this paper was based on the subject's ideas as expressed through his quotes.

"'In short, my paper is based on the criteria of validity and truth. What higher standard or criteria is there in academia, than this? I would appreciate it if you would read my paper again.' And he did.

"So, from that experience I said to myself, 'I will never grade a student of mine on my likes and dislikes. If the student's paper used the criteria of validity and truth, whether I like it or agree with it or not, they get the grade. Period.'"

"Dr. Castle, did you get the grade?" Ms. McCormack asked.

"No. He patronized me, he gave me a half grade increase. Ironically, my daughter, who is studying and working for the Human Rights Commission in Belfast, and whom you will meet I hope, had exactly the same experience in her college career. Her instructor didn't agree with her conclusion, so he marked her down."

"Did she fight it like you did?" another student asked.

"Yes, with the same outcome."

"Did she go to your college or university?"

"No. So you see, the problem may be universal."

"Where did she go?" Ms. McCormack asked.

"I hate to admit it, but a rather prestigious university.

I don't want to come right out and say, so I will simply say a major university in a neighboring state."

"For real?"

"Yes, for real. Now lets get back to any questions about what you heard tonight. Are you totally confused?"

BARB'S GIFT

When Eoffa and Barb got to Belfast they only had one day to see the city. The night they arrived, Eoffa called Denny and "reported in." She asked if they might be able to meet for lunch or a drink later. He said either would be fine with him. They agreed that she would call him about noon and they'd make arrangements.

After stopping at a bakery for coffee and a scone, they headed for the city center. They did a little shopping, stopped for a quick coffee before heading for the Human Rights Commission offices.

Since it was a Friday things were rather relaxed because anything they were working on seriously would really have to wait until Monday so as to have the rest of the week if needed. Friday was for wrapping thing up, or relaxing after a hectic week. So things were casual and hassle-free.

Barb met Deirdre and the rest of Eoffa's friends in the office. When Brice Dickson had a minute she introduced Barb to him and they chatted for a few minutes about her impression of the North of Ireland.

Eoffa wanted to stop at her desk and check if there were any messages for her. When she finished and turned to ask Barb something, who should walk over but Mr. Mark Prestin. With a broad smile and his hand extended, he introduced himself to Barb.

"I'm usually not this forward," he said, "but your cousin would probably not introduce a relative of her's to me since I'm the pariah of the Human

Rights community here. I work in conjunction with the Royal Ulster Constabulary, the police force here in Northern Ireland."

He waited to see if Eoffa would contradict his comment of "I work in conjunction with" the RUC. To his relief, and satisfaction, Eoffa let it slide by once again. He took this to be a good sign on several levels.

Before he could relish too much satisfaction, Barb said straight faced, "You failed to say your name. Is it a state secret or is it Mr. Pariah?"

What Prestin thought was, *My God, sarcasm runs deep in this family*, but what he said was, "My name is Prestin, Mark Prestin."

Barb replied, more to Eoffa than to Prestin, "Did you mention him to me before?"

Eoffa's answer was emphatic, "No."

Barb commented, "No, I didn't think so. RUC, huh? No wonder," she said lifting one eyebrow and staring quite intently at him. "RUC," she said again with disdain.

Turning to Eoffa, Barb said in a barely audible whisper, "Plain clothes. Probably Special Branch."

Eoffa responded in a hushed tone, "Probably."

Deirdre and the rest of the girls standing near the door didn't hear the last exchange but were all laughing at Prestin's expense because of what was said between Barb, Eoffa and Mark. He blushed noticeably.

This one is smart, beautiful and deadly too. I'm actually happy for them that they do not live in Belfast. They wouldn't last long here. Eoffa is protected by her accent and status, but if they were citizens here, they would be in trouble, constantly.

He stopped to think about what he just thought. *It sounds like I was just describing a police state, one of the old soviet republics or satellites. My God.*

Eoffa said to Barb, "It's time for lunch. Deirdre, can you join us? Anyone else?"

Only Deirdre could go, "I'd be happy to."

Prestin said, half kidding, "Me too, I'm available."

Everyone, whether going or not, was silent and just looking at him, when he started to explain that he was only kidding. But to his and Eoffa's surprise, Barb said, "OK, if you're buying?"

Caught off guard, again, Prestin smiled and said, "Of course. Where are we going?"

Eoffa said light heartedly, "Some where expensive. You can use your RUC PR diner's card. The problem is, it's probably only good for gruel."

Everyone, including Prestin laughed. As they headed out the door, Eoffa excused herself and said she'd catch up. She phoned Denny and made plans for seven-thirty that evening.

———•◦•———

Lunch was at a pub with exceptionally good food and a nice selection from which to choose. Deirdre and Barb had a glass of wine, Eoffa had a Guinness, while Mark had a Smithwicks. The talk was light and Prestin was eager to hear Barb's impressions of the Ulster.

"You mean the North of Ireland?" she corrected him.

"There is clearly a drop in military and police presence since I was here last. The Nationalist community has a bounce in their step. The place doesn't seem so downtrodden. They have taken the imitative and are lifting themselves up and out of their, how should I put it Eoffa, so as not to sound offensive?" Barb asked.

"Ghettos," Eoffa said flatly.

"First, that's not quite accurate. Next, you'll not bate me into one of your one sided debates, Eoffa. If she doesn't beat me up a couple of times a week, she gets ornery," Prestin said with a smile.

Deirdre laughed and said, "It's true."

Eoffa responded, "Deirdre, you turncoat. If he is beaten like a dog it's because he asks for it. Any attention is attention, right Mr. Prestin?'

Shaking his head, but smiling, he said, "Right."

Barb asked, "Mr. Prestin, do you crave my cousin's attention?"

Everything at the table stopped and everyone held their breath. "Yes. I suppose I do. Don't I?" Prestin asked looking directly at Eoffa.

It was Eoffa's turn to blush.

Before she could come up with a smartass comment, Prestin followed up his question with, "I think we could make a smashing couple. They say opposites attract. If that is true, we were made for each other.

Deadre, you are a neutral observer, what do you say?"

Pushing his stool closer to Eoffa, Prestin asked. "Don't we make a handsome couple? How about it Barb? Let's say I quit working PR for the RUC and disowned my Protestant heritage, my Loyalist leanings, my Unionist voting pattern, couldn't we be a couple? Deirdre? Barb? Eoffa?"

Again silence until his smile disarmed everyone, and he said, "That would be one for the ages."

"If you were really interested in someone like my cousin, would you, could you, do all of those things? Out of love?" Barb asked playfully.

"For the right woman, absolutely."

"You'd be like Faust, selling your soul for the experience of love, the ultimate experience of life,"

Barb taunted.

"Not selling my soul, buying my redemption I suppose, right Eoffa?"

"Yes, I suppose. Selling one's soul, paying for redemption, two sides of the same coin. The crown's coin in this case," Eoffa commented trying not to look into Prestin's eyes.

"Well said Eoffa," he admitted.

Deirdre raised her glass and said, "I'll drink to that."

Barb responded, "Let's all drink to that." What she thought as she looked at Eoffa was more to the point, *lets drink to Eoffa and Mark.*

Deirdre had to excuse herself and return to work, and Barb said she had to go to the ladies room, leaving Eoffa and Mark alone for a few minutes. Barb said, "Eoffa don't come to the powder room with me. Stay here so he doesn't skip out on the bill. I'll be back shortly." She gave Eoffa a wink as she passed her.

"She's part of your family alright. I know a thousand blokes though, who'd love to meet her, prejudices and all," Prestin commented.

"What prejudices?"

Prestin did not respond.

'You like American girls?" Eoffa inquired sarcastically.

"No, not all American girls. If the truth were known, I just like one American girl."

"Anyone I know?"

"Yes. Quite well."

"Don't play with me, who is she?" Eoffa playfully demanded.

"You know perfectly well who it is. For some time I've been . . . ."

Eoffa cut him off. "Are you going to say me? Really? You don't know even half of me. What you do know is some of my family history. For all you know, I have a dozen boyfriends back home waiting for me."

"Do you? Be honest, do you have boys lined up waiting for you. I wouldn't doubt it."

"I have my studies and my internship here first and foremost. Those are my commitments. Those come first. Nothing will interfere with those commitments," Eoffa said emphatically.

"Whoa, commitments," Barb said as she returned to her stool. "Is he asking you for a commitment Eoffa? How presumptuous. Does he have any idea how many lads are waiting for you back in America?"

Both Eoffa and Prestin broke up laughing. Barb asked, "What's so funny?"

"Nothing. I was just telling him that I had oodles of men waiting for me back home. You just confirmed it," Eoffa laughed.

"Let me ask you something, Mark, may I call you Mark? How do you think you would line up with all the boys back home?" Barb teased.

"You girls are relentless. You tease, you insult, you embarrass, you gang up, you are hopeless."

"And we take no prisoners," Barb grinned and winked again at Eoffa knowing full well that Prestin saw it.

Prestin did insist on paying the bill, saying as they left the pub, "Now both of you owe me."

"When you are in Hartford we'll buy you lunch," Barb said playfully. "Or maybe when Eoffa's parents, grandmother, and my mammy come over in a couple of months, they could treat you to a meal. I'm sure they'd love to entertain a PR man for the RUC."

Prestin just looked at Eoffa, the she said, "Probably not."

"I could be available," Prestin said without much conviction.

Eoffa said in a hushed tone, "RUC and Special Branch at that. Right!"

Barb asked, "What was that comment?"

"Nothing," Eoffa said.

The three of them stood quietly and awkwardly for a few seconds.

"Let me ask the two of you something that's serious. Is Deirdre a colleague of yours Mark? I mean, is she RUC and Special Branch too?" Barb asked.

Prestin was taken aback. "I don't think so."

Eoffa was silent for a moment. "What would make you ask?"

"I don't know, just a feeling. I don't trust her and neither should you cousin. I just have a feeling," Barb warned. But it was Prestin who was seriously taking the warning. *If Deirdre was Special Branch, was she watching Eoffa, or him? Jeffries would do that sort of thing. Spy on his own.* Prestin looked at Eoffa with genuine concern on his face. Eoffa felt something uneasy also.

"My da says Barb's mother is 'fay,' has the gift. Maybe her daughter is too," Eoffa said with a smile. But all three of them sensed Barb might be correct.

Eoffa finally said, "Thank you," to Prestin.

Prestin was clearly upset by Barb's accusation, and now he was also disappointed. He'd expected a "See you next week," or "Next time, my turn," something relating him to the future, their future. But just a "Thank you."

Barb gave her "thank you" to Prestin and again warned him about Deirdre. Then she said it was interesting to meet a PR man for the RUC, "a real oxymoron," and she also said cryptically, "Good luck." She gave him the wink, turned, took her cousin's arm, and the two of them walked away from him while talking and laughing.

Their wholesome attitudes attractiveness, and delightfulness, made them stand out in a city and a Province still haunted with darkness. They truly were the happiest and most attractive girls in Belfast.

———————◆•◆•◆———————

"Barb, it is very good to see you again."

"You too Denny. I hear you have a full-time job watching over my cousin here. Uncle Rudy must owe you big time, or you owe him," Barb said.

"That goes without saying, and Eoffa here is just adding a wee bit to the debt."

"She says you are her guardian angel."

"Sweet Jaysus, God and all his saints and angels must be on holiday then. I've been called a lot of things, but guardian angel has never been one of them," Denny laughed.

"That's not how I see it," Eoffa chimed in.

Denny became very serious and reflective and said, "Eve Conlon's wee daughter, like Rudy's, all grown up. I feel so old."

"Like uncle Rudy, you may be getting gray and slower, but never old," Barb said with an ingratiating smile. A day doesn't go by, at least when I'm around, when Uncle Rudy doesn't talk about 'Denny.' It's Denny this and Denny that, Denny and I went here, Denny and I went there, Denny introduced me to this one and that one.

"When we ask him what the two of you boys did together over here, he clams up and just smiles," Barb reported.

"Some times we'll be driving along, or on a walk, or even in church, and da will start to laugh to himself. Me mother will say, 'Rudy, what are you laughing at?' He just keeps his peace and says, 'Nothing.' But we know it's something you boys were about. We all just know," Eoffa added.

"When uncle Danny comes they sit in the back garden and they tell stories whispering so the rest of us won't hear, we hear your name come up, and they start to laugh like schoolgirls aunt Barbrie says.

"Some day he'll tell us, she promises. I hope some day you'll visit and you'll all tell us what went on. It will be grand, to hear you tell it and to finally know."

"Not to change the subject, but tell me about Paul and Eve and young Paulie," Denny said to change the subject.

They had a bite to eat and a few rounds to drink, as they talked about the families. They were all comfortable because every one was family or considered family. Again and again they invited Denny to Hartford. Again and again he said he would come the first chance he had. Money was not the problem he assured them. There were just some loose ends he had to tend to. Then they would have to put up with him for weeks if not months. "Well, it will seem like that long," he assured them.

"One last thing before we go. Barb like her mammy Eve, are 'fay,' Denny. Barb thinks my 'office friend' Deirdre, the one whose purse you saved, is Special Branch too. Maybe watching me, or Prestin, or both of us. More importantly, she knows from that incident that you are IRA and still active. You've got to be careful Denny, especially careful.

"I'll be watching out at work, and I'll be keeping an eye on her. But Denny, you really have to be careful," Eoffa warned.

"That's my middle name," Denny said with a smile. "How do you think I've lasted so long on the outside?"

"Luck," Eoffa said. "As my da says, 'Dumb fucken luck.' My da has told me things, uncle Denny."

———————◆•◆•◆———————

On the following Monday Mark Prestin approached Eoffa at the Commission office and asked, "Your cousin made it safe home?"

"Yes, she called to thank me for a great holiday. We did have fun, although it was a short stay."

"The two of you certainly seemed to enjoy yourselves and one another's company. I enjoyed our drink together," Prestin said sincerely.

"Thank you again for lunch, and that goes for Barb as well. She enjoyed herself at the pub."

"Well, next time it will be her turn to buy, isn't that what she said?" Prestin teased.

"Barb flirts and says a lot of things as she is beating a haste retreat and knows she will never be held to account for it," Eoffa explained.

"Never?"

"Do you see it in the foreseeable future?" Eoffa asked incredulously.

Prestin was quick on the reply, "I hope so. I'm planning on it as a matter of fact."

"Don't hold your breath. My da would be the lesser of the evils. Barb's mother is the enforcer of the family. You can be glad she's in America now. She takes no guff and she wears her opinions on her sleeve for everyone to see. She's honest to a fault. I'm named after her, but the Irish form," Eoffa explained.

"I have a little more information for you. Friday at the usual place?"

"This is becoming a habit. Are you purposely dragging this out just so we can meet?"

"Yes," was his answer. He just grinned and was clearly unabashed and blunt in his admission.

Quietly, very quietly, he whispered, "You know I like seeing you." As Eoffa quickly looked around to see if any one was watching or in earshot, he continued, "and I like being alone with you."

"Look, I told you this is business. You give me information and I stay quiet about who you really are."

"That too," Prestin whispered, obviously enjoying Eoffa being on the defensive, being nervous, and rattled somewhat. He had to laugh to himself.

She was staring hard at him. Not with a hateful gaze, but threatening all the same. Finally she said to end this encounter and the potential attention it was arousing in the office, "Alright, same place, same day, same time."

His smile of satisfaction was cut short when she continued, "In the mean time, keep your distance or I'll terminate this PDQ. I'll also pass on what I know about you to not only the staff here, but to **them**."

So much for thinking you were on top, feeling you were in the driver's seat, you were finally in control, Prestin thought in a dejected mood.

The rest of the week he threw glances toward Eoffa, but not once did she return the favor, not once.

He had opened up to her, told her how he felt, and she had deflected his admissions, and now as cold as a fish, she refused to nibble at his attention.

—•—•—•—

Jeffries studied the young man as he entered his office. He seemed disenchanted, or distracted, or confused maybe.

"Mr. Prestin, you look like you lost your best friend. Personal I hope, and not professional?" Jeffries said in a distinctly aloof voice.

"Oh, nothing sir. I thought I had a date this weekend, but I just found out that it fell through. So, personal, not professional."

"Do I know her?"

"No sir, I'm sure you don't. Someone from out of town. I'll survive, and probably be better off for it. I suppose it would have been a waist of time."

"Speaking of time, what's with Ms. 'Cashel,' nee Castle?"

"She is clearly on to something, sir. She has constant parleys with Dickson. She stays close to the office though. But she is close lipped and as I reported earlier, I can't get close to her or her desk. She avoids me like a plague and if I wander toward her desk, either she or her friends put up a warning as if a gale were blowing in off the ocean."

"Possible a replacement for you. You aren't too attached to the place are you? Maybe you've worn out your welcome," Jeffries pondered.

"Yes sir, possibly. If I can't get something concrete in the next few weeks, bring in a fresh PR person. Maybe a woman would work. Most of the staff in the office are women at this point. Their field workers are by and large men, but at the Commission itself, it's a sewing circle," Prestin explained. He knew Jeffries would like the slight put down on the female staff.

"Yes. I suppose you are right. Stay put for a few more weeks, then we'll pull you out and replace you with someone who might fit in as one of the girls," Jeffries said with satisfaction, as if the idea was his own.

"A woman may be the answer. You don't suppose 'Cashel' is a lesbian do you?"

"I don't think so. At least I've seen nothing to suggest that sort of thing."

"That would make it easier. Catch her with her female lover. Dickson wouldn't care, the liberal taig. But I think her family and her reputation would suffer irreparable damage and humiliation. It might even affect how her work is perceived, by the police, the courts, and the news media.

"I'll have to think this one over. In the mean time keep and eye on her and keep your ears open to any talk of her being a lesbian.

"Well, good work Prestin."

With that, the meeting came to an end. Ms. Eoffa 'Cashel' was going to get an ear full this Friday night, and Prestin was pretty sure it would take the wind out of her sails.

EOFFA'S DILEMMA

Denny occupied a new table at the pub on Friday night, located next to a vacant booth he was hoping Prestin and Eoffa would use. He had to shoo some people away from the booth, but there were plenty of vacant tables. He also had resuscitated an old disguise. He was bearded, new glasses and wearing a new leather jacket and hat.

Fortunately he saw none of the friends he had acquired over the past few visits. That could have been a problem. He didn't even see the usual bar keep until half an hour after he had been seated.

Prestin came in and headed for the privacy of the booth. Denny had to smile to himself. Just minutes later Eoffa showed up, looking like a Hollywood movie star. Prestin nearly fell out of the booth as he stood to greet her.

"You look stunning."

"I'm sure it's the poor lighting," Eoffa said seriously.

"In spite of the lighting, you look wonderful. What would you like to drink?" Prestin asked.

"A Guinness would be great."

"Guinness it is." He caught a waitress' eye and ordered two of the drinks.

"I'll get right to the business at hand. There are two issues we need to discuss. The first involves a couple of Paras who have begun to talk out loud about 'Bloody Sunday.' The military have tried to silence them; first by peer pressure, then threats of demotion, then deploying them far away from Ireland and the UK to God knows where."

Eoffa asked a logical question, "Aren't they due to be discharged? I mean, if they were not officers, they are ready for being mustered out, aren't they?"

"Indeed they are. That has contributed to the army's paranoia about what they might say. In fact they seem to have been sought out by a couple of newspaper and book writers. They are telling different stories from the ones the Widgery report told.

"Peter Taylor, the famous documentary maker, if you recall put out a three part television documentary, one titled *Brits*, and he again recalled the Sergeant-Major of Support Company contradicting the official version. He saw no gunmen, no nail-bombers, no weapons. Apparently there are a couple of other Paras who will corroborate his testimony.

"There is going to be another official Inquiry. The lid will be blown off the Government's position. The British Military, especially Wilford and your man Kitson, will be featured. Kitson is old, he will stall with the usual verbiage about the Paras: they are professionals, they are 'even handed,' they did not 'go about their duties in an excessively forceful way,' and that anyone who sees the One Paras as representative of 'toughness and brutality, I think they are mistaken.'

"He's old, he represents the old school, the old boys network, empire and all that sort of thing. He'll write out a manuscript and ply his opinions instead of facts, he'll verbally testify while clearing his throat and projecting his chin while puckering his lips, and he'll never once admit that One Para followed his published instructions from his book.

"He sees himself as the 'Last Lion,' now that Churchill is gone. He sticks up for empire and those who defend it and punish those who attack it. The ungrateful Irish have been in his crosshairs for decades."

"So you are telling me a new report will substantiate it was a massacre, but that the 'godfather' of that sort of tactic will get off Scot free because he's the embodiment of the failed empire?" Eoffa asked with disdain.

"Unfortunately, yes."

"Don't you think there is a difference between Aden and the North of Ireland? Do you think the One Paras legally had a responsibility to act according to the crown's law on the crown's streets and public areas? And don't you think that Kitson is as responsible for shooting innocent people in Derry, just as much as officers were responsible for policy, instruction, and expectations, as Nazi officers were for their men when the committed atrocities all across Europe? And as I recall, the Brit judges weren't always the ones calling for the death penalty at post World War II trials. Gee, I wonder why?"

"I know you know why. We did a lot of the same sort of thing in India and other places, and closer to home, like Ireland. It's the pot calling the kettle black," Prestin admitted.

"Thanks for being objective and honest," Eoffa said.

"A year, six months, maybe even a month ago, I may not have admitted it. But today I admit it," Prestin admitted.

"Why is that?" Eoffa demanded.

Prestin took a big breath, and said, "You."

"Me?"

"Let's not go there now. I have another issue for you. Take a long pull on your Guinness and get ready for this one. It's a beauty.

"Once again this is so confidential that I could not just be jailed, I could be shot for sharing it with you. I am nervous to be talking about it here. I wish we were some place really private."

Eoffa interrupted him by asking, "Like your apartment or bedroom?"

Once again he was exasperated with her flippant attitude.

"Please Eoffa, this is serious. Your attitude could make me think that you don't understand or care how serious this is. Let me say again, I could be in real trouble if they knew, and it would not just be me. There are laws that could have you end up in a high security prison until you were well beyond your child bearing years" he said with a slight smile to show her he in fact knew she was aware of the gravity of what he was doing for her.

Denny, eavesdropping on the conversation, couldn't have agreed with him more. But he also knew Eoffa understood the danger involved in the nature of this clandestine meeting. He was also aware that this confident, maybe overconfident, woman led her to be what her da would probably have called a "smart-ass."

She smiled weakly and said, "I know, I'm sorry. It won't happen again. Honest."

"I'm holding you to that."

"Back home a guy would say he was going to hold that **against me** for half an hour."

"Jesus, Eoffa, you just did it again. Five seconds after you promised to be serious."

"Aye, we taigs are slippery. We are liars, hypocrites, duplicitous, and smart asses. I'm playing with youse, and I do know how serious this is for the two of us."

Denny nearly choked on his drink when she said, "smart asses."

Shaking his head, Prestin was ready to continue. But in the back of his brain he noticed that Eoffa was no longer hurtful in her "smart ass' comments. This time they had a new tone and they were playful, to the point of self-mockery. Some thing had changed in their relationship.

"My boss is an old 'friend' of your father's. His name is Jeffries, and he clearly has it in for your father. Since you are now here, his obsession now extends to you. Since you are here you have become his main target. I have no doubt he has listening and recording devices on your telephone. I'm sure he opens your posted mail, watches your flat, checks up on your friends at the Commission, and I'm sure he has you followed.

"I have no doubt that the bearded man right here is one of **them** and he protects you. In hindsight I believe he has been to every one of our meetings but with a different disguise, right?" Turning to Denny, he said, "Your build and stature gave you away.

"I also understand that prior to each meeting some of **them** have intercepted the Special Branch boys and disrupted their attempt to follow you.

"The look on your face tells me you didn't know that. Well it's true."

Motioning to Denny, Prestin said, "Why don't you join us."

Denny picked up his non-alcoholic drink and joined them in the booth. "Have I been accurate so far?"

Denny just nodded his head.

Turning to Denny, Eoffa asked, "Why didn't you tell me?"

"I've men in here watching us even now and two more outside. Two interrupted the tails that were following you Eoffa. It's been like this from the very beginning. Your da and me fear for your safety. Your man here's friends are nasty people. We've delt with their lot for decades and centuries, present company excepted," Denny said with a smile and a nod.

Prestin smiled, as much in relief as satisfaction. He continued his story.

"About a month ago a good friend, from my primary and secondary school days, took me out for lunch. He warned me that the 'woman your working on at the Human Rights Commission is under tight surveillance. Everything. I happened to come by a pub in the inner city a weekend some time ago and I saw you with this American girl. I knew who she was immediately. I also saw how you looked at her. Be careful. I've no doubt your chief is on to you too.'

"That was a sobering warning. I've been particularly careful as of late. I keep reporting to Jeffries that you are aloof and want nothing to do with me. I've suggested that you probably have a strong hunch at what I'm up to at the Commission. That's why, Eoffa, I've kept my distance and not tried to contact you out of the office."

Denny said, "Wise man. Eoffa and I appreciate your discretion."

"At our last meeting," Prestin continued, "Jeffries said that since I was making no progress at getting to you, Eoffa, nor have I been able to get at your notes and desk, that he was taking me off your case and reassigning me elsewhere. As if that weren't bad enough, because you seem to disdain any men, he thinks you might be a lesbian."

Eoffa's head jerked back and she gasped, "What?"

Denny just laughed. "These fucken Brits. They cast us in their own perversions, they do it all the time. Prestin, you tell you man that's why the Nationalist population has caught up and surpassed the unionist numbers. Because we are all homos and lesbians."

Prestin had to laugh himself. "I know, it is absurd. But he's going to increase his efforts to see if that is the case and he's thinking of replacing me with a woman. I suspect that if she is not a lesbian herself, she is willing to play the part and try to test you, Eoffa, and trap you in a compromising and embarrassing situation. If their plan works they would expose you, your family and the commission to ridicule and all the rest. So that's Jeffries plan."

Eoffa said emphatically, "Well it's not going to work because I'm not a lesbian."

Prestin said somewhat sheepishly, "Whew, that takes a load off my mind."

Eoffa reached out and punched him lightly and gave him a smiling frown.

"If this were not so serious, I would ask you to prove it to me," Prestin smiled. Even Denny had to grin at that one.

"When will you be replaced," Denny asked?

"A week or two. Why?"

"I want to check a few thing with a friend."

"And I want to be in on the conversation with my da," Eoffa demanded.

Denny asked, "Are we going to have something to eat before we break this meeting up?"

"I'm in no mood to eat," Eoffa said.

"What would you like, I always buy?" Prestin asked.

"Are you sure Eoffa? Your man is buying. I'm partial to the 'shepherd dip,'" Denny smile.

"I'll get three in case you change your mind, Eoffa."

"Can we trust him?" Eoffa asked Denny.

"Aye, I think so. He's in love with you. Second, every thing he said figures. He also made me and hasn't sicked the hounds on me. He also told us plenty of information. Last, he isn't nosy about my name, unless he already knows it," Denny said raising his eyebrows.

After a relatively quiet meal, even Eoffa eating a little shepherd's pie, Denny excused himself for a moment to make arrangements for an escort home for Eoffa.

"Are you playing us, Mark?" Eoffa asked genuinely.

"Absolutely not. I'm in love with you and I'd never betray you. Everything I've told you and have done in the past several weeks have been in your best interest. Your cousin knows how I feel, do you at least accept that much?" Prestin asked pathetically.

"My friend isn't absolutely sure of you. After I leave, be careful. He'll probably want to talk to you."

Denny returned and announced, "It's all set for you Eoffa. I'll be in touch, then we'll talk to your da. Safe home.

"Prestin and I'll remain for a minute. I'd like to talk to him"

Eoffa said her goodbyes, and gave Prestin a genuinely concerned look. "See you on Monday," she said to him as she left.

"On second thought, let's go for a walk. It's a nice night," Denny said.

It was obvious they were not alone. At least two men were up close behind them. After a block, they passed at least two other men who were just hanging around a corner and watching walkers, vehicle traffic, and parked cars.

"Prestin, I don't need to introduce myself and my friends. You know who we are, and I know who you are. So my first question to you is, who are you?"

"I'm with Special Branch, a special unit, working special cases like the Human Rights Commission and Eoffa Castle. I was raised in a unionist family and community, and after university I went through the RUC Academy. I did well in my course work and exercises, so I went into Special Branch. After spending about nine months doing nothing, I was told to report to Mr. Peter Jeffries. He told me my assignment with the Commission. When Eoffa's father started coming with his students and Eoffa herself showed up, they became THE targets of surveillance. Because of Eoffa's position, Jeffries said I could kill two birds with one shot. That's pretty much the story."

"Why are you talking to Eoffa now?"

"She and I sparred for some times, she always getting the better of me. I was really attracted to her, but she just beat me up every opportunity. Then, after an exchange of punches, she said I could make points with her if I'd supply her with certain information.

"I was falling in love with the woman. I knew it would never work, being who she is, her da and her mother's family. But the more I saw her and the more I started to listen to her and follow up on what she had to say, the more doubts I had about what we were doing in the Province.

"Doubt about that, growing attraction to her, what a combination. Greater changes of heart have been made by lesser motives. I really love that girl, and what I'm trying to help her with is redemption and surrender to her, and you and her family. I've been on the wrong side. If she were to accept me, if her family were to let me prove myself more, I'd do anything to have a chance at winning that girl's heart."

Denny put his arm around Prestin's shoulder and with the other hand he put a revolver to his side, and said, "If you betray her or anyone else in her family, or **us**, you are dead. Oh, and it won't stop there."

"Look, I'm willing to betray my country, my service, my family, all for her, and indirectly for her family and you boys. I know as a couple we are a long shot, but I'm willing to take the shot. What else can I say or do to make you believe me?"

"Eoffa and I will talk to her da, and Rudy will have a plan. She'll set up the next rendezvous. We are watching. Don't fuck with us."

Jeffries came along with Sergeant Galoway to the meeting. He didn't always tag along. He had better things to do with his time, he assured himself. But he felt he could sometimes get a better read from and agent by watching the body language and expressions as reports were made, than merely reading a written report of the interview.

This was the case in this instance. Time and money had been spent on this operation and virtually nothing was coming of it. He had a suspicion that maybe the key agent had muffed it, or had gotten soft on the subject, or simply had given up the chase. But whatever the reason, Jeffries wanted to hear and see the analysis of the second agent on the operation that was unknown to the first undercover plant.

The second agent might have not just a report but also an analysis that could explain the absence of success from the primary agent. They were close to the subject under scrutiny and the primary agent. Maybe they had sensed something improper as to approach. Or, something improper as to technique. Or, God forbid, something improper as to the relationship between agent and subject.

His agent, Mark Prestin, was an exemplary officer. Top of his class, excellent internship, stellar performance in the two previous operations. But in this last one, with Miss Eoffa Castle, or Cashel, or by whatever name she fancied, he was off his game.

By all accounts, she was witty, intelligent, and attractive; God forbid, maybe she had seduced the boy. He would let agent number two, Deirdre Palm, report, and if this possible seduction did not show up in her report, he would suggest the possibility to her.

The meeting was at lunchtime on Friday, so time was limited. The bakery was in the neighborhood of the Commission office, but far enough away that no one else from the office would stumble upon them.

Galoway said to Ms. Palm, "Good to see you. Let us pay for lunch. We'll drop you off around the corner from the office to help you get back on time.

"I think you know Mr. Jeffries who heads this operation."

"Yes, of course. So good to see you again sir."

"Yes, it's been a while. How have you been?"

"Quite well sir. Enjoying my first real undercover work," Deirdre Palm said in a whisper, looking around as she spoke in a hushed tone.

They were sitting far enough away from everyone else in the shop so there was little fear of anyone actually hearing what they said if they kept the conversation tone low.

Sergeant Galoway began by asking, "Well now Deirdre, tell us about Eoffa Cashel. What is she up to these days? Our man Prestin hasn't been able to tell us much, so what about you?"

"I'm afraid that I have very little to tell either. She is a rather private person, and she huddles with Dickson at least once a day, she never shares what they talk about or what she is working on specifically. As I've reported, she is working on 'Bloody Sunday,' and 'Patrick Finucane,' but beyond that I haven't a clue."

"Does she go out during the day to meet anyone? How about at night?"

"She stays around during the day. As to her nights, she never says anything about that, socially or concerning work," Deirdre reported.

Jeffries interjected, "That's what Prestin has reported also. Several times the team we had tracking her on the weekend has been interrupted and we lost her for several hours. We believe the traffic problems have been deliberate, intentionally blocking our people so she can get away.

"Then she returns to her flat hours later either by cab or on foot. We've interviewed the cab drivers but they report various pick up places that often seem bogus to us.

"Her flat has produced nothing of interest, and neither has her phone," Jeffries explained.

"She used my phone at least once, but I don't know who she called and I can't remember exactly how long ago it was either," Deirdre reported.

"We may be able to check that call if we have the time and date," Galoway said hopefully.

"What can you tell us about Prestin's presence in the office? He seems to be trying, but he is not successful with Cashel, is he?" Jeffries asked.

Deirdre explained, "It's not for not trying. She is clearly rude to him, not so much for what he says or does or offers to do, but who he is. Being the PR man for the RUC has targeted him for her. She takes every opportunity to embarrass and belittle him. He has been a gentleman and Cashel just targets him for insults."

"That is pretty much what he has claimed," Jeffries concurred. "Has he tried to meet her outside of work?"

"We all went to a pub one Friday after work, he was more than his gracious self when a verbal dispute broke out between them with Cashel leveling a diatribe about Irish emigration and the like.

"She walked out of the pub and several of us tagged along for support, my self included so as to build up trust. It was the night I nearly had my purse swiped and supposedly an IRA man stopped it. I reported the incident to Mr. Galoway, along with the IRA man's description."

"So there is no chance that Prestin has met with her officially or unofficially?" Jeffries inquired cautiously. "She hasn't seduced him, has she?"

"Dear me, I wouldn't think so. He tries to get on with her, professionally, and she rejects his friendship every time. I'm sure it is a genuine dislike on her part. As you are aware I'm sure, her father and mother were involved with the IRA and Republican movement and she is sympathetic with all of that too.

"As far a Prestin is concerned, how he could really like the woman is beyond me. She belittles and insults him constantly. I can tell he just holds it in but would like to thrash her if he could. She's so insulting to him and the service, the RUC. No one knows he's with Special Branch but me," Deirdre explained.

"Right, that's very helpful. Oh, there's no chance she's seeing anyone is there? I mean romantically?"

"Not that I'm aware of. She seems to be a loner. That's why I'm a little surprised she goes out on the weekend and the tails loose her. I can try to find out where and with whom she's going and seeing," Deirdre said.

"No chance she's a lesbian?" Jeffries couldn't help asking.

Deirdre was clearly caught off guard. "No, I don't think so. I've never seen any evidence of that sort of behavior, nor have I gotten any sense or vibes of that sort of thing. But I'll watch and listen for it."

"Good. Well that's it. Galoway will bring you back now. Good work and tell Galoway straightaway if you discover anything before your next scheduled meeting."

Later that day Galoway reported to Jeffries that Eoffa used Deirdre's phone to call a number in the United States. "That US number was to the Rudy Castle residence."

"Too bad it wasn't a local call. We may have been able to pick up a still functioning IRA man, or a whole damn unit."

———————•◦•———————

The IRA man reported to Denny about 14:00. The hunch turned out to be a pot of gold. They had recognized Jeffries when he went into the bakery. They also knew Deirdre, but not the second man. He was tall and bald except for a fringe just above the ears circling around the back of his head. They managed to get a photo of him exiting the shop with the woman though, for the files.

"Deirdre met with Jeffries and another man for about thirty minutes. Then the unknown drove her back to the Commission and dropped her off about a block away. We got the unknown's picture."

"Good work. This confirms our suspicions, and throws oil on the water. Make sure I get the photo for the album," Denny instructed.

"Right."

"I'll have to tell Eoffa that her cousin has the 'gift,' from her mammy. What a stroke of luck. If young Barb hadn't shared that insight with us, we all might be fucked," Denny thought.

Eoffa always took the taxi home on Wednesdays. The driver, Denny, had vital news.

"Deirdre is confirmed Special Branch, reporting to a Jeffries, an old friend of your da's, and another fellah. Your cousin and your auntie have the gift and it probably saved us some time in prison."

"I've not behaved any differently than before to Deirdre, but I've been vigilantly watching her. I don't think her primary interest is myself, it's Prestin.

"Prestin and I still ignore each other no more no less than before, so as not to let on we know about her. He wants to meet. Maybe we should break the weekend pattern and find another place than the pub," Eoffa suggested.

"I'll get you tomorrow after work. We'll lose whoever is tailing us. We'll pick him up near the Europa Hotel and we'll head for a safe house in Andersonstown. Can you get the message to him tomorrow?"

"It's short notice, but yes."

"Short notice is sometimes good. No opportunity for the opposition to plan. Here you are. I'll wait till you are in. Oh, your rooms are probably bugged, did I tell you that before?"

"Ten times."

———◆———

"Well 'boys and girls,' only a week left before we're off to Ireland. Any last minute questions? No heavy raincoats. Plan to layer, as Tracy has suggested, and bring a half dozen of the ninety-nine cent rain slickers," I said for the fiftieth time.

"You said no travelers checks, right?"

"Well, if you must, OK, but you will find many merchants don't want to bother with them. That only leaves banks and hotels. You aren't staying in any hotels, and they often only serve hotel guests, so be advised," I said again for the hundredth time.

Tracy leaned over to me and asked, "Is that true?"

"Which part?"

"Any or all of it?"

"Hell I don't know."

Tracy exhaled in an exasperated way, and said to the group, "The general rule of travel is, 'More money, fewer clothes and incidentals.' So be advised of that too."

"Very good. Is that true?"

"Yes it is," Tracy said emphatically.

"Are you getting pissed off?"

"Pissed off? No. Excited? Yes. These 'boys and girls' still believe everything you tell them, so stop making stuff up, please. It just makes more work for me when I have to explain the truth to them later."

"Why? It's what I do. It's who I am. I'm teaching them a valuable lesson. Don't believe or trust anyone over thirty. At least at face value," I said with a grin.

"Mr. Castle, when can we start calling you Rudy?" a young coed asked.

"Once we are on the bus and off campus."

"Can I ask you a question about the course material?"

"Egad. There is a brown nose in every group. We know who ours is."

Every one laughed, including the brown nose.

I waited around the college until eight that night, then called Denny from one of my colleague's office phone. It was one in the morning in Belfast; it was inconvenient for him to hang around the monastery that late, but it was essential for privacy and a clean line.

"I've a plan but it can wait until I'm there," I said.

"We need a couple of plans, don't we? Do you have a couple of ideas or one all encompassing plan?" Denny asked.

"Yes." Then I hung up. I thought, *come on Denny, I'm so tired I don't know if I'm foot or horseback, and you're asking too damn many questions.*

Denny just stood there holding the phone as it went dead. He then thought to himself, *He's tired and I'm asking too damn many questions.*

LET THE GAMES BEGIN

Eoffa had gotten the same message about a plan from her da, and no more details. She had explained that she intended to tell Dickson about Deirdre being RUC. She would not explain how she knew, and she would ask him not to expose and dismiss her for a while yet. I agreed.

"But what if Brice doesn't agree?"

I said, "Have him talk to me before he does anything."

Eoffa went about her daily tasks the rest of Thursday, and she went in to talk to Brice Dickson, as she motioned to Prestin with her eyes and a slight nod of her head, to follow.

No one in the outer office seemed to notice the three of them gathered in Dickson's office. Eoffa didn't beat around the bush.

"Brice, Prestin here is not the only RUC person in the office. I cannot explain how I came to this knowledge yet. I will disclose who it is if you want me to, but I'd rather not for now. My da is working on a plan.

"He will be here in a week with his students and he wants to talk with you before anything is done about the plant.

"I'm finishing up a report on 'Bloody Sunday' and today Mark and I are going to meet about Finucane. We believe the plant is spying on Mark as much as on the rest of us and our work here."

"You have been busy, Eoffa. Thank you for keeping me informed, and I will not expose our 'friend' until after I hear from your da, in person," Dickson said.

"Could you walk us to the door and say, 'Would you two please be civil to each other?' That will help explain why we were both together with you, getting a dressing out if you will."

On the way out Eoffa slipped a note in Prestin's hand. Dickson pretended not to notice. He thought to himself, *there are games, in puzzles, in an enigma going on around here.*

Everyone got the mild reproach as Dickson ushered the two of them out of his office. Prestin read the note at his leisure at lunch and then thoroughly destroyed the note.

At the safe house in Andersonstown, they got down to business immediately. Denny asked if they would be more comfortable if he were not present? Both agreed he could and should stay.

"The 'Stevens Report,' back in 1990 said that although 'collusion' has existed for some time between the security forces and loyalist paramilitaries, it was non-the-less restricted to a hand full of security people and never 'institutionalized' nor 'widespread,'" Preston explained.

"But, in the Pat Finucane case, it was clearly targeted on that man: for the RUC, the Special Branch, the British Military, and specifically the UDA. Although the lid has been kept on much of the 'Steven's Report,' just a summary has been published to date. The recent killing of William Stobie, a UDA man and a Special Branch agent, who was killed by the UDA for fear he would talk about the Finucane murder, indicates there is more to the story than is in the official 'Report.' Stobie supplied the gun to Ken Barrett, also a Special Branch agent, who pulled the trigger on Finucane. These two Special Branch agents were part of Tommy Lyttle's UDA gang, and Tommy was also a Special Branch agent.

"The collusion was in fact 'deep' if not widespread and institutionalized as the Chief Constable of Cambridgeshire reported. The RUC, and especially Special Branch, were in collusion branch, trunk and stump. And you wondered, Denny, why I've had a change of heart? It's not just Eoffa, it's everything I stood for. She and what she stands for is true and what I stood for was a lie," Preston confessed.

"Well, to return to Finucane. It brought down the intelligence agent who set up the murder, Brian Nelson. But what a few people know, maybe a dozen at most beside you, is that Stobie made a tape. In it he explained who, when, where and the why of Finucane's murder. The names I've mentioned of the UDA-Special Branch operatives, you know. But Stobie names others, out of the UDA

"The UDA and other groups have released hundreds of files of targets, IRA and Sinn Fein targets, supplied to them by the British Military and RUC, thus being assured they were 'legitimate' targets. They subsequently released two thousand more files.

But this is just the tip of the iceberg."

Eoffa perked up and said, "The British Military, huh. Kitson was long gone by that time, but I wonder if some of his disciples were applying some of his teachings in killing Finucane. I'd love to know the names of the military jerks involved."

Prestin nodded his head affirmatively, then continued his story. "Stobie named names in Stormont and Whitehall who were also involved. He provided not just names but also dates of meetings and the amount of financial help forth coming from these sources."

Denny asked the obvious questions, "How did you come by this information about a tape and then what is on the tape?"

"The childhood friend who warned that Eoffa was under surveillance also told me his boss opened up one night after a few drinks. He said he was in possession of a secret so secret that he had to confide in somebody.

"I asked him if it was in connection with our work? He said it was and it wasn't. He was slobbering all over the place. He was talking about his marriage, his wife, and his two daughters. Wanted to know if I would take one of his daughters out? Did I have a friend I would trust with the other daughter?

"Finally he told me he was one of a few who knew of and the were a bouts of a secret tape made by the criminal, just killed, William Stobie.

"I told him he should keep that under his hat, and he laughed and said it was under his hat because he trusted me. I said to him, 'you've got to keep quiet about that.' He just smiled and said, 'mum is the word.' The next day at headquarters, he acted normal and all. Like nothing had happened.

"He says to me, my friend, what should I do about him? He's going to blab and let the cat loose. I'm asking for your opinion?" Prestin explained.

"I said, 'Is the tape secure?'

"My friend said, 'Yes, right in the Special Branch's safe.'

"I said, if I were you I'd let it slide this time, but if it happens again, I'd report him.'"

"Any chance of seeing the tape?" Denny asked wistfully.

"No. Only two people to my knowledge have access to the vault. But the important thing is, Eoffa, there is a tape that incriminates and indicates people in politics, the military, and the security services, besides the UDA in Pat Finucane's killing.

"Besides access to it being a problem, if it's existence is exposed I can see some one destroying it," Prestin warned.

"So we're no further ahead today than we were before," Eoffa claimed.

"Maybe not," Prestin said. "If Stobie knew, maybe others knew, or know, as well."

"You're man Brian Nelson knows, but he'll be killed if he talks, or they think he'll talk," Denny warned.

"Lyttle, Barrett, and Nelson know something, but they are as quiet as the grave. And the grave is where they'll be if they talk; they know that. But he's right Eoffa, others must know. Maybe if some one from the Human Rights Commission went to visit his family, maybe other names would come up," Denny suggested.

"I would need Dickson's OK on this," Eoffa said.

"And a small army for protection," Prestin added.

"Thanks for the heads up on the tape, Mark," Eoffa said. "I just don't know what will come of it. I don't know who specifically we can go after who hasn't already been identified and prosecuted."

"Sorry I can't do better for you, but Special Branch won't help and will probably deny any tape. Brice Dickson should be happy to know such a tape exists. Warn him to be careful with that knowledge. Having it destroyed is the least of the trouble the security forces could do. They've murdered people for as much," Prestin warned with genuine concern.

"And less," Eoffa added.

———————•◦•———————

The students loved their accommodations at Ti Cuchulainn. They also found the local pub in Mullaghbane. All was well. I had rented an auto for three weeks and the second night I headed up to Belfast to meet up with Eoffa and Denny.

I parked near Eoffa's flat, went in, and was impressed. She obviously had picked up and cleaned.

"Your mammy would, will be impressed," I complimented.

"Thanks da, it took all day."

We left and started our walk. I noticed a shadow immediately. We turned a corner, entered Denny's cab and were gone in a flash. He drove around for a while, but we ended up at the "Felons Club."

"They let anybody in, you don't have to be a felon any more, as you know," Denny explained.

We found a corner and I said I'd come and talk to Brice on Tuesday.

"My plan was simple: we hire a Dublin security company to install a camera, we plant a phony folder on Eoffa's desk, we film Deirdre, detain her, get her on tape condemning Jeffries for betraying Special Branch. A simple sting operation.

"Next, we inform Jeffries that she has implicated him in this illegal penetration of the Human Rights Commission, and selling secrets. We won't have to wait too long to see what he proposes to do."

Denny smiled. "Seems simple enough."

"They will go after Eoffa, so I propose that we wait until the last week I'll be here with the students so you can go down to Dublin and wait for your mother and auntie Eve. If Brice accepts, I'll handle the negotiations. It will be on me, not Eoffa," I explained.

"We can get a film crew together to do the interview with Deirdre, no problem. The question is where will we do it?" Denny asked.

"We'll burn her at the Commission offices, then we'll trick her at some apartment," I answered.

"This will give Jeffries a heart attack."

"No, this next bit will. We offer to trade Deirdre's tape for a look at the William Stobie tape!"

"Da, you're kidding, right?"

"Rudy, there is no way he'll agree to do that. Even if he does have access to it," Denny explained.

"I'm sure he won't. But if we can get on tape that he acknowledges such a tape exists, it's as good as we can hope for. Now we've got to assume he is one of them in the know. We'll have to assume he is in the loop, and next we catch him flat footed and burn the bastard before he has time to rationally respond."

"He'll come after you Rudy. It could mean the end of your program here in the North," Denny warned.

"I'll just send somebody else. And, this would be worth it, don't you think?" I asked rhetorically.

We sat there sipping on our drinks. Only Eoffa was having a drink with alcohol in it. Old Sean Mac Stiofain would have been pleased. The old boy had been the first Chief of Staff of the Provisional IRA, wouldn't allow drinking of alcohol before an operation. He was old school, and I'd cut my teeth under him. Denny had too, and he abstained always. So, no alcoholic drinks, for us any way, until we were home free.

———•◦•———

My meeting with Brice was what I expected. He was hesitant at first. When he came around he was cautious, but he was willing to "trap the rat," as Denny called "Operation Deirdre" in his crude moments. I did not tell the whole operation to Brice, specifically the part about detaining Deirdre and filming her talking about Jeffries, probably while she was under duress.

That same Tuesday, Denny contacted some friends in Dublin who were experts on security equipment.

"They are good on both sides of security," Denny explained. I just looked at him, and he smiled as he raised and quickly lowered his eyebrows twice. I knew immediately what he meant, but I didn't derive it from his usage of the English language or facial expression. I just knew. "They could break security very professionally, or they could install it very professionally."

That same evening of the longest Tuesday in my life, I met Mark Prestin. Denny arranged the meeting, the pickups, the drop offs, and the pub. Everything was quick, efficient, and professional.

Eoffa and I were already there when Prestin walked in. I think every patron was one of Denny's men. No one looked at any of us. They didn't have to, they were not just aware and conscious of our presence, but they were guarding us and scrutinizing us every minute. I never saw any of then look directly at us though. Denny had taught these men well.

"Eoffa, have you told me everything you can about this man?"

"Aye."

"He's in love with you? That I can understand. You are as lovely as your mother. But I have to ask, and you can take your time in answering, how do you feel about him? Do you love him?"

"Yes he loves me. He is willing to turn his back on everything he stood for here: his family, his church, his friends, his job, his culture and his politics, for me. He says I converted him. He's doing what he's doing for repentance and love."

"Do you love him? Have you spent any normal time with him?"

"I think I love him. As to the second question, No."

"Every time you've been with him Denny and his crew have been there, right?"

"Aye."

"And he's RUC, actually Special Branch, and the top of his class? And he's been seduced by you?"

"Da, I've not seduced him in any physical way. I treated him like a dog. I lectured him like a student. I've been rude and ugly to him. But he says he's willing to betray every thing for me and my beliefs."

"And you believe him?"

"I did. If you have questions about his sincerity, then so do I. If you don't believe him, neither do I. If you think he's lying, then so do I."

We sat there for several minutes without a word. Then in through the door came Denny and Mark Prestin. The vibes in the place were instantly hostile. Denny's group were like a pack of wolves that just found a sheep, all alone without its shepherd.

Denny turned to the bar. An empty stool and plastic container of spring water was waiting for him.

"Mr. Castle, I'm Mark Prestin. I know this is going to sound absurd and embarrass your daughter, but I love her."

He just stood there looking at us. First at Eoffa, then at me. I let this go on for about fifteen seconds. Then I said, "Shut up and sit down."

"I'm going to ask you some questions. You'll only answer the questions. The answers will determine if you live or die, not whether you will spend time with my daughter, you understand, you spying 'Nairac.'?

"Did Jeffries put you up to this charade?"

"No, sir"

"Stop that sir shite."

"Yes sir. Sorry sir. Umm, sorry."

"Who put you up to it?" I scowled at the "sir" bit.

He hesitated for an instant, looked at Eoffa, and said, "She did, your daughter, Eoffa Castle."

Although it was a good answer and I sort of believed him, I said, "Don't insult us."

"I'm not trying to insult any one. I was . . . ."

I cut him off, "I didn't ask you a question, so don't manufacture an answer to a non-question.

"Who do you report to?"

"Jeffries."

"You report to Jeffries, but he didn't put you up to any of this?"

"Well, my job was to spy on the Human Rights Commission under the pretext of being a RUC Public Relations representative."

He wanted to say more, but I cut him off. "So Jeffries did send you and you report to him as well?"

"Yes, well, he sent me to spy on the Commission, but not to lie to Eoffa or you."

"But you did lie telling them you were a PR guy. Wasn't that a lie?"

"Yes, that part was."

"So you are a liar?"

"That was my job."

"Exactly. You are a trained liar. Where does it end?"

"I've not lied to Eoffa about any of the information I got for her. I'm not lying when I say she changed me. I'm not lying when I say I love her."

I looked over at Eoffa. She looked miserable. I looked at Prestin for a few seconds. Then I motioned to Denny. Although his back was to me he instantly spun around and came over to our table.

"'Nairac' here deserves a ride. So get this piece of lying shite out of our sight."

Two of Denny's boys were right there to help lift Prestin up. They each had an arm.

Denny said in a truly menacing voice, "Don't make this any harder on yourself. Just come along peacefully. Don't make a scene."

I felt Eoffa tense up, and for an instant I was sure she was going to protest, but then her shoulders dropped, she exhaled, and resigned herself to Prestin's fate.

In ten seconds the four of them were gone. I reached over to take her arm. I expected her to jerk it away and for her to curse me. But she did neither.

Taking her arm I said, "I believe him."

She stared at me in disbelief. "They are just taking him to his apartment. I'm going to bring you to him. You need to spend some time with him, alone. Not all night. I'll be outside, waiting, and in about two hours you'll come down and I'll drive you to your flat."

"Da, I don't know what to say."

"Don't say anything about this to your mother, at least for a while. Come on, its time to go."

———————◆•◆•◆———————

Denny's team provided security; they swept the neighborhood of Prestin's flat, they patrolled the area on foot, and they monitored cars passing in front of his address. As I said before, Denny had taught them well.

Prestin did not resist Denny's squad when they bundled him off in a car. He seemed totally defeated and resigned to his fate. Eoffa had left him out to dry and die. It was only when they pulled up in front of his apartment did he wonder what was happening.

Denny turned from the front seat to face Mark and said. "You failed Rudy's test. Every one fails Rudy's tests when he wants them to" he smiled. "He did interrogation in Vietnam, he rigged the outcomes to fit his needs. He was a terror, so he was. But you passed Eoffa's, go on into your flat, her da is bringing her to be with you to sort things out. You'll have two hours. Don't exceed two hours, Rudy won't tolerate it.

"Remember this for the rest of your life, young man, you owe your life to Rudy Castle. If he wanted you dead he'd do it himself. He's funny that way.

"Your phone is bugged; by your friends at Special Branch. Unplug it. It will piss them off, but fuck em."

"Do you also have a bug?"

"Now, would I tell you if we did? We do know you've never called to report a meeting with Eoffa, so you passed that test. The question is, have we tapped your phone or your headquarters?" Denny smiled, raising his eyebrows up and down a couple of times.

Prestin got out, went into the foyer and waited for Eoffa. He only had to wait a minute. She went in and he led her up to his flat. Once in the apartment he took her coat, put his arms around her, kissed her and said, "I love you, I really do. And every thing I've said is true. I've been a fool for years believing blindly all the lies I've been told, and turning a blind eye to all that I should have seen."

"Enough of that, what about us? How do you see us? What are your plans for us?" Eoffa asked.

"I'll help do what your da has planned here, then I'll come with you to America. I'll get work there, I'll do what ever you want me to. I'll become a Roman Catholic, I'll do whatever it takes."

"I want to believe you. I think I love you. I've never really been in love before, so I'm not sure what I feel is real love. I feel strongly about you, for you, but is it love?" Eoffa confided.

"It could be infatuation I suppose. I hope it's more than that," she said.

"What more can I do to convince you? What else could I do? Just tell me," Prestin pleaded.

"We are going to take it slow, we are going to get to know each other, trust each other, learn from each other. Will this virtually kill your folks, your parents?"

"They'll be hurt, for sure. But I am the apple of their eye and they will get over it. When they get to know you, they'll understand my actions."

"The way you put it they will blame me for what you are choosing to do. I don't want them to think that I trapped you, forced you in any way, or manipulated you, because I haven't."

"You are right, of course. Your mother and auntie are not here yet, correct?"

"That's right."

"What if we go up to Newtown Crommalin on Saturday, spend the night with my parents and come back Sunday afternoon. They'll get to meet you, and you'll be able to wow them with your American charm."

"It's awfully short notice, I'll have to make sure my da doesn't need me. I'll also want to get his OK. I'm still his 'little girl' you know. He also just suspended your death sentence," Eoffa teased.

"Don't I know it, Denny told me to remember for the rest of my life that I owe your da my life!"

"He wasn't kidding," Eoffa said with a grin.

The rest of their time together they talked of likes and dislikes related to food, drink, colors, animals, artists, music, literature, clothing, musicians, architecture, styles, weather, sports, and public displays of affection.

"Before you go, can I really kiss you passionately?"

Prestin asked.

"You mean with tongue and a little, and I mean a little, groping?"

"Aye, exactly."

Before he could make his move, Eoffa had him on the floor and was all over him. Just when he was ready to jump in whole heartedly, she was up on her feet, and said, "That was nice. Maybe it's love."

She waited for him at the door, gave him a little peck of a kiss, and they walked back through the foyer. She reached out and touched his arm, said good night, and ran to her da's car. He just stood there, more in love than two hours ago, than an hour go, than fifteen minutes ago.

Eoffa explained the reason for the visit to his folks. I had to agree with her argument, and saw no reason for her not to go.

"Separate bedrooms," I said.

"I'm sure his Presbyterian parents will see to it, da."

I had lectures set for Wednesday and Thursday at Ti Chulainn Center and so particulars were left up to Denny. His "security crew" from the Republic came in on Thursday night and placed a surveillance camera and had it set to go with the push of a button.

Friday the Human Rights Commission got a surprise. A new PR person, Ms. Elisabeth Trimble, a distant relative of David Trimble, the Ulster Unionist Party leader and First Minister of the Stormont government in the North of Ireland, replaced Mr. Prestin.

Prestin came in to say his goodbyes to one and all. He shook hands and introduced Ms. Trimble to as many as he could. When she was introduced to Eoffa, she shook her hand and lingered holding on to for it an awkward minute. Eoffa remembered the questioning of her sexual preference. She didn't know if there was such a thing, but what she just experienced could certainly be a lesbian invitation.

Eoffa took her lunch break out of the office and met Prestin at a car dealership a short distance away. They were on for tomorrow. Denny would drop her off at his flat for their get a way to his parent's home.

"I'm excited about this," Eoffa said to Mark's great satisfaction.

"I wish I could kiss you right now," he admitted to her.

"This weekend, if your parents don't mind," she teased.

"I don't care if they mind," he said with a grin.

———•◦•———

Eoffa called me and explained the new development at the Commission.

"It might be better to throw suspicion off him. We are set to go. You'll get a registered envelope, or what ever they call it over here, on Monday. I've really doctored it up. Your Ms. Deirdre should crap her pants when she sees it. We'll be recording it all. So have a good time tomorrow and Sunday. Ask his parents where the nearest Catholic Church is you and Mark can attend on Sunday morning."

"Probably not, although he said he'd become Catholic, Roman Catholic, for me."

"That's just fine, but there have never been any Romans in Hartford, or Michigan, or North America to my knowledge. We do have pizza parlors and shops whose owners and relatives may have been from Rome though," I kidded.

"What's with the 'Roman' stuff, da?"

"It's their way of claiming that Catholic's real allegiance is to a foreign potentate. They are not loyal subjects."

"And they believe that?"

"Supposedly. Paisley surely does."

"And people wonder why there is such a religious divide here in the North," Eoffa said in exasperation.

"Eoffa, honey, have a grand time and wow his parents. Oh, ya, separate bedrooms."

"Love you too da."

———•◦•———

"What a pleasant surprise it was when Mark called to say he was coming and bringing a 'beautiful American,'" his father William Prestin said as they got out of the car in the driveway. "You can just call me 'Billy,' every one does, except Mark here. This is Grace, Mark's mother and my wife for nearly forty years now."

"I am very pleased to meet you. I know this was short notice, and Mark has probably been so busy that he failed to mention he was seeing someone. Probable concerned it was a colonial girl from America," Eoffa said playfully.

Mark just watched her, both his parents noticed. She was a beautiful American as he claimed on the phone; so clean, healthy, and perfect posture, and with such an American accent.

"Let me get your valise and we can go in. Do you need to freshen up, Eoffa?" Mark asked.

"No, I fine actually. I can get my grip, and yours is so big and heavy, you can't manage both comfortably."

Grace said, "Eoffa, what a beautiful name. Is it Spanish for Ava?"

"It sounds that way, doesn't it? But it's actually Irish for Eve. My mother's family is from Belfast, and my auntie, her little sister, is whom I'm named after, aunt Eve, but in Irish," Eoffa smiled.

"Charming," Grace said.

"From Belfast," Billy said, "where may I ask in Belfast?"

Eoffa was smiling as she looked at Mark who was grinning from ear to ear, "West Belfast, off the Falls not far from Clonard Monastery. Are you familiar with that area," Eoffa asked innocently, but Mark knew she was teasing his father.

"Only from the news so many years ago," Billy said straight faced.

"Of course, the 'Troubles.' Well it seems to be winding down, thank God," Eoffa said.

"Yes," Grace said.

"Let's hope so. We've more important things to do than fight over religion," Billy interjected.

"And Fair housing, and jobs, and gerrymandering, this is the twenty-first century after all," Eoffa countered.

"Here we are," Grace said. "Let me show you to your room."

Once out of sight, Billy said to his son, "Feisty, and opinionated, isn't she?

"She is that, and she has been proven correct making those opinions facts, in fact. She's also from a Republican family of Catholics," Mark explained.

He knew his father wanted to ask, but didn't, "*Then why in the hell are you with this woman?*"

Mark did everything he could to keep politics, religion, unemployment and the IRA out of the conversation. Bye and large he was successful.

Eoffa and Grace got on brilliantly. They talked food and cooking mostly.

Eoffa had to catch herself a couple of times and reword statements such as, "Well, if Mark comes to the US he could bring one back for you," and, "When Mark comes to visit me possibly you could come along and I could show you," and so on.

Billy was very quiet, according to Mark on the drive home. "He was studying you. He was watching me, but studying your every move. He watched my mother take to you, but he studied you every minute."

"He didn't like me nor approve of me. But he was very polite. He's from a generation that just can't conceive of the protests and condone the changes of the recent past. I understand. When your folks come to visit, they'll see us intermingle with Catholics, Protestants, Jews, Moslems, Hindus, and atheists. That will be an education for him. You are prepared for it, aren't you?"

"With you, all things are possible, probable, and acceptable," Mark said.

"Boy, if you'd just stay this way," Eoffa commented.

The rest of the trip back to Belfast was spent reliving some of the conversations, comments and moments, that were funny, embarrassing, and challenging to them this weekend, but especially to Billy.

Eoffa was thinking, *Poor Billy, he knows he's not gaining a daughter-in-law, with us living over in the US, he's loosing his son.*

For that Eoffa felt a ting of sadness. The man sitting next to her truly did love her if he was willing to have his father, who he had been close to previously, go through the loss of his son.

———◦•◦———

"A special delivery for Mr. Eoffa Cashel," the deliveryman announced. "You have to sign for it here."

Eoffa ripped it open, read it for several minutes, went into Dickson's office, shutting the door behind her. After nearly half an hour she returned, followed by Brice who congratulated her before returning to his office.

The "Operation Deirdre," or "Trap the Rat," in Denny's vernacular, was under way.

Deirdre said, "Something big I take it?"

In a very quiet conspiratorial whisper Eoffa said, "Aye, really big. A big shot from the RUC, actually Special Branch, finally came through for me. I had some dirt on him and he finally admitted the existence of something for me. This will blow the Finucane case sky high.

"I've got to meet with another source here in a bit. I'll fill you in on all the details later. After lunch I'm having Brice lock this up in his safe."

"Good for you, Eoffa. I know how much this means to you, with only a few days left in your internship," Deirdre said sounding very sincere.

"I only wish our RUC PR man, Prestin, was still here. I'd have loved to see his face when this story broke. Brice will have all the news services here, newspapers, TV, radio, from the North, the Republic, and the BBC. This one will be the big one for the Human Rights Commission."

Eoffa opened up the envelope again and read through it all again. She could see that Deirdre was nearly beside her self, trying not to be nosey, but trying to catch any little gesture, no matter how trivial.

"Boy I wish that wanker Prestin was here," Eoffa said out loud.

Brice came out of his office, Eoffa came over and met him, and the two of them left together. As part of the plan, Eoffa was secretly to catch the train for Dublin and to stay out of the way for a few days.

Deirdre was following their movements, and hoping that Eoffa would be so excited that she'd forget to take care of envelope. That was exactly what happened.

Several of the office girls also got up to go out for lunch. Some one was always in the office at lunchtime and Deirdre said it was her turn to watch the shop during lunch. It was at this point that Elizabeth Trimble came in.

"Sorry I'm so late, Mondays," she said painfully! "I need some coffee."

"It's right over there, help yourself," Deirdre said as she leaned over to Eoffa's desk, taking the envelope and putting it on her own desk.

When Trimble crashed at her own desk with her cup of caffeine, and Deirdre was sure she would not be coming over to bother her, she positioned her chair so she could see the front door. There were some photos of Jeffries with some unknown men who appeared to be paramilitaries. There was one of him with the former IRA man, Jerry Kelly, now with Sinn Fein. There was another one with Brice and Gerry Adams! He had associated with the IRA and Sinn Fein, thanks to a computer photo-shop program. To Deirdre, Jeffries had apparently sold out Special Branch.

Deirdre was not going to share this info with Ms. Trimble, even though she was also with Special Branch. She could be in all of this with Jeffries. He had appointed her to this new position. She was his girl.

The photos were disturbing enough, but the documents were more so. Jeffries described the UDA man and Special Branch agent, William Stobie who'd been killed because he'd threatened to talk about the Finucane murder, as having made a tape about the murder. Jeffries had written in this document:

> "Stobie had made a video about who killed Pat Finicune, and who else was involved. Several Senior men in Special Branch and the RUC were named. He also kept notes as to dates and places of meetings to discuss Finucane's killing.

> "Stobie also identified several persons high up in MI5 and the British Special Branch, Scotland Yard. He recorded name, places and times of meetings.

"Stobie identified senior members of the British Military, especially British Intelligence (FRU, Force Research Unit) and the Military Reconnaissance Force (aka MRF, Military Reaction Force), dates, times and places of meetings.

"Stobie listed many Conservative MPs, and many UUP and DUP Stormont assembly—men, the times, dates and places when they met and discussed 'getting rid' of Pat Finucane.

"Stobie catalogued several senior civil service personnel who participated with all the groups mentioned above. He identified dates, times, and places of these meetings.

"Stobie identified several meetings where combinations of these groups met to discuss the elimination of Pat Finucane in particular, but other troublesome Republican defending solicitors as well. He identified people, places, times, of these meetings."

Deirdre leafed through several other documents that Jeffries had typed up discussing several very delicate topics like 'collusion,' Jeffries called it 'cooperation' between the RUC, the FRU and MRF with the UDA.

He also said he, Jeffries, could identify the infamous "Colonel J" from the Brian Nelson trial.

He was willing to share this info with Eoffa since he was shortly going to go "missing." Jeffries said Eoffa would have to deal with her own government, the US government, to get the tape. He said what followed was to be kept confidential by Eoffa, or he would see that her dad's life was made miserable.

He had arranged to sell the tape to the Americans. What he was expecting was $5,000,000 and participation in a witness protection program in the USA for himself and any four relatives he identified, beyond himself.

Deirdre just sat there, periodically looking at the door to ensure she would not get caught reading the papers. Then she rose, took the envelope contents over to the copy machine and made copies of them. She put her copies in her purse, returned the originals to Eoffa's envelope and placed the envelope on Eoffa's desk. She had bought the faked summary by Jeffries hook line and sinker.

She wrote a note saying she had been taken sick and had to go to her flat to recover. She taped it to Brice's office door and headed for the street. Once outside she looked around, and headed up the road.

It was at this point that Denny's people "collected" Deirdre, hustled her into a car, blind folded her and took her to an apartment for safe keeping. I was there waiting for them.

Prearranged dialogues were made for her to hear by her captors. Her fear increased as they continued to refer to her as being "expendable," as a "fucken spy," and, "better dead than an embarrassment to us."

She was becoming more terrified by the minute. No one would be looking for her since she left a sick note, Denny explained.

Denny, behind his fake beard and eyeglasses began to grill her; a pillowcase was pulled over her head, even though she was still blindfolded.

I gestured "Why?"

He just shrugged his shoulders. "Saw it in a movie."

I whispered to Denny, "Why the disguise on you?"

"For you my friend. For old times sake."

I began to laugh quietly. I whispered, "This is serious shite."

Denny nodded his head affirmatively and started:

"Jeffries informed us some time ago you were a Special Branch bitch. We know it all. We know everything about you, and you are expendable, you understand that don't you?"

She just sat there and whimpered. Denny raised his voice, "You are expendable, do you understand?"

A very weak and muffled, "yes, was heard."

"We have you on film reading private mail to Ms. Cashel. Then we have your copy, the copy you made of Ms. Cashel's mail. You are finished. We can hold a news conference and disclose what you did and what you are.

"You are an embarrassment to your service. If we don't shoot you, they probably will."

I shouted in a Belfast accent, as I cocked a Colt 1911 45 caliber loud enough for her to hear, "Shoot the fucken cunt."

Denny intervened, "No wait. I think I know how she could help us and fuck that asshole Jeffries who is planning to screw all of us."

"What?" I exaggerated for effect. "Why the Americans, just for the money?"

"I guess," Denny said. "Jeffries has contacted them for some reason, maybe just the money and protection, and made arrangements with the Americans. He's going to give them Stobie's tape and they are going to pay him and hide him. He also sold Deirdre here to us, knowing what we usually do to cunts like her and that Elizabeth Trimble. Aye, we know the truth about her too, Deirdre, the cunt."

I interjected in an irritated voice, "So what the hell? Let's just kill both of them."

Denny was silent for a few seconds, but then said, "Deirdre, would you be willing to make a tape we could send to the Americans, exposing Jeffries as a first class shite who betrayed you, Trimble, us, and who knows how many more, for his own gain. Would you do that? I'll guarentee you'll live and we won't expose you to the news media.

"We'll make a tape and tell him a copy will be shown to the news media. We'll tell him we've called a news conference to expose him. We'll tell him we have proof of his duplicity. That should fuck him up."

"You don't have the authority to do that," I said in an angry voice. "Just shoot her, and then we can find Jeffries and shoot him."

Deirdre was shaking at this point. Denny yelled, "Get him out of here, get his gun, and guard him till we are finished and gone."

"Well, will you do it? Get even with Jeffries and save yourself?"

With no hesitation, she said quite clearly even through her fear, "Aye, I will."

Denny asked rhetorically, "How or where do we start?"

"Just start filming. I'll expose him as a unprofessional, selfish, egotistical, 'me first,' wanker. You can ask questions as they come up," Deirdre said.

"OK, start filming."

"My name is Deirdre Palm and I am a Special Branch agent. I was sent to the Human Rights Commission as an undercover agent. I was to report on what the Commission was about, what they were focusing on, who they were talking to, and who they heard from. I was also to spy on Eoffa Cashel, but we knew her last name was Castle. She is an American whose father has crossed paths with the RUC on several occasions. Mr. Jeffries has a special hatred for her dad, Rudy Castle.

"There was another agent, Mark Prestin who was passed off as a PR man for the RUC in the Human Rights Commission, but he too was an undercover agent, doing the same thing as me."

"Is Prestin still there at the Human Rights Commission?"

"No, Jeffries moved him out because he was getting nowhere with Cashel. He was supposed to get close to her and burn her and her father if possible. Her dad brings students here to study the 'Troubles,' and the

'Belfast Agreement.' Jeffries hates him, and so he hates her too. Castle's wife is a Catholic from Belfast, and her brother is the famed sniper Danny Conlon."

"So Jeffries obsession with Castle and his family is personal. They've not done anything illegal that the RUC is aware of?"

"Aye, exactly. It's personal. The replacement for Prestin, Elizabeth Trimble, is supposed to make a lesbian pass at Eoffa Cashel. Jeffries thinks because she didn't fall for Prestin, she must be a lesbian. He hasn't a clue about reality."

"Hmm. You saw the material in Cashel's envelope. Do you think Jeffries would use something as important as Stobie's record to benefit himself?"

"Absolutely. He has a reputation in the department as an egotist and as being ruthless. He looks out for himself, and only incidentally for the country. He's no Loyalist. He's selfish."

I kept writing questions for Denny.

"Would he be one in the know about Stobie's tape?"

"Oh yes, he'd know about the tape. He was leading the investigation on Stobie [Denny and I looked in astonishment at each other, we did not know Jeffries headed that investigation]. He's one of the important men in Special Branch. The Stobie tape is locked up and safe. He knows the whereabouts and has access of this certain safe and its content, I've no doubt. He always strutted around, bragging and tooting his horn. He acts and says he is so important.

"It would kill him not to be in the inner circle. He has access. The tape is his key to retirement, a comfortable retirement with a lot of money in California or Hawaii I suspect with a new identity."

"So there is no doubt in your mind he'll sell the tape, and kill anyone to prevent the transcript from getting out, all for his personnel gain?"

"I will say categorically, Jeffries has the tape and is selling it to the Americans for $5 million and protection in a witness protection program. Proof exists, but I am not in a position to disclose who has the proof, provided by Jeffries himself."

"Thank you Ms. Palm, you just bought you life and your freedom. We'll cut you loose soon."

Denny and I went into the next room, and I said, "Get your editing crew working on it. You know what it has to say. She cooperated and gave us what we needed.

"You were great Denny, and your crews. I'll be in touch. I've got to get back to Mullaghbane. It's been a hell of a day. We'll never get the tape, if it really exists, but Jeffries reaction could determine that it does exist."

"I wonder how close you were, Rudy, on that faked summary of Jeffries?"

"I'd be willing to bet on a good day, that we were pretty close to the truth."

"A good day Rudy. This was a good day, and one to add to your legend."

"The legend can wait, and it needs a rest."

"There's no rest for the wicked, and you, Rudy, are one wicked man, so you are."

The film technicians put the film of Deirdre's condemnation of Jeffries together in a few hours. She was kept comfortable, but she was also kept until midday on Wednesday when she was released along the Falls. She looked like hell, but some kind souls were willing to help her. They paid for a cab to bring her to her flat. She really did look sick, so when Brice Dickson called her to see how she was feeling, staying home again for being sick, she said she still felt sickly and she wasn't lying.

I walked into the Special Branch Headquarters, passed through the security screening area, and asked for Peter Jeffries. "No I don't have an appointment," but I said, "I'm sure he will see me without one."

He came out to, well not "greet me" exactly, but to "collect me."

"It's been a while Jeffries, things going all right for you?"

"What the hell do you want, Castle?"

"To catch up on what you've been up to, that all."

"That's it. Get the hell out of here."

"I have something for you," I said as I reached in my breast pocket. He panicked, thinking I was about to produce a gun. I couldn't have gotten a gun past swcurity.

"Not a gun, something more lethal." I handed over the small tape and said, "I'll wait for you at the Human Rights Commission with my daughter. Just the two of us, and you. You can ask me questions about the tape. Come alone, you'll be watched as will the area surrounding the Commission the rest of the day. See you at 18:00. Come alone," I reminded him.

TRAPPING THE BIG RAT

At closing time for the Human Rights Commission, every one was filing out when I came into the offices and told Brice everything had gone according to plan, and that Jeffries would be here at about six.

"He thinks he'll be meeting Eoffa and myself, but it will be just me. The camera will be running. I hope to get him to admit to Stobie's tape. That's the best I think we can do," I explained.

"And why here?" Brice asked.

"The camera, and what a backdrop if he admits to the tape. You can have it for the press," I explained.

To my surprise, Mark Prestin came by looking for Eoffa. I indicated that she was safe down in Dublin, and that I was waiting for Jeffries, so I would appreciate his leaving the area.

He asked when Eoffa would be back and I told him probably tomorrow. Brice said he would leave and told me how to set the alarm and lock up. Then he was gone.

Clearly Mark wanted to say something about his interrogation and time spent with Eoffa.

Denny had the security tape machine ready. We hoped Deirdre didn't call her boss and blow our plan. That was the loose screw in the whole operation.

Denny was hiding in Brice's office with several of his crew canvassing the area outside.

Mark and I went in and I sat at Eoffa's desk and waited. We were talking about Eoffa when Jeffries showed up forty-five minutes early.

"What a surprise. Mark Prestin cavorting with Rudy Castle, why am I not surprised. Where is your daughter?" Jeffries demanded.

"Safe," I answered.

"Are you in on this, Prestin?" He asked Mark.

"No," I quickly responded. "He was here talking to Dickson and followed me in when he was told who I was."

"I find that difficult to believe," Jeffries said as he pulled out a small caliber semi automatic.

"Is that necessary?" I asked.

"After watching your movie, I think it is."

"That video makes some serious accusations. Why not let Prestin go so he is ignorant of the business at hand?" I suggested.

"No. He's a party to this I'm sure. He will have to pay for his involvement."

"OK, it will be on you. Your boss has a tape made by a Special Branch agent about the Pat Finucane murder. It was unknown to exist. When it's author, Will Stobie was murdered because he threatened to talk, the investigator in his murder apparently found the tape. He's kept it under raps, but now its out in the open. It is also reported that Jeffries here is selling the tape to the Americans for a lot of money and a new identity," I reported to Prestin.

Mark played along, and said, "Boss, I can't believe you'd sit on information like that. Did you?"

Jeffries didn't acknowledge Mark's question.

"Why the Americans? Money and new identities? Was Deirdre Palm right?" I asked.

"I won't honor that accusation with an answer."

"The Finucane family demands justice. Getting it from Special Branch would go a long way to mend fences," I pleaded.

"They can wait until hell freezes over."

I looked at Prestin and said, "What an ass. That was not just cold, it was pathetic."

"I'll tell you what's pathetic, a kidnapper bating two Special Branch men to come to the Human Rights Commission after hours, and the young agent lunging to get a gun away from an American IRA terrorist, and getting fatally shot."

Jeffries produced a second gun at that point, and he continued, "Then I had to shoot the infamous Rudy Castle, and everyone who lived, lived happily after."

Everything stopped as Denny stepped into the doorway of Dickson's office and shouted, "What's going on, should I call the Peelers?"

Jeffries shot wildly toward Denny who retreated back inside Brice's office. Mark made an injudicious decision, and lunged at Jeffries. His boss was backing up, and tripped backwards, but he was able to put a bullet in Prestin's shoulder.

Jeffries was sitting on the floor, with his back leaning against Eoffa's desk. "Your plan was to shoot me and my daughter, right?"

He remained silent, then said, "Certainly you. I'd shoot your daughter first just to watch you suffer."

Denny reappeared in the doorway again, and Jeffries was totally concentrating on him when I smashed into him, sending us crashing into the desk and moving it back several feet.

I ended up with Jeffries gun. I laid on my back, figuring the two of us were out of the camera's view.

I shot the camera, smashing it to pieces, thus ending any recording.

Mark was clearly in pain and bleeding. I found the second gun and motioned for Denny to get Prestin into Dickson's office. I said, "Call for an ambulance." Denny appeared in the doorway again as the shot rang out.

———————•◦•———————

The RUC determined that Jeffries committed suicide. Denny had assured me that the tape would support most of what we told the police, so it was our word that satisfied the police.

I reported that after Jeffries shot the camera, both he and I each had a gun and were faced off against each other.

"Admitting his stupid plan to kill me and my daughter, Jeffries became despondent, raised the gun to his head and shot himself," I testified.

Denny said, "Just like he said." The film crew concurred.

Even Mark said, from his hospital bed at the Royal Vic, "That sounds right. I was in pain and in the other room, but what Castle described sounds correct."

Jeffries, holding the murder weapon, his own automatic, was very convincing to the RUC investigators.

Denny claimed he was at the Human Rights Commission checking on the camera. I said Prestin and I were there looking for Eoffa. Both Denny and I had to spend some quality time at the RUC headquarters that night and again the next morning, repeating our stories several times. But the investigators concluded that the preliminary evidence suggested and supported suicide.

Denny produced a copy of the surveillance tape that caught Jeffries in actions and words, thus corroboration our story. The RUC was satisfied with our account of the tragedy.

Barbrie and Eve rescued Denny and myself from the police headquarters. There were hugs, kisses, and the now old question, "Rudy, are you all right?"

"Aye. Denny keeps me safe."

"My God, you two!"

"Rudy, what of Stobie's tape?" Denny quietly asked.

"The RUC big wigs have moved it or destroyed it by now. No chance of ever seeing it now," I whispered.

"Where is Eoffa?" Barbrie asked.

"At the Royal Victoria Hospital, visiting some one who got shot," Eve answered. "Let's get a cab and get her."

"Fine by me. You hungry Denny?"

"I am that, Rudy."

"Denny and I have some thing to tell the two of you that is very serious," I said.

Denny stopped in his tracks. "Rudy!"

"We've got to explain who it is she is visiting," I explained. Denny let out a sigh of relief. But Eve picked up on his relief immediately. She kept quiet, but I knew she was going to follow up on Denny's 'sigh' in the future.

I didn't talk about the new circumstances until we were in the cafeteria of the Royal Victoria Hospital.

"Your daughter, our daughter, did some sterling work for Dickson and the Human Right Commission on 'Bloody Sunday' and the Pat Finucane murder."

"That's wonderful, Rudy," Barbrie said.

"Barb mentioned she was really doing some fascinating and important work, when she got home. But she said, Eoffa was working too hard and too much," Auntie Eve commented.

"All of that is true. But she got an awful, and I mean an awful lot of help from a RUC man. Actually, she turned him, maybe 'converted' him is the right word," I said looking at Denny.

"Aye, that's the word," he agreed.

"She converted a Special Branch young man, and in the process, they fell in love with each other."

"Jaysus , Mary, and Joseph, you've got to be putting me on," Eve burst out.

Barbrie was quieter but equally astonished, "Rudy, are you serious? RUC, Special Branch. What is she thinking?"

Denny was totally contemplative, probably deep in prayer. I continued to eat my bangers and toast, and finally said, "He's the one who got shot, for Denny and me."

Denny remained silent but shook his head, "yes."

"Fucken Special Branch," Eve said with real distaste.

"She's converted him, the whole nine yards: he gave up his boss, the Special Branch and RUC, his family up in Antrim, Presbyterianism, Unionism, Loyalism, all of it. He turned his back on his family, whom she has met, for her. She belittled him, mocked him, treated him like a dog."

Eve interrupted me, "Good on her."

I continued, "But he fell in love with her and she with him. Funny thing love, some times opposites attract. Look at Eve and Paul."

"What in God's holy name does that mean," Eve demanded. Denny just smiled, sensing that the issue now was my comment and me. Eve went on and on about my "smart arse" comments. I corrected her, you are an American now, get it right, it's **smart ASS** comments, **smart ASS** comments.

"Now when we get up there, don't make a scene, just remember how in love your sister was with me and how you opposed it, Eve."

"You were trying to seduce my virgin sister, you big yank, army vet, man of the world, and all. And here's poor Barbrie, all innocent, and this American wanker drooling all over her."

"Eve, for God's sake, calm down. Look how it turned out," Barbrie observed.

"That remains to be seen. Lets go up and see for ourselves," Eve insisted.

"Make her behave," I said to Barbrie.

"She will."

Denny and I just stood back and let nature take its course. Eoffa hugged her mother and her aunt, then she introduced them to Mark Prestin. An elderly couple were standing there also. They were introduced to all of us, William and Grace Prestin, Mark's parents. It was all very awkward.

William Prestin was very reserved, as were Denny and I. We just listened to the women talk, and we men just eyed each other and sized each other up.

After an eternity, the Prestins said they were heading home and Denny announced he was headed home as well.

"We'll be heading home in three days too, I announced. I noticed that Eve had slipped out, so I asked, "Where is Eve off to?" I hoped not to ambush the Prestins. We were in West Belfast, Conlon territory after all.

"She'll be fine. Come and listen to your oldest daughter and her . . . ." Barbrie hesitated, looking for the correct word.

"We are not lovers, he hasn't given me a ring, so 'boyfriend' will do just fine," Eoffa concluded.

Mark smiled and asked, "Will you marry me?"

Eoffa blushed, looked at Barbrie and myself, then back at him and said, "yes."

"I'm Eoffa's fiancée. In a month I've gone from her whipping dog to her fiancée," Mark said with satisfaction.

"Listen to me. Enjoy it for now, because it can change in a second. It can reverse very easily," I warned. "The bed one day, the dog coop the next."

Barbrie gave me a swipe with the back of her hand, saying, "Mind yourself and your manners, Fido."

We all laughed.

———— •:•◆•:• ————

"Denny," Eve called out near the elevator. "I'll ride down with you and we can stand out side so I can smell the Belfast air, and dust, and soot, and mold, and mildew, and grime, and grease cooking."

Denny knew he was in trouble. "How is your brother?"

"Just grand."

"He's married now, right?"

"Aye, to Megan Kelley, from Hartford. She's expecting their first."

"That is grand."

"Denny, explain the 'gasp' when Rudy said he had something serious to tell us."

"All I will say is this. You're brother-in-law is a magician. He trapped that wanker Jeffries, tricked him to acknowledge an import piece of evidence in the Finucane case and he filmed it. Brilliant, so it was."

Eve scowled and said, "And what else?"

"He got his old nemesis, Peter Jeffries of Special Branch."

"And what does that mean?"

"Ah, he got him to acknowledge the evidence of a tape he withheld."

Eve was getting impatient. "What else?"

Denny stood there like a trapped criminal surrounded by coppers. "If I tell you and he finds out he'll never trust me again."

"You've my word, I'll not tell what you tell me."

"After Jeffries shot your man Prestin, Rudy wrestled the guns from Jeffries. He came to your niece's office to kill her and Rudy. He hated Rudy so. He wanted to hurt him so bad. Rudy was fed up, and while I was helping Eoffa's man, it appears that Jeffries committed suicide. He put the gun to his head. Rudy said, 'you have been found guilty of crimes against the Irish people and Humanity. You are condemned to die.' The gun went off, it was a case of suicide all right. Even the RUC bought it.

Rudy never flinched. He made the world a better place last night, starting with saving his daughter's life, and her friend up there. Prestin owes Rudy his life, twice now."

"Twice?"

"Rudy interrogated Prestin trying to trip him up in front of Eoffa. He succeeded, but felt Prestin was sincere in what he'd done for Eoffa and his 'repentance' for being a Special Branch agent and in his love for Eoffa."

Eve took it all in, stepped forward and gave Denny a hug. "Thanks, and I'll not say a word."

"Rudy knew what he had to do, and he didn't flinch."

"Aye, our Rudy is solid all right."

"The boy up there is all right, Eve. He loves Eoffa, and he got shot trying to help us. He's been a big help to Eoffa too. Go light on the lad. There will be time to give him 'shite.' Sorry, you Americans say 'shit.' Right?

"Fuck off, Denny, and thanks," Eve said with a smile.

------ ◆•◆ ------

"I, well Eoffa and I told my parents I was going home with her, if it's all right with you Mrs. Castle. Oh, and Mr. Castle of course," Prestin said looking first at Barbrie, then at me.

"We'll be OK with it, and it might be best for you to get out of the North for a while. Eoffa's auntie might take some time to warm up, but she'll come around," Barbrie warned.

It was a done deal, I just stood there and smiled.

Prestin was released from hospital that afternoon. He had to report to Special Branch to make a final report on the shooting and to fill out forms for his leave of absence for rehabilitation. He made sure that his paychecks would still be deposited into his account at the Bank of Ulster.

He met Eoffa at his flat, told the proprietor that he was leaving Belfast, so he'd be moving out of his flat on short notice. He was leaving the furniture to offset the security deposit that was returned by the proprietor. So far so good.

Eoffa helped him select about a half dozen appropriate shirts and pants, a sports jacket and two suits. One pair of shoes, and overcoat, and "that was it," she said. "The rest is for the Knights of Columbus Charity." Everything Mark was bringing to Hartford fit in one suitcase.

We were staying at the Europa Hotel, and we splurged on supper. Denny and his wife Mary were there of course.

I proposed a toast, "Next year in Hartford." Only Mark and Eoffa got it and laughed.

"It's a twist on a Jewish, or Israeli toast. It was a joke," I explained.

"Republicans support the Palestinians," Denny explained, to the nods of Barbrie and Eve.

"Aye, that's right, we are in the North of Ireland and everything is political," I joked again. Everyone just stared at me, including Eoffa and Mark.

Eoffa made the joke with, "And this is coming from Rudy **Castle**." Everyone laughed at that. Eoffa continued, "Denny, next year in Hartford! Hartford, Michigan, via Chicago." We all toasted that. Denny and Mary couldn't make the trip this year, as we all understood. But he promised they would next year.

Mark's passport was good for another five years, not that he'd need it. We made arrangements for him to fly home with us to Chicago on the same Aer Lingus flight as the rest of us were taking.

"Eoffa and cousin Barb will owe me a lunch in Hartford this year," Mark claimed. Only Eoffa seemed to get the inference behind this comment.

The 'goodbye" to Denny at the train station was somber and joyful at the same time. Denny drove me down to Mullaghbane in time for the bus ride with the students and Tracy to Dublin.

"I feel badly that I didn't get a chance to see Brendan again. I would have liked that," I bemoaned.

"Aye, I'll stop and see him. He'll understand and have a great laugh at the latest escapade," Denny explained. "He'll have full satisfaction when I tell him about Jeffries, how you tricked him, and his end, especially the end."

Tracy was glad to see Denny again.

"Are you not married yet Tracy? No. Then I still have a chance," he teased.

We said our goodbyes, and I said to Denny, Next year . . . ."

"He said, "In Hartford."

Tracy asked full of excitement, "Really?"

"You heard him," I answered as we pulled out on the bus.

"I expect a full report," Tracy said.

"Everything I report is usually full," I said. "The question is, full of what?"

"Exactly. Are you tired?"

"A little."

"I'll give you an hour, then you report, OK?"

"Why are all the women in my life so bossy?"

"You love it. I don't think you would want it any other way."

AN AMERICAN HOMECOMING

In Dublin five 'new students' joined us for the trip to the US, replacing five original ringers, three male students and two females. Students were told that the original ringers were staying on to travel on their own. With all the excitement no one seemed to notice their replacements. I always made sure they joined the line at the end when the rest had gone upstairs at the airport to eat breakfast or lunch. The new folks didn't appear to anyone as being part of our group. Mark was not the only refugee from the North on this trip home.

The night before we were leaving for Chicago, we called Maya and told her to get Sean Kelley's big van, "We've a surprise."

"Barb and your mother want to come too," Maya said. "So I was already planning on it. Young Barb says she thinks she knows what the surprise is, but she won't tell us.

"I suspect it is a 'who,' right?"

"We've also got some girls from Saintfield, remember?"

"Emma and at least one friend."

"Make it two. It's like we are running a camp for displaced girls from the North of Ireland"

"Be careful uncle Rudy, we outnumber you."

"That's the plan. All the beautiful fertile Catholic girls of the North."

"But we're not all Catholics."

"You will be when you marry a good Catholic boy and start cranking out little Catholics."

She was abrupt, "Good bye uncle Rudy, we'll see all of you tomorrow."

———————◆·◆·◆———————

I tried to sleep on the flight home. But sitting between Barbrie and Eve made it impossible.

"I can't stay angry at Eoffa for her choice. I'm also warming up to the Prod pup. He does seem genuine.

I guess I'm OK with it," Eve was saying to Barbrie.

"Good Eve. I understand your hesitation. But he is a good lad, even Rudy says so."

"Jaysus, Barbrie, if Rudy said Hitler was OK because he fought the Brits, you'd agree because Rudy said it," Eve said shaking her head as I opened my eyes.

"In spite of fighting the Brits, he was all bad," I teased.

"That's right, Rudy!"

"We agree then. Thank you for agreeing with me. Eve you are so easy to wind up. You are so predictable. By the way, have you noticed the smoke coming from that motor out your window?" I asked.

Eve nearly came out of her seat in spite of the seat belt. Barbrie elbowed me and said, "Rudy, that's not funny. You know she's terrified of flying."

"Damn it Rudy, that's not funny," Eve said in a threatening voice.

"Quite the contrary, it is funny."

———————◆———————

I drove the first leg of the trip home, through Chicago, taking the Skyway south and east out of the city. "We'll bring you back to Chicago for a couple of days, Mark," I said to no one in particular.

Everyone was so busy talking I'm not sure a soul but Barbrie and my mother who shared the front seat with me, heard much of what I said.

"Mom, it seems like I keep bringing back refugees."

"Aye, isn't it wonderful. I'm so happy you do. I truly love it. I love them all. And you too, Rudy. I just love you all."

"In a couple of weeks we will go up to De Tour to gather up five ringers. Five. But after the last three weeks I know the need is still there."

"Good on you, Rudy. Your granda is proud of youse," mom commented.

"Aye, but I'm getting tired. More tired every trip."

"Well, stop all the extra curriculars," ma laughed.

"It's curricula, mom, curricula."

"You say potato, I . . . ."

I know mom, but it's different."

"So says you."

I was too mentally tired to argue.

My daughter Emma chose this time to inform me of a new development that would cause me more consternation.

"Oh, da, I've talked to Professor Dickson, and he said I could intern for the Human Rights Commission next year, so you can all come over to Ireland to fetch me. Won't it be great?"

"Honey, great isn't the word for it," I said. "It doesn't come close!"

———•◦•———

Two days later at home in Hartford, out in the back yard under the old tree, I said to my mother, "Every year I bring back an interesting group. First Barbrie and Eve, then Danny, Maya and "little Eve," the Saintfield girls, and. now Mark, a former RUC, Special Branch man. I feel like the Pied Piper

"Every year it seems to be getting more personal and I seem to be getting more tired. I'm wondering if it's time to retire, let someone else take over the program. The college won't let Tracy do it. She's the logical one, but her degree is in another area than History. But as you know, she runs the program."

"Rudy, only you can decide if it's time to call it quits."

"When you put it like that, it doesn't sound good. 'Call it quits.' Ouch, that sounds like I'm quitting. I'm not quitting, I'm retiring."

"Is there still work to do? If you quit before it's done, then it's quitting, isn't it?" mom asked.

"The work will never be done."

"How can you quit then with a clear conscience?"

"It's someone else's turn. I'm thinking about retiring, I'll still help. But I won't be so active. I have too much to lose with these women to take care for. I'll stay in the background."

"OK,' she commented accusingly. "If you say so. It sounds like you've convinced yourself."

"I haven't made a decision yet. I need to talk to Barbrie, Denny, Tracy, you. Then I'll decide, and only then."

"That's the thing to do," she said. I detected the hint of a chide in it though. She wouldn't look at me. Finally she said, "If not you, who? Really Rudy, who?"

I wouldn't look at her nor would I comment. She sensed that now I was tired of sparring with her.

When Barbrie was not listening, my mother whispered, "Eve says you have some wonderful stories to tell us from this years trip. I can't wait to hear them. She said some are not for anyone but me to hear. That means they are good, really good. Good on you Rudy, good on you."

"I'm more concerned with the people still hurting there and still threatened by the past in general and their past in particular. In some ways, it's not over yet. So Ireland just keeps sending people to us."

"Rudy, it will never stop, even if the 'Troubles' stop. It's Irelands gift to the world, her people. That is the truth and the mystery behind the saying, **Erin go Bragh.**"